City of
Sin and Virtue

Andrew Stevens

To Tyler Stevens

Thank you for always believing in me

Prologue

Chicago 1922

Katherine O'Donnell hated most things. Her ever-growing list materialized as she strolled through Chicago, walking to meet the outsider who invited her to their impromptu gathering.

She hated how her curls defied her every attempt to tame them.

She hated her painful choice of shoes.

She hated the chill and the mugginess in the air.

Honestly, the longer she lived in Chicago, the more she hated the dilapidated city.

She hated how debris rolled freely, how mud covered every stone, sign, and building. The cracked sidewalks and abandoned buildings reminded Katherine of the beauty her city once held and how it fell further into disrepair, and it repulsed her.

Once Katherine was proud of Chicago, she remembered a time when she could walk through the streets and not worry about stepping in shit, but those years were far gone.

That same disdain for the city clouded Katherine's mind as she made her first slip up of the evening, sinking her foot ankle-deep into a mound of unidentified sludge. Katherine did not restrain herself from swearing as she kicked the unknown filth from her once cream-colored Chanel pantsuit, throwing the sewage back onto the street. She glared at her pants, wishing she could intimidate the stain from the hem and now brown left shoe. Both were unsalvageable.

Bystanders atop nearby stoops pointed and laughed at her blunder.

A scowl promptly ended all amusement.

"Idiots," Katherine hissed, memorizing the faces of those who laughed the hardest, wanting to remember them when she returned with her bat. Her wildness growled in hunger at the thought of shattered kneecaps and broken fingers. It tugged at its mental leash, begging Katherine for action, needing Katherine to give in to her feral nature. Images of broken bodies collapsing atop one another flashed in her mind and tugged Katherine's red lips into a smile. Her hand itched for her gun.

Not tonight.

Not now, at least.

Katherine resumed her stroll forward with a flick of her heavy red curls, paying no attention to the men who stepped from their stoops or appeared from the shadowed alleyways. To them, she was an easy mark, a lost lamb dressed in affluent clothes and luxurious jewelry, stumbling through the dangers of Chicago.

Best to ignore them.

Katherine's wildness grumbled at her disinterest in confrontation and bloodshed. She reaffirmed her decision with a casual over-the-shoulder glance.

Three men. No weapons.

Well, no guns.

Two carried baseball bats, while the third held nothing.

If they're criminals, they aren't very good ones.

Katherine showed no concern for her safety as they trailed behind her.

The heavy weight of her father's gun brought her the reassurance that allowed her to stroll through the slums of Chicago without fear. Her name alone afforded her the protection she required most nights, but people were hungry and hungry people were desperate.

Katherine paused at an intersection, looked at the signs, and crossed the street, moving deeper into the forgotten tenements of Chicago. The men behind her dispersed, choosing to stay in the well-lit areas while Katherine traveled further. But her mind was elsewhere as she traveled to her engagement.

Could this indeed be a trap?

She scoffed at the idea, though the preposterous notion did thrill her. Who would be brave enough—or dumb enough—to try to lure Katherine O'Donnell, queen of Chicago, into a trap?

Who indeed?

When the invitation arrived hours earlier, Katherine, at first, was appalled by the idea of being summoned. Few knew where she lived, and even fewer had the conviction to command a meeting. That someone would consider coming into her city without a proper introduction and then summoning *her*. It wasn't just absurd—it was insulting.

At first, Katherine thought of tossing the letter into the fireplace and waiting for this perpetrator to make a proper introduction. But as she read and reread the invitation, she felt almost . . . drawn to meet. The strokes of the handwriting, the tone, the word choice; it seemed so familiar and yet foreign. Katherine accepted the invitation, if only to meet the courageous, imbecilic person.

She prepared herself as she would any meeting—a clean suit, fresh curls, and a fully loaded gun. Every fabric and powder added a layer to her armor. Whether the invitation brokered peace or declared war, Katherine prepared for either.

Against her will, her colleagues arranged a vehicle and chaperone to accompany Katherine.

"Another safety precaution," they had assured her.

She fervently declined both.

Yet not ten minutes into the walk, Katherine regretted her hubris, cursed her choice of footwear, and dreamed of the plush cushions of a vehicle. Even more so now that one of her favorite pairs of shoes had become dyed the color of shit. But the pain in her feet did not hinder Katherine's stride. She kept a moderate stroll and arrived precisely as planned, fifteen minutes after the prearranged time.

She might have even missed the building if not for the brass numbers that shined through the ivy and moss that claimed the face of the abandoned place.

Katherine sighed.

The structure was more frame than it was building. The third and fourth-floor walls were gone entirely, exposing the wooden beams. The floors where walls still stood were rotted and held shattered windows. Much of the roof was missing. The spaces deemed 'salvageable' were claimed by plant life, covering them with all manner of creeping vines. The first floor was primarily whole, with an enormous iron door fixed into decaying wood.

Katherine counted the days until they tore down the slums and the city erected something more modern.

"Such a peculiar place to meet, but roaches hid in the most disgusting places," Katherine thought aloud. Did they think she would be scared?

Katherine turned from the building. Her eyes roamed the streets, seeing not a single soul. With her back to the designated meeting space, Katherine's hand fished into her inner jacket pocket, withdrew her gun, and checked the barrel. She knew it to be full, but the memory of her father's first lesson resonated through her.

"Knowing your ammunition count is most important when entering a dangerous situation. You must know how many bullets you have to use, so you always have one for yourself."

It was her father's hardest lesson. One that still weighed profoundly on Katherine's mind.

"Family before self," she said, repeating her family's mantra before she turned, climbed the steps, and approached the iron door.

Bang. Bang. Bang.

Three heavy raps announced Katherine's arrival. The noise echoed through the building and exited through a gaping hole in the roof. The sound of water overpowered her knocks as it declared its arrival. Kathrine turned to the east. A curtain of rain rushed down the paths she had just traveled, drenching everything in its course, seeing Katherine as its next victim.

"Jesus, Mary, and Joseph—if I get wet, this meeting will be over before it begins." Katherine's gun and her wild side agreed. Katherine raised her hand and knocked three additional times, but with more force and less patience. Before her knuckles made another attempt, the door opened.

Expecting to be greeted inside, Katherine stepped forward. Her face met the surface of a rough wool coat. The smell of cheap cigars and body odor quickly invaded her nose. She retreated from the smells and looked up at the scowling face above. The man's vacant expression and scarred face showed a history of fighting. His wide jaw and crooked nose made an already ugly face more unpleasant. Katherine showed no hesitation in returning his scowl. She crossed her arms and tapped her foot, waiting for the man to move. He remained a silent obstacle.

"Now, are you going to move, or am I expected to stand outside all night?"

Silence.

Katherine huffed; her eyes caught the sight of the encroaching rain.

"You have two choices; you can either—"

"Christ Almighty, George! Let her in! Let her in!" A female screamed from the inside; her order cut off Katherine's threat, but the man moved.

Katherine raised a victorious eyebrow and crossed the threshold a second before rain assaulted the place where she just stood. But her triumphant entry faltered when she gazed at the familiar insides.

A bar?

The door led to the first level of a two-story interior. The top level, where Katherine stood, held stacked tables and chairs cluttered together and covered with dusty white clothes. Large crates were scattered throughout the entry, making Katherine weave around the boxes as she stepped further inward. Several boxes were opened, revealing the shiny bottles nestled within beds of packing straw.

Alcohol?

Katherine leaned toward one of the opened crates, rotating the bottle within. The label on the amber bottle read clear as day. Whiskey.

Very interesting.

The door slammed behind Katherine, interrupting her examination. Her red hair flew as her neck snapped over her shoulder, glaring at the guard whose sour face gave just a hint of amusement. Her scowl deepened.

Stepping away from the crate, Katherine descended into the lower level, the dining area. Her hands grazed the banister. Dust painted the tips of her fingers. A small group of people with backs turned spoke softly to each other, surrounding the only uncovered table. An older gentleman worked behind the bar, boldly placing alcohol on the back shelf.

Katherine waited at the base of the stairs, watching the group interact without giving her notice, but after several long moments of watching, she spoke, "Is someone going to greet me, or do I expect the meeting to be held without formalities?"

The group of people muted themselves and departed.

Rarely was Katherine surprised by the men who hosted these meetings. Always the same—nasty, white, decaying skeletons more interested in forcing her out of the city or into their beds than a true partnership. They saw her as an obstacle, and Katherine saw them as an annoyance. One she typically remedied with a bat or bullet.

But to her shock, it wasn't an aged crocodile.

It was a woman—a Black woman.

The woman gracefully raised from the table, like Aphrodite emerging from the seafoam. Every movement seemed purposeful—choreographed—even her beaded dress moved to an unheard rhythm as she approached. Before Katherine could react, the stranger's arms extended, wrapped around Katherine, and forced her into a hug. Katherine's body tensed. She attempted to dislodge herself, but the woman's arms tightened. Over the years, Katherine grew numb to the pawing, clammy hands of the gentleman, but this hug disturbed her more than any 'accidental' grab.

"Katherine! I have long been waitin' to meet you!" The woman rocked them back and forth overly familiarly. When they broke, the stranger held Katherine's shoulders in the same iron grasp as she looked down at her with large innocent brown eyes, staring at Katherine, searching her features for something that Katherine did not understand. Katherine noted the height difference, with the woman standing at least six inches taller—even with the help of a three-inch heel.

"Can I get you a drink?" She swooped a glance over Katherine, noting the mud-covered heel and the splatters along the hem of her pants. "You didn't walk all that way, did you? You must be dying of thirst!"

Katherine began to decline, but the woman had already started to order.

"Alfred! Rob Roys. Make it two!" she said, flipping up two fingers.

"Yes, ma'am," the older man croaked.

"Here, sit, sit, sit!" She took Katherine's wrist and brought her to the single table. Katherine flexed her hand, unsuccessfully trying to break from the woman's hold.

Jesus, Mary, and Joseph. Why is she so strong?

"Give us some room. Shoo! Shoo! Shoo! Shoo!" She waved the guards away, sending them to the walls of the sunken dining space. "Us ladies have important business to discuss." The stranger settled in her chair and slapped her hands together. "Gee, I just can't believe it. I came such a long way, but seeing you here just made it all worth the trouble! I'm just so excited!" She shook like a child on Christmas morning, a constant excitement running through her.

"Georgia?" Katherine asked, unable to miss the Southern accent. The woman snapped her fingers in response.

"Mississippi." She corrected. "I guess those years of lessons were a waste. Nothin's harder than gettin' rid of an accent." Her inflection adjusted slightly as the woman leaned into her words, choosing to embrace her accent instead of hiding it.

The two women went silent, choosing to gaze at one another as the sound of the older man mixing their drinks filled the space. Katherine pulled on her mask of solemn observance while the woman continued to bounce, rather annoyingly, in her chair.

She wasn't much younger than Katherine, less than a handful of years. The woman's smile stretched across her apple-shaped face, remaining as a tight grin. Her black hair was tightly curled and pressed around her head, held in place by a headband. A sheer lipstick colored her lips, matching her beaded dress.

The shuffling of the bartender ended their silent stare-off as he offered drinks to each woman. Katherine pushed her glass away while the other woman impatiently swiped hers.

"I prefer not to drink while I work," Katherine said flatly, but forced a smile to appear friendly. The sweetness bridged the gap of the sour taste she typically left during meetings. The woman shrugged her thin shoulders.

"Oh, sug', I can't work without drinking."

With a single gulp, she drained the glass. The older man stumbled forward, ready to refill her drink, but the woman dismissed him with a wave of her hand. The Southern stranger leaned back in her chair and crossed her unbelievably long legs, as if she knew Katherine longed for her shape. A waterfall of diamonds spread across her dark skin as the beaded dress split along her upper thigh.

A little glitzy but pretty.

Against her better judgment, Katherine spoke first, if only to move the meeting along. The hour was late, and Katherine had things to do.

"If I knew we would remain anonymous throughout this engagement, I would have worn one of my party masks." She looked at the woman's dress again. "Perhaps something a little more *flashy*."

"Well, pardon my bad manners. My grandmother would tan my hide if she knew how I was treatin' you. It's just been one *hell* of a night. There's so much to do, and I just got so gosh, darn excited to see you!" She smacked her thigh, punctuating her excitement. "I thought I would have to use a more forceful approach to get you to meet me."

The woman's eyes glistened as she laid the threat gently between them. Her cheerful voice made the warning seem less dangerous, but the unspoken meaning underneath was clear, and Katherine's lips twisted at the corners.

And so we begin.

Katherine found the art of conversation most enjoyable. She loved watching the tapestry of her counterpart's true intentions unravel as she tugged and pulled. It took years for her to temper her urges for blood and violence and find interest in something less volatile. Though it did not force blood, Katherine's tongue was as sharp as any blade and just as painful.

"Abigail Edgefield, a pleasure to meet you finally."

Abigail's fingers danced along her long-beaded necklace. Her brown eyes tightened, transitioning the welcoming host into a calculating gaze that examined Katherine's every movement. Katherine returned her intensity, not fearing the woman's intrusive observation.

"And you"—Abigail pointed—"are Katherine O'Donnell, king, I mean, queen of alcohol and drugs for all Chicago and the surrounding cities." Abigail's lips widened into an intimidating smile as she rattled off Katherine's resume, enjoying the shock that crept through Katherine's stoicism as she listed her most personal affairs.

"I know who I am," Katherine interrupted. "The question is, who exactly are you?"

"Just a friend—or someone who would like to be your friend. That is, if we can both behave."

A brave claim.

"But between the two of us, I rarely like to be good." Abigail leaned forward. Katherine tensed, expecting a pulled gun or another attempt at physical contact, but instead, Abigail grabbed an ice cube and sucked on it.

Katherine sat straighter.

"*Friends*," Katherine said, chewing on the word. Her eyes moved to the guards, who seemed almost bored by the meeting, staring at the ceiling instead of paying attention to their boss. "Someone who wanted to be *friends* would have come to me with a proper introduction. Someone interested in *friendship* would have held a formal meeting. To me, all of this doesn't appear to be very *friendly*."

Abigail shrugged once more, giving yet another nonanswer.

Katherine stretched her arms, nonchalantly moving one into her jacket's inner pocket as if reaching for a cigarette. The movement was casual. One practiced to boring perfection. Abigail showed no regard for Katherine's actions, focusing on the beads of her necklace until the tip of Katherine's finger brushed the handle.

In the blink of an eye, Abigail's gaze tensed, emptying the warmth in a blink. Their rigidity froze Katherine to where sweat sprouted along her back.

"I wouldn't do that, darlin'." Abigail threatened.

Katherine's lips parted, eager to return the taunt, but she released a horrific gasp for air in its place. She couldn't breathe. Her mind forgot the gun and went to her throat, pawing at herself to force air into her lungs. Her cheeks reddened as her body screamed for air. Katherine released her throat, slamming her hands on the table,

13

shaking the two glasses. She tried to inhale, but an invisible grip halted any effort.

Breathe! Breathe!

Abigail's face contorted with enjoyment as she watched Katherine struggle for air.

"Now, let us be cordial, Katherine." The phantom hand released with Abigail's words, and air flooded Katherine's lungs as if it were a gift for her obedience.

"Just two ladies having a friendly chat. No need to get serious." Abigail smiled.

Katherine's heart galloped like a horse, thundering in her chest. She took several shallow breaths to slow her pulse while Abigail relaxed as if nothing unusual had occurred.

What the hell was that?

Katherine's face faltered. Her mask of confidence and contempt slowly slipped as anger simmered under the surface.

Who the hell is she?

Abigail looped and loosened her necklace around her fingertips, tightening until the tips of her dark fingers turned red. Katherine realized why Abigail had no concern about hiding a weapon.

Why would she need to worry about concealing a weapon when she had something she could wear so publicly?

"I think we can have a civilized conversation, don't you?" Abigail peeled away the venomous look and fell back into her cheery-eyed host persona.

"Yes," Katherine answered through tight lips.

The room's atmosphere altered as she held Abigail's gaze. The space crept towards Katherine. The guards seemed closer. The ceiling seemed lower. And for the first time, Katherine felt like an animal brought to the slaughter, a queen who unknowingly walked to the guillotine. This was not a conference for peace but an execution. Her mind replayed every bit of information she gathered—every window, every door, and every potential escape route.

One entrance. Maybe one in the back or upstairs. Six men, counting the one behind the counter. Eight bullets.

If she wanted to get out fighting, she would need every bullet.

Best-case scenario, she would take Abigail out first before anyone reacted. Worst case, Katherine would be dead before she even pulled her gun.

"Answer me this, Katherine," Abigail said as she lowered her eyes toward her empty glass. "What makes you angry?"

"What?" Katherine replied, shocked by the unexpected turn in the conversation. "What kind of question is that?"

"An easy one," Abigail teased as she released her necklace and circled the rim of her glass, collecting the condensation on her fingertip. "So, what is it, Katherine? What fills you with a deep hatred so hot that you could raze this hellish city?"

Confusion spanned Katherine's face.

Why would she ask such a question? Was she crazed?

Abigail lifted her eyes, and fear swarmed Katherine.

Abigail wasn't mad; she was something far worse. The wildness inside of Katherine withdrew further into her, recoiling from the danger she now sensed.

The once harmless eyes that welcomed Katherine transformed before her. Spots of red appeared beneath Abigail's brown irises, like blood vessels bursting; the tiny droplets diluted the color, collecting and changing the brown into a bloody red.

Katherine's father's voice spoke to her, uttering a word she had never heard before. *Run.*

"Is it men? The police? This godforsaken city? If I were you, I would have burned Chicago to the ground and left without a care. Set everything aflame until it transformed into a glorious inferno." Abigail leaned in her chair and stretched her arms to the ceiling. Her fingers danced on invisible strings, plucking one after another. "Maybe something less material and more spiritual?" Her voice peaked. "Did the good Lord take away your mother? No, not a mother." Abigail tilted her ear to the ceiling as if a voice beyond this world whispered the answer to her question. *"Father."*

Goose pimples erupted along Katherine's body.

Run, Katherine! Run quickly! Her father shrieked.

"What I wouldn't give just to dip into that mind of yours and see—"

"Enough!" Katherine barked, silencing Abigail's ravings. The fearful sensation that entrapped Katherine wavered, and it was her time to act. She threw herself from the table, withdrew her gun, and pointed it directly at her opponent. "I'm leaving NOW!"

Abigail raised a thin brow as if to challenge the gun.

Katherine held steady while Abigail observed her, and the guards ignored her.

Don't stand down. Katherine's father whispered his words of encouragement as she tightened her finger around the trigger, ready to pull.

For the second time that evening, Abigail stunned Katherine.

Instead of a fearful "Okay," Abigail threw her head back and laughed.

The surrounding men remained silent as their boss released a high-pitched squeal of enjoyment. Her demented giggle slowly transitioned into a horrible cackle, becoming a sound that scraped against Katherine's brain and burrowed into her bones, a sensation far worse than any physical pain Katherine had ever endured. It wasn't just painful—it was unholy. The sound felt like acid rain, assaulting every inch of her mind, burning away at her soul until nothing was left.

"You are so entertainin', Katherine. I knew you would be a fighter. That's good. You'll need to be one for the future I see for you—for us." Abigail spoke to the ceiling. She shook her head back and forth until her face fell level, and Katherine saw what Abigail had become.

"Jesus Christ," Katherine gasped.

"Not quite. Think lower."

Scarlett flooded Abigail's gaze. The crimson color swallowed her brown irises and widened until they consumed her eyes' whites.

Katherine had seen evil in her life, men who killed children, raped women, and burned entire buildings to the ground, but this was her first demon.

"I don't think such a weapon would be much use here, Katherine." Abigail laced her fingers within her necklace, showing no fear of the gun or death.

"What do you want from me?"

Her father's lessons raced through her mind. Katherine's eyes darted around the room, searching for her next step.

Where is your exit? What can you use? What does. . .

Quick as a viper, Abigail shot from her chair and latched onto Katherine's hand. For a moment, Katherine thought Abigail would force the gun from her hand and turn it against her, but Abigail pressed the tip into her sternum, almost daring Katherine to pull the trigger. Her scalding hands tightened around Katherine's fingers. She winced, feeling her fingers bend, a hair away from snapping.

"I'm not afraid of death, Katherine. Are you?"

Abigail's deranged voice rang through Katherine's mind, ripping through her confidence one syllable at a time. "Do you fear the Grim Reaper? Of the day he will ride toward you with his sickle and horse of shadows?" Katherine tugged at her gun, but Abigail clasped it between her collarbone. "What do you think waits for you on the other side, Katherine? Do you think someone like you, who murders and cheats and steals, would be welcomed through the pearly gates?" Abigail tilted her head. "Think those Sunday services and hollow confessionals will be enough for you when the time comes? Think those saints you worship will come to your aid on the day of reckoning?"

Katherine lost herself in her opponent's red eyes as Abigail's questions brought the fears that Katherine tucked away. Katherine felt herself drowning beneath their intensity. The deep wells of blood reflected every fear that Katherine could imagine.

"But why choose fear, dear Katherine? When rage tastes so much better?" Abigail's question was the match that ignited the wildness contained within Katherine. The red fed Katherine's monster, begging it to attack.

Remain in control. What is the plan? Her father's voice begged for her to remain calm. He knew what Katherine became when she gave in to her darker appetite. Abigail released Katherine's fingers and raised her hands, accepting whatever fate Katherine dealt her. She placed a finger on the gun's tip, lifting it toward her manic smile.

Give in to it, Katherine. Enjoy it. Let it be free. A foreign voice spoke to her. It stroked her wildness as it begged for freedom. *Be the wild monster your father forced you to hide.*

Katherine stared into the eyes of her enemy and released.

Something passed through Katherine as she tightened her grip and pushed the gun into Abigail's chin. Katherine freed herself from fear, seeing images of blood and violence—images she wanted to make a reality.

Sensing the change in Katherine, a nearby guard reached his hand into a pocket.

Before he could touch his firearm, Katherine unloaded her first bullet into his head.

Seven left.

"Death comes for us all—some sooner than others," Katherine bit back as she returned the gun to Abigail's chest.

Abigail showed no remorse for the new body on the floor. She seemed almost . . . *excited.*

"Been so long since I had a friend to play with. We are going to have such fun!"

"What. Do. You. Want?" The hammer pulled back, ready to fire a second bullet, though Katherine did not know if it would harm whatever stood before her.

"Darlin', I just wanna be friends," Abigail said with her sickly sweet voice before she turned away from Katherine. She strolled to her seat without worrying about the weapon that could easily fire into her back. Facing Katherine, Abigail's brown eyes rose from their bloody depths, a change that extinguished Katherine's fury.

Katherine wobbled. Her dark thoughts seemed drained from her mind, taking with it the will to fight.

"Such a delicacy your wildness is, Katherine. Such deep wells of hatred and anger hide beneath that proper face," Abigail said as she sucked the tip of her finger. "You are a flavor unlike any other, which is expected. We have so much to talk about. So many plans to make. An entire world of people to see." Abigail motioned for Katherine to sit.

Abigail's hands returned to her necklace, patiently waiting for Katherine to obey, but she remained a statue surrounded by monsters.

"Do you think we could be friends, Kat?" Abigail tilted her head to the side. "Do you think we could be the *best* of friends?"

Katherine did not feel the hunger to fight as she looked at Abigail. She swallowed a mouthful of air and contempt for the woman. Abigail, seeing the dryness of Katherine's lips and the pale color of her skin, slid the glass of alcohol toward the empty seat.

"A peace offering."

Katherine licked her lips. Her mouth was so dry, and alcohol had never looked more appetizing.

Sorry, Father.

It was the first lesson of her father's that Katherine broke. She took the glass, tipped it back, and swallowed. The alcohol didn't give her the courage Katherine desired, but it reassured her of one thing— she was still alive.

"Another?" Abigail asked.

"Yes."

Abigail's smile grew as she raised two fingers to the bar.

"I knew I was going to like you."

"I can't say the same about you," Katherine said and quickly added, "and never call me Kat. It's Katherine."

Abigail nodded. "Yes, ma'am."

From the corner of her eye, something rustled. Katherine turned her head and watched as the supposedly dead man stood. He brushed his jacket and touched the bleeding gunshot wound on his forehead. Blood flowed down the guard's face and onto his clothes. He noticed Katherine's shocked expression and smirked.

Katherine turned to the smiling Abigail as she reached for her second glass. She added another item to her mental list of hated things: Abigail Edgefield.

Chapter 1

Las Vegas, Present day

Robert and Rebecca spent their final evening in Vegas at a bar—well, sitting at a bar or running down the boulevard searching for another one. The city's extra-wide walkways gave them the freedom to trip, stumble, and laugh. Like moths to a flame, they moved from one bar to another, searching for another drink, another taste, another story.

The twins drew the occasional side-eye from their drunken antics, neon pink cowboy hats, and matching "I Get Slotty in Vegas" shirts. Rebecca picked the hats. Robert, the shirts. Their relationship was a never-ending ping-pong battle of jokes and humiliation. Their unsightly, matching outfits complemented their nearly identical faces. A pointed nose cut between a pair of gray-blue eyes. Their thin lips stretched into large, comical smiles. Rebecca's smile twisted somewhat menacingly while Robert's kept a reasonably kind and flat appearance. Rebecca was four inches taller and 5 minutes older than her brother, two facts she reiterated ad nauseam. She used her slightly taller body to her advantage, resting her head atop Robert's, requiring the additional source of stability.

"That one!" Rebecca chorused, unhinging herself from her brother and pointing to the flashing neon sign: Two for One Margaritas—a prime reason to frequent a restaurant. She turned to her brother, expecting to see him salivating at the thought of reasonably priced alcohol and tacos, but she found him staring down at his phone.

I should have taken that damn thing the moment we left.

The dark cloud within his phone leaked into the world as Robert stared unblinkingly at his messages. Rebecca became concerned. She desperately hoped Robert hadn't texted *her* and wished, even more, *she* had not texted him. Before suggesting a final night of debauchery, Rebecca knew her brother would go one of two ways with tequila.

Unfortunately, it appeared that Robert had sunk into the deeper end of the depression pool.

"Robbie, just forget about her," Rebecca said as she stepped toward her brother, causing a block in traffic flow. "Hellooo?" Rebecca asked sarcastically, attempting to steal his attention. She looked at the screen and watched as he scrolled through past messages.

Rebecca's anger flared, and she plucked the phone from her brother's hands.

Robert blinked. And then blinked again.

He stared at the space between his fingers for several seconds before his glossy eyes turned from his hand and scowled at his sister.

Haphazardly, he lunged for his phone. "Becca, give it back."

Rebecca chuckled at his pathetic attempt.

He lunged again. "Becca, give it back!"

Robert dove for his phone a third time and missed yet again. Rebecca spun gracefully out of reach, giggling continuously. With every drink, Rebecca grew faster while Robert reduced to a sluggish pace—a trait Rebecca was not afraid to use to her advantage. She evaded Robert's attempts, bumping into the surrounding pedestrians without care. They shouted at him and cursed at Rebecca. To them, she was yet another crazy in a city of senseless people.

Rebecca ended her teasing with a tap on her brother's shoulder. He twisted to meet her foolish smile. She wagged a disobedient finger. "Do that again, and your phone goes straight into the nearest fountain."

Come on. Say something.

She needed him to say something. Make some snarky remark. Tackle her to the ground. She would've been happy with, "I'll toss you in after it." Rebecca wiggled a manicured brow and hoped her brother would take the bait and play.

Instead, his face fell, his shoulders tucked inward, and Robert turned away. Rebecca's smile sank. Had she gone too far?

"You can be such a bitch sometimes." Robert shoved his hands into his pockets and stomped away from the bar and his sister.

She had—in fact—gone too far.

25

Rebecca's heart sank at seeing her brother so depressed. But what he needed now wasn't pity; he needed a swift kick in the ass.

Rebecca inhaled, pushed out her chest, straightened her back, and marched after her brother as he floated away.

"It's not his fault. It's not his fault. It's not his fault."

She repeated the statement until her anger cooled, blowing annoyance out of her chest. She knew Robert wasn't to blame for his shift in his demeanor, but it didn't make it any less annoying.

Rebecca sped up to her brother, tucking her arm through the space between his elbow and body

"It's just one of my many, many, many AMAZING qualities." She looked down at his profile.

Come on. Just a smile. Just one.

"What are big sisters for?" Rebecca added.

"Don't you mean older sisters?" The corner of Robert's lips tugged, teasing a smirk.

He'll be fine.

Rebecca sighed. Robert would *be fine*. He would always *be fine*. They would both always *be fine*. But Rebecca didn't want him to be "*just fine*"; she wanted him to be great. She wanted him to thrive. Rebecca wanted him to be free. He had taken his share of the pain in their life, and Rebecca needed to be there for him, especially if nobody else would.

But right now, what she really needed—what they both really needed—was another drink. Rebecca's buzz was wearing off, and to save the night, she required an obscene amount of cheese and the largest margarita the city could offer.

First, she needed to have an uncomfortable conversation.

"Real talk, Robbie." Rebecca unlooped her arm and stopped walking. Robert continued onward until Rebecca took hold of his shoulders and turned him to face her. "Why are you going to let her ruin tonight? If you wanna call someone a bitch, then we need to talk about Victoria. Now, SHE'S a real bitch."

"Be nice, *Rebecca*," Robert said, using her full name. The burgeoning smile died as he twisted free of her arm and stared at her.

"No, *Robert*," she said, matching his tone. "I'm gonna call a spade a spade and a clown a clown. And she is, in fact, a clown!" Robert turned to walk away. Rebecca gripped his shoulder and spun him back toward her.

If the gentle approach won't work.

"I'm not letting her ruin the last night of our vacation. So, I'm gonna need you to buck up, put on your big boy pants, and stop thinking about that bleached bimbo and have fun with me."

Robert crossed his arms as if to say, "Or what?"

Rebecca released Robert and groaned in annoyance. What did he have to be so infuriating? Rebecca pushed her fingers through her tangled curls, shaking out the knots and her frustration.

"She's trash, Robbie! I don't see what you see in her! You're such a great guy, and if it's her prerogative, then she can ruin her life—not yours."

"She's not all bad," Robert said as he rubbed his watch. Rebecca's eyes widened, knowing the spot that hid behind Victoria's 'gift.' She knew why he rubbed the site.

Never again.

Rebecca pledged never to let her brother feel so lost or alone again.

"Robbie, please, just listen. You know she wasn't good for you." Rebecca cradled her brother's hand, feeling her protective nature spike. "You have to agree that it was for the best. I'm sorry she hurt you. I really am. But after everything she put you through. You know it's better this way."

Robert's lips tightened in thought. He considered Rebecca's words but showed nothing on his face. Rebecca wished she knew what went through his mind when he thought of Victoria. He held everything so close to his chest, hiding his emotions and his fears from everyone, even her. Rebecca wished he would just exhale for once in his life.

The two stood like stones in a river, unmoving as the water rushed pass them. Other people sent scowls at the 'careless' pair standing in the middle of the walkway, but Rebecca would have waited an eternity if it was what her brother needed.

Finally, Robert nodded

The worry inside of Rebecca eased but did not vanish. She would always worry about him. But that was what older sisters did; they cared for their younger brothers when the world wouldn't.

"Excuse me!" A voice snapped behind Rebecca. "Can you two move?"

Rebecca faced the thin woman, and her eyes came alive with rage. "Can you see that we're having a moment?"

The woman screamed in terror and fled.

Robert snickered. He knew the look his sister gave the woman. Medusa incarnate, he called it.

His sister possessed a glare that could curdle milk and frighten even the nastiest bully. For Robert, that was his breaking point. He erupted with laughter and pushed his sister away—lovingly, to say the least. Rebecca eyed the woman until she vanished from sight, silently thanking his sister for her aggressive way of loving him.

"Why are you crazy?" He walked away from her, shaking his head at his ridiculous sister. "Still in the mood for margaritas?"

"Is that even a question?" Rebecca grinned, twirling toward the Mexican restaurant with thoughts of melted cheese dancing in her head. "You're paying!" she announced, before looking over her shoulder. Robert raised his hands in surrender and smiled.

He'll be fine. Just give him time.

Chapter 2

Rebecca witnessed the hardships her brother had endured the previous months. Finding out his piece of trash girlfriend was cheating on him with his supposed best friend was two swift sucker punches to the gut and ego. Two heavy hits Rebecca wished she could return to Victoria with interest.

It worsened when Victoria weaseled her way around 'the issue,' warping the narrative, so Robert became the bad guy. She twisted the events around Robert like a python, choking him until he believed her version even more than the truth. Everything became so chaotic that Robert couldn't figure out what he wanted. So, he left, or more specifically, Rebecca liberated him. While their parents urged—quite firmly—for him to take her back.

"It's what would be best for the family," their mother had insisted, worrying more about optics than her child's happiness.

It disgusted Rebecca how their parents saw 'the issue' as they labeled it. Their father agreed with their mother and urged Robert to move on from 'the issue.' While Rebecca openly abstained from their relationship, seeing Victoria as a gold-digging tramp. So Rebecca did everything within her power to keep them apart, much to Robert's secret appreciation.

*   *   *

The morning the winnings arrived; Rebecca was at her rope's end. Dodging their parents' phone calls, consoling Robert, and keeping him away from his phone was a full-time job—and an exhausting one at that. She wasn't sure if it was fate or simply good luck, but it was the escape that they both needed.

An all-expenses-paid trip to Vegas, courtesy of a contest Rebecca couldn't *quite* remember entering. All she needed to do was accept it, no strings attached. Her mental wheels turned with a crazy thought as she read the details. It was an outrageous idea, but one she knew she could make a reality with a little finessing. It only cost Rebecca a few hours on hold with the airline and the hotel. Her first-class ticket and expensive suite were exchanged for a pair of business class seats and a modestly sized room right off the strip with two queens.

It would be a perfect vacation for her and the ideal escape for Robert. All she needed to do was convince her brother to go, which was more difficult than it should have been.

She announced their trip the morning of the flight with a horrible off-key rendition of "Waking up in Vegas." Robert immediately formed an excuse, talking about work and his 'responsibilities.'

Rebecca, knowing her brother, was already one step ahead of him and his excuses.

She mimicked a phone at her ear and spoke. "Oh, hello, Mr. Robertson. It's Rebecca, yeah, John's daughter. I know it has been some time. I just wanted to let you know Robert came down with food poisoning and won't be coming in the next few days. I know, I know. That's what he gets for eating gas station sushi." She forced a hollow laugh, one very similar to Victoria's.

Fake but believable.

"I know! Exactly! I didn't want my parents to worry, so if you can keep this—oh perfect, thank you so much! I'll make sure to come by and say hi at the Christmas party. Have a great day; tell Babs I said hello." Rebecca crossed her arms, bowed, and raised a challenging brow. "Anything else you wanna throw at me?"

Robert sank into the couch cushions. Rebecca was exhausting. "Why are you a Bond villain?" He sighed.

"I prefer evil genius, but I guess that works, too." Rebecca shrugged her shoulders. "Just call me Becca Big Tits." Rebecca pushed out her lips and made a comical/seductive look.

"Wouldn't you need big tits to be called that?" Robert teased, pulling his blanket over his face.

"Ungrateful!" Rebecca shrieked before landing a slap on the back of Robert's head.

"That hurt!" Robert yelled from beneath the blanket.

"It was supposed to! The flight leaves in two hours! Be ready in thirty!" Rebecca marched up the stairs to her bedroom to gather her luggage. Robert rose from the couch.

"Guess we're going to Vegas." Though he complained, he couldn't deny that he was just the tiniest bit excited about an escape.

Two hours later, the siblings were packed, snacked, and ready for a weekend, where they could ignore their problems.

At certain moments, Robert seemed to lose himself in the fun. They ate. They drank. They did something *very similar* to dancing. The weekend was a whirlwind. Rebecca kept the two moving at a pace where Robert was too busy to even consider the problems at home.

If only it had been as freeing for Rebecca.

When the plane landed, Rebecca felt a tickle—a slight tingling-—in the back of her head. A sensation that told her to look. The first time she looked over her shoulder, Rebecca thought it was nerves, but at the thirtieth time, Rebecca thought she was going crazy. At moments, the sensation would surge as if someone was just inches from reaching out to her, but nobody was ever there.

Rebecca said nothing of the weird impression to her brother. She didn't have the heart to plague Robert with her imaginary problems when *genuine* issues weighed him down. But the feeling felt less fictional as the phantom tickle transformed into a heavy pressure, constantly forcing her to search. Rebecca spent the weekend with one eye over her surroundings and one on her brother, collectively driving her insane. She struggled to tuck the worry away, but as they approached the Mexican restaurant on their final night, Rebecca found the source of her *imaginary* tickle to be very real.

Two emerald eyes caught Rebecca's attention as she crossed the street, leading the two of them to the food and drinks they desperately wanted. When their eyes connected, Rebecca felt the force develop into something far greater than anything she had experienced previously. The green-eyed woman acknowledged Rebecca with a dip of her chin, but Rebecca could not move.

Robert cluelessly pointed at the seats on either side of the green-eyed woman. "You think she'll move over if we ask?"

Something in Rebecca flickered to life as the woman studied her. Her green eyes were the kindling that ignited a small flame inside Rebecca. Vigor infested her body the longer their gazes remained connected. Harsh, unbridled strength coursed through her. Freed from the exhaustion brought by the long weekend, Rebecca felt alive.

"Mm, those look good!"

Rebecca's heart throbbed violently, beating faster and faster as she stood under the woman's gaze. Her predatory eyes beckoned them forward, but Rebecca needed to escape.

Only one plan came to mind, and it was a dumb one.

"Tag!"

Robert turned just in time for Rebecca's hand to meet the side of his face before she ran away without further explanation.

Robert cradled his now throbbing head. "What the hell, Becca!" He shouted. "What about the drinks?" Robert called as Rebecca cut through the crowds of tourists. "Becca! What about the cheese?" Rebecca did not respond and forced Robert to chase after her. "Lord, help me."

The green-eyed lady watched unamused as Rebecca hid within masses. She pursed her lips, slid from the chair, and vanished into the crowds, following behind.

Robert chased after his sister, trailing far behind her as she moved between cars, pushed through crowds, and jumped over one very perplexed dog. He continuously shouted after her, begging her to stop or explain or, at least, slow the fuck down!

But she answered none of his questions.

All she knew was that she needed to get away. The farther she ran, the less tangible the woman's gaze became. With every turn, the firm sensation on her neck became an itch, then a tickle, and finally, the impression became like a faraway breath on her mind.

With one final turn, the sensation vanished. The cool alleyway welcomed Rebecca; for once, she felt unwatched—she felt safe. She leaned into the wall at the far end, embracing the solitude and the cool bricks against her overly energized body. She felt like she was on fire, unable to resist the need to move.

"Becca . . . what the . . ."

Rebecca looked up, seeing her brother appear at the entrance of the alley. He sucked in a deep breath, walked a few steps, and then exhaled far too quickly.

"Oh, God . . . I think . . . I'm gonna hurl." Robert braced himself against a trash can, and the tequila took its revenge.

Rebecca smiled, laughing slightly at her brother. "Sorry, I just—"

A pair of shadows appeared at the alley's entrance as if they formed from the darkness stretched along the bricks. Their large frames blocked the light from the street and drenched the corridor in obscurity.

"Ugh!" Rebecca screamed, grabbing the sides of her head as pain assaulted her body like a spike driven into her head. Rebecca fell to her knees in pain as something repeatedly forced the pain deeper into her skull.

"Robbie. . ." Rebecca croaked. Her lips parted, but her voice muted. She reached for whatever the green-eyed woman had ignited within her, but a voice appeared within the agony and chastised her.

None of that, my sweet child, the chilled voice whispered within Rebecca's mind. *Oh my, she's already waking you up—none of that, my dear. Let me fix that for you. Let us extinguish that flame.*

Like turning off an internal switch, the voice dowsed Rebecca's spark, and exhaustion washed over her.

A chill filled her limbs and spread throughout her body, freezing her mid-motion. Her arms froze outstretched, reaching toward her brother for help. As ice formed in her veins, her vision became blurry. Her once racing heart slowed, beating its death march rhythm slower and slower. Unseen fingers danced along her spine, sending frosty splinters across her body, completing her stillness.

Sweet, sweet child, the voice whispered, *we shall have such fun with each other, relieving you of your darkness with agonizing penance.*

Rebecca fought through the pain, using her last vestige of defiance to call out for her brother.

"Robbie. . . help me."

Robert lifted himself from the wall and saw his fallen sister.

"Rebecca!" He called out, running toward her without noticing the shades who descended behind him.

One rushed toward Rebecca while the other went for Robert. Robert turned. The first attacker's fist flew towards Robert's stomach. He raised his arms to block, but was too slow. An arm smashed into Robert's body and sent him flying into the nearest wall. His head snapped against the wall with a sickening sound.

Crack

A horrible ringing filled Robert's mind as nausea slammed into him. The world twisted and turned, becoming a kaleidoscope of confusion for Robert's addled brain. The men moved like they had no legs. They swarmed Rebecca like they had no bodies.

"Becca, run! Run, Becca!"

The shades turned what Robert thought to be faces but saw only unshaped darkness. Why couldn't he see them? Was the concussion that pressed behind his eyes already so great that it changed the world? Robert shook his head to clear his mind, but it only worsened his eyesight.

Was Rebecca . . . flying?

Robert couldn't distinguish what was real and what his concussion created. He steadied himself, but unconsciousness ate away at the edges of his vision. He didn't have long before he succumbed to his injuries.

A van screeched to a halt at the entrance to the alley. The side door opened, and hands extended, reaching out. The shadows drifted beside Rebecca as she floated, passing Robert without concern for retaliation.

Robert stumbled forward with arms raised.

"Let her go!" Robert lunged forward, punching Rebecca's captor, and . . . missed?

But he didn't miss. He hit the man.

Robert knew he had hit him, but also somehow didn't. Robert fell forward, falling through his enemy as the force of his attack drew him downward. The shadow grabbed Robert before hitting the ground and lifted him into the air while Rebecca floated away.

"Jesus Christ!" Robert screamed as he stared into the unmade face of the thing in front of him, slamming and kicking his limbs against the shadow. Nothing connected. The thing laughed a deep chuckle before it twisted and threw Robert to the opposite end of the alley as if he weighed nothing.

Robert's shoulder *popped* as it took the brunt of the impact.

Pain kept the darkness from consuming Robert's vision as his arm fell limp to his side.

"Becca!"

Robert watched helplessly as the darkness of the van wrapped around his sister, pulling her beneath its inky surface. The kidnappers merged into the obscurity of the vehicle, becoming but a figment of Robert's imagination.

Ache pulsed through Robert's body, urging him to remain still, but his desperation forced him to crawl. His hand dug into the cracked bricks, pulling him forward. The van door slammed shut, and Robert howled an animalistic sound of pain.

"Rebecca ..."

Robert reached out with his good hand, stretching toward the van as it pulled away. Blood dripped down his forehead. The warm fluid drained into his eyes, painting his world red. Robert blinked to clear his vision but could not find the strength to reopen his eyes. The pressure within his skull became too great, and Robert was forced to surrender.

Chapter 3

Robert slipped in and out of unconsciousness.

Voices spoke to him, but he couldn't hear them. Hands prodded him, yet he felt no pain. His eyes were opened, yet he could see nothing. He tried to speak, but no words came from his lips.

Is this Hell?

Was his first thought. It had to be Hell. Every part of Robert hurt; his head, his back, his heart.

Was this my punishment for not saving Becca?

Robert allowed himself to float through the sea of pain, listening to his sister call for help over and over and over again. And no matter how often Robert heard her call, he could not save her.

*   *   *

Robert's eyes opened late the following day, and he could see—partially. His vision was blurry, and the room was unbearably bright, but his eyesight refined the more he blinked. To his surprise, he wasn't in Hell, and he wasn't dead; he was in a hospital room, and everything aggravated his pain. The beeping machines, the blinking fluorescent lights, the weird smells; it all added to Robert's already horrible migraine.

"Hello?" Robert coughed. "Hello?"

He braced himself on the bed railings and lifted himself upright. His left shoulder screamed at the pressure, while his internal injuries begged him to remain still. Robert's hands searched the bed and found a call button. A nurse entered shortly after, accompanied by a police officer.

"Look who's finally awake," the nurse chirped. "Here, let me help you with that." She adjusted the bed, allowing Robert to sit comfortably. "How are we feeling today?"

"Horrible," Robert grumbled. "Where's Rebecca?"

"Who?" The nurse looked at Robert's chart. "Says you were brought in by your lonesome, honey. Is there someone else hurt out there?"

"My . . ." Robert swallowed as the pain hit him again. His eyes were forced shut, and the room spun.

"Let me go get something for that pain. I'll be right back. This is Officer Morrice. She has a few questions for you, but only if you're up for it."

Robert responded, moving just enough so his migraine wouldn't worsen. He listened as the nurse left the room and gently closed the door. His eyes remained shut until the room stopped spinning. Robert opened them and found the officer sitting beside him with a notepad.

"They brought you in pretty banged up. You say there is someone else out there? Rebecca?"

Robert nodded.

"Is that your girlfriend?"

"Sister." Robert coughed.

"Is she hurt?"

"Yes. No. I don't know."

"Why don't you start from the beginning?"

Robert thought of the night and told his story.

The cop kept a straight face as Robert spoke. She didn't comment about the shadow men or how his punches passed through them. Robert hated how ridicules he sounded, but it was the truth . . . at least he thought it was the truth. He knew he was drunk the night prior but not far gone enough to imagine people.

At the end of his story, the officer stood. "If you'll excuse me." She left the room, shutting the door before she talked on her radio.

Robert sunk back into his bed. "They must think I'm some nut job." He turned to the window and stared into the city. Robert looked to the door, hearing the cop's voice raise and lower as she talked. "Please don't send me to the psych ward." Seconds of silence turned into minutes, which felt like hours, as he waited for the officer or the nurse to return. He grew antsy with his time alone, knowing that Rebecca was farther gone every second wasted.

After twenty minutes of alone time, the officer returned with a wheelchair.

"If you would come with me, Robert. My captain wants to get your story down on an official report."

The officer eased Robert into the wheelchair and rolled him down the hallway and into a nearby vacant office.

The room was empty except for a table and a singular chair. The walls were bare, and the room smelled like peroxide. The intense odor infuriated his migraine and made Robert dizzy. The officer placed a notepad and pen on the table.

"Write every detail so we can have this as evidence. The captain will be with you in a few."

Robert nodded, and the officer shut the door. Robert filled eight pages before the door creaked open.

"Hello?" Robert asked as the door opened.

A foul smell seeped into the room and quickly filled the office. Robert gagged at the scent as it overpowered the odor of bleach and peroxide. The door opened wider, and the smell intensified as an obese officer appeared in the doorway. His broad build plugged the doorframe while his gut protruded nearly a foot in front of him like a beachball hid beneath his shirt. The shirt's buttons seemed ready to burst, straining to contain the man's stomach as it bounced and jiggled towards Robert. The horrific scent radiated from him, growing stronger as the officer settled in the opposing chair.

"Robert?" the large man asked.

Robert nodded, attempting not to breathe. His odor was worse than anything Robert had ever smelled, like old socks soaked with curdled milk, left to bake within a locker room.

The chair groaned beneath the officer's weight. His gut pressed into his side of the table and spilled atop a portion of it. Dark curly hair sprouted between the gaps, stretching toward the many stains that covered the shirt. He lifted a hand to scratch his stubbed chin, revealing years' worth of sweat stains. Robert stared in confusion at the officer's tan, pimple-like face and beady eyes. Gel or grease smoothed back the officer's hair.

"I was waiting for Captain Russo," Robert said, trying his best not to inhale through his nose.

"That's me," the large man grumbled, taking a bite of his cream-filled donut. Robert's eyes followed the filling as it dropped onto the captain's gut. The officer showed no care for the missing food or the stain. Just another layer to his unkempt appearance. "They say your sister's missing?"

"Taken," Robert corrected. "She's not missing. Someone took her."

With that remark, Robert launched into his notes and retold the events of the night before. Captain Russo said nothing as Robert told his tale. His eyes remained disinterested and unfocused until Robert mentioned the shadowed men and the weirdness surrounding them, knowing he sounded like a psych patient.

Captain Russo choked on the last bits of his donut and seemed almost surprised at Robert's description. "What did they look like?"

Robert sighed and recapped the last details he had recounted just moments before.

"That will be all we need from you today, Robert," Captain Russo said abruptly, cutting off the end of Robert's story. "We'll take it from here. Usually, these things work themselves out in a few days. People show up all the time." Captain Russo shrugged his bulky shoulders and leaned forward. "Just let me take that notepad as evidence, and we will follow up with you in a few days." Captain Russo reached out, but Robert leaned away from the captain's hand and off-putting words.

"A few days?" Robert repeated with disgust. "Works themselves out? You make it sound like she ran off with her boyfriend or a group of friends. I had the shit beaten out of me, and they threw her into the back of a van. Tell me, Captain, how do you think that would just *work itself out*?"

The captain's dark eyes focused on Robert. The constant pressure behind Robert's eyes intensified, bringing the concussion-like haze back.

"You don't need to worry about this. We got this." The captain's voice became less annoyed and more reassuring, relaxing even. "Why don't you just go back to your hotel? Relax. Go get something to eat. Don't worry about your sister. Put it behind you." Everything Captain Russo said seemed so enticing. "Just leave everything to us. You can trust me. Just go home and *relax*." Captain Russo's tone became carefree as he made his suggestions—like a melody. A lullaby that pushed Robert to sleep.

Just relax, said a voice in Robert's mind.

A peaceful scene played for Robert, one of him lounging in his hotel room with a beer in one hand and a slice of pizza in the other. No worries about his sister, about his parents, about Victoria. It seemed so serene, so peaceful, so . . . *relaxing.*

"Doesn't it sound so much better than worrying about this craziness?" Officer Russo waved his hand as if he could push away Robert's problems. "Just give me that paper, and we can have you on your way. Hey, I'll even give you some donuts for the ride home. Free of charge."

Captain Russo leaned slowly toward Robert, who remained still, trapped in the serene picture painted by the officer.

"That's a good boy—just relax. *Relax.*" The word was like a weighted blanket pinning Robert. "Your sister will be fine."

"My sister will be fine." Robert parroted the captain's words. "My sister. . ." he began to say, but his sluggish mind could not finish the sentence.

"Exactly. Now just forget everything and move on. Don't worry. Just relax. *Relax and forget about last night.*" The captain's hand hovered just an inch from the notepad.

"Last night."

Robert thought of the attack and felt a gentle tug within his mind, and like a sweater, his memory unraveled. Moment by moment, the night came undone. Robert stared deeply into the officer's grotesque eyes as he loomed over Robert, like a creature approaching its sedated prey.

The night before played like a movie in Robert's mind. Each memory came to the screen of his mind's eye and then rapidly erased. Robert felt as each was taken, pulled from his psyche, and forgotten until only the final moment remained; Rebecca screaming out to him for help. His sister's terror radiated through the empty hallways of his mind, begging for Robert to save her, though he could not remember why she was so terrified. Something tugged on the memory as it had pulled the previous ones; Robert held it. He needed to know why she called for help and why he couldn't remember saving her. The moment felt too vital for him to release.

"Robbie!" her voice cried out.

Robert battled the calming haze. The vision of leisure resurfaced, trying to take the place of his sister's terror.

Release Robert. Rest Robert. You Deserve it; the voice urged. The vision was so enticing, so relaxing, so peaceful. Everything Robert wanted in his life. A moment without stress or worry. *Just be at peace, Robert. Accept it. You earned it. Worry only for yourself. Just forget Rebecca. Forget about your sister.*

"No!" Robert screamed, shattering the serene vision. Robert pushed away from the table, throwing the wheelchair back and creating distance between him and Captain Russo's extended hand. Robert stood, fighting through the pain.

"What . . . what did you do to me?" Robert asked, feeling the gaping hole in his memory. Something was gone. An entire night was gone. "Why am I here?" Robert twisted, examining the small office. Pain shot through him, forcing him to double over. "Fuck! Why does

47

everything hurt?" Robert clutched his stomach, feeling like a truck had run him over. He remembered little; that he woke in a hospital bed and had been talking to an officer about something . . . something important . . . what was he talking about?

"Where is my sister?" Robert realized she was not in the room with him. He remembered them drinking early in the afternoon, celebrating their last day on vacation, but after that, everything went black. The night before was an empty space in his mind, filled with his sister's cry for help.

As he looked at Robert, the officer at the table smiled. The relaxing fog pushed at Robert's mind again, but did not break through a second time. Robert felt the captain's intrusive gaze, but the vision of relaxation did not reappear.

"What did you do to me?"

The captain continued to stare.

"*Just trying to help you relaaaax.*" The captain spoke as if music played underneath his words. His gaze intensified. The browns of his irises darkened and spilled into the whites, muddying them until his eyes were wholly the color of filth. Two stagnant mud puddles stared at Robert, craving to drag him beneath their murky surface.

The relaxing sensation that tempted Robert returned tenfold, forcing the tips of his fingers and toes to grow numb. The lack of awareness crept up his legs and arms, causing his body to go limp.

Robert fought the encroaching numbness, holding it off and standing even as Captain Russo focused his filthy eyes on Robert.

A look of surprise broke through Captain Russo's hungry gaze. He leaned back into his chair, placing his hands atop the roundest point of his gut, and laughed.

"What are you?" The captain inquired, searching Robert's face with his repulsive eyes.

"What-what do you mean?"

"What. Are. You?"

"I don't know what you mean." Robert's mind raced, still trying to recall the night before.

"I'll just have to push a little harder." Captain Russo braced himself against the side of the table. "I'll make you give me the answers I crave one way or another."

The numbness washed over Robert's legs, inching its way toward his torso. He felt his legs giving out. He wavered back and forth as he remained standing through sheer will.

"Captain, are you there?" A broken voice called from his radio.

The split second where Captain Russo looked away from Robert was all he needed to escape from the room, run from the floor, and race out into the city. Every step was painful, but fear empowered his body to keep moving. Robert expected to hear sirens or screams of officers behind him as he ran, but the sirens never sounded, and no officer gave chase. Robert ran shoeless through the streets of Vegas, wearing nothing but a hospital gown. It was nearly a mile away before Robert felt safe enough to sit. He collapsed onto a bench, realizing he had held a notepad the entire time.

"Rebecca," he breathed, reading her name throughout the sheets. Her terrified scream echoed in his mind, unattached to any event or thought. He couldn't believe what he had read, but it was his handwriting. But why couldn't he remember any of it?

Every moment was outlandish. Shadow men? Floating? Punches that went through people? Every line seemed more ridiculous than the one before it. He couldn't believe it was true, but what other option did Robert have? He reread the notes several times, hoping that a word or an event would reawaken his memory.

He needed to remember.

And he needed to find his sister.

Chapter 4

Six months.

The time passed in the blink of an eye, yet every day that Rebecca was 'missing' seemed like a lifetime. Robert was the only person who knew she wasn't just missing. It was six months of dead ends, false hopes, and empty promises from the police—police who seemed more interested in Robert than putting any actual workforce toward finding his sister. The interaction with Captain Russo troubled Robert, giving him even more unanswered questions.

"What was he?"

The simple question haunted Robert as he racked his mind for an answer. Robert asked himself the same question: *What* was he? But the *he* that Robert referred to wasn't himself, but the man who stole his memories and erased the night from his mind. Robert couldn't explain how or why he did it, but he knew Captain Russo to be the culprit.

Three days after the incident, Robert's and Rebecca's parents arrived.

Their mother came dressed in black and wailed like a banshee. Any person who consoled her received an altered version of the story—a tale of her missing daughter and the man who'd snatched her. Robert corrected her once, but realized it was safer for his mother to live in her fantasy. His father said nothing. He gave Robert a curt nod after they landed and pretended Robert did not exist. It was abundantly clear that they blamed Robert for his sister's abduction.

Robert later learned that Captain Russo paid for their flight and invited them to assist with the investigation. Against Robert's pleading, his parents went to the police station and returned as entirely different people hours later.

They acted as if Rebecca wasn't missing. His mother seemed more interested in shopping, while his father just wanted to sit and watch television. Robert questioned them about their encounter with the captain. Neither displayed any holes in their memory, only an ambivalence toward Rebecca's disappearance and a desperate need to return home and relax. They booked a return flight for the following morning, spending less than twenty-four hours in the city. Robert's mother purchased him a ticket, requesting him to return and make amends with Victoria.

Robert passionately insisted on staying and searching for Rebecca, especially if they would not help. In retaliation, his parents issued him an ultimatum. If Robert stayed, he would do so without their blessing or support—financial or otherwise.

His parent's lack of concern in finding Rebecca furthered Robert's resolve to stay. So they left as they arrived, judging Robert and his choices.

In the days that followed, Robert received several calls, emails, and text messages from his parents. Each begged him to come home and allow the officers to do their job.

"They know best. Just let them handle everything."

"Just come home and relax; you are working so hard for something already being taken care of."

Their messages were like lines from a poorly written script, empty of emotion, and played on a constant loop for several weeks. Robert wanted to scream at their brainwashed rantings, but he held his tongue. He knew Captain Russo somehow wormed his way into their minds, as he attempted to do with Robert. But unlike Robert, Captain Russo somehow squatted inside his parent's brains, feeding them lines like mindless puppets. When their last message came, Robert felt he could finally begin his search for Rebecca.

* * *

"Robbie, help me!"

In the second between sleeping and waking, Robert thought the last six months were a dream, that he hadn't moved to Las Vegas, that his sister wasn't missing, and that his life wasn't in a constant downward spiral. For just a split second, Rebecca was safe, and he was home.

Most mornings, Robert would wake up, half expecting to see Rebecca in the corner of his room, screaming his name. Some mornings, when the haze would be incredibly thick, he would half see her in the clothes draped on a chair. Robert would see her lounging and laughing at how she startled him awake. But when the fog cleared, he would see only clothes and remember that Rebecca was still gone and Robert was alone.

"It was just a dream," he reassured himself, knowing that admitting it took another chip out of his heart. "It was just a dream." He pushed away the nightmarish sounds and reached for his phone, knowing disappointment followed. The black screen showed his reflection, a sight Robert wished he hadn't seen.

Dark circles surrounded his eyes. His cheeks were both somehow sunken and swollen. The late-night shifts, fast food, and constant drinking affected his skin, leaving it blotchy and red. His hair was longer than he typically kept, curling against his shoulders. Robert tapped the screen, not wanting to look at his reflection any longer.

Robert wasn't sure which was worse, his reflection or the empty voicemail.

"Nothing." Carelessly, Robert tossed his phone towards the end of his bed. It bounced twice and hit the floor. He winced at the sound. "Please don't be broken," he said before he fell back into bed.

An internal battle followed as he began the list of "what-ifs" that plagued his mind. What if the detective found Rebecca and just hadn't called? What if he had news and didn't call Robert? What if he found Rebecca and didn't have the heart or will to tell Robert the bad news? The voice of reason said the detective would reach out to Robert if he found Rebecca or had any leads.

But what if he didn't?

Robert's anxiety outweighed his better judgment. He stretched for his phone, silently thanked God for his unshattered screen, and dialed his detective.

The phone rang once, immediately went to voicemail, announced it was full, and then hung up on him.

Robert sighed and began yet another uninspired day.

The shower was depressingly cold, and the pressure was terrible. Better than usual, but nowhere near what he had back home, remembering what it felt like to have a shower that could scald off the top layer of his skin. He downgraded his closet to a handful of T-shirts and jeans, selling off his suits for rent the second month he was in Vegas.

Once upon a time, Robert was supposed to be at a desk in a dress shirt and tie by eight o'clock. Now, effort was a slightly clean shirt, and if he was at work before noon, he was early. Robert checked his phone at the thought of time and grunted.

"Looks like it's a bear claw kind of morning," Robert said before leaving his apartment and walking across town.

In the six months since Robert unofficially moved to Las Vegas, he'd spent his entire savings, sold all of his valuables, and worked as a bartender in potentially the least frequented bar in all of Nevada. Fortunately, he lived close enough to walk, though it took nearly thirty minutes. But with little money, a car or a daily taxi was entirely out of the question, not that walking was indeed a safe option.

Naked City, as the locals labeled it, was home to drug addicts, prostitutes, crime, and now, Robert. Police were sparse and only showed when it was exceedingly necessary. But it was cheap and cheap was more important than safety.

It shocked Robert how close he lived to civilization. Ten minutes into his walk, the run-down, forgotten buildings transformed into gleaming skyrises and flashy casinos. Homeless men became tourists, and prostitutes changed into celebrity impersonators, posing and working the strip. The space between the two versions of Vegas housed aged hotels, new shops, and one particular coffee shop—his boss's favorite.

"Hello, Robert!" an overly cheerful barista shouted, ignoring the customer who stood at the counter.

Smile back.

Why was it so hard to just smile?

"Morning," Robert responded with a forced grin. The muscles on his face reformed, but everything seemed so unwilling to move into place. If he were being honest, it felt like a grimace, but the barista didn't seem to notice. The employee gawked at Robert, looking over every customer that approached her.

When it was Robert's turn, the barista leaned onto the counter and batted her long lashes. Her blonde hair fell in perfect ringlets across her shoulders. She hung on to Robert's every word as if his order was something deep and meaningful. Her hand softly grazed Robert's as he handed her the money. Her eyes remained on Robert, even as she pulled several bear claws from the case—adding in one free pastry—and filled up two cups of coffee. He accepted both and tucked his change into the tip jar. Her eyes lit up, seeing the tip as a sign of interest, not a compliment of her service.

"Thank you, Robert!" Her high-pitched voice chirped.

Her lips parted, ready to answer a question she hoped Robert would ask.

"Have a good day, Kristie." He quickly turned from the counter and rushed towards the exit, unable to see her smiling face fall.

"See you tomorrow!" She shouted after Robert as he rushed through the front door.

It wasn't that Robert didn't find Kristie attractive. And it wasn't like Robert wasn't lonely most nights in his six-hundred-square-foot apartment. He just felt . . . wrong about the idea of moving on with his life while his sister was still missing.

The thought was enough to make his stomach churn, and his heart fall. His hand massaged the empty place where his watch once sat. A faint tingling, like static electricity, buzzed around his wrist whenever he touched the spot, a constant reminder of his past and the debt owed to his sister. He wished he could stop, but his nerves were no longer under his control. The more he touched his wrist, the more anxious he became and the more memories he conjured.

Stepping into an alley, Robert leaned against the shaded brick and grabbed hold of the wall. If Robert occupied his hands, he couldn't feel the electricity. He inhaled and exhaled, counting his breaths until he no longer thought of his past failures.

"Deep breaths."

It took ten minutes for Robert to release the wall. He looked at his phone and saw the time. His stomach twisted again.

He wasn't just late. He was very late.

"Fuck."

Coffee and pastries would barely compensate for his tardiness, but Robert had little money to spare. Robert hoped his boss would be in a cheerful mood, but even Robert wasn't THAT delusional. But that was hope—delusion with a much prettier label.

Chapter 5

Neglected came to mind when entering the Rusty Nail.

"Nestled within the heart of Vegas. It is a unique hole in the wall, bringing the old city's charm and mixing it with the new. A true forgotten gem," as the ad in the tourist's guidebook read. Yet, the Rusty Nail wasn't a glorified hole in the wall—it *was* the wall, decrepit, forgotten, and in desperate need of a fresh coat of paint. Or torn down, dealer's choice.

"You're late," Nathan grumbled from his corner of the bar. A single-top table buried beneath piles of outdated newspapers and fast-food wrappers. Robert raised the coffee and shook the bag of pastries. Nathan raised a grayed brow, snorting his response before looking back at his newspaper.

Employed for another day. Hooray . . .

Sometimes Robert thought, would being fired really be that bad? But homelessness didn't seem alluring.

Robert crossed the empty bar, dancing between the stacks of newspapers surrounding Nathan's table before placing the coffee and the full bag of bear claws in the singular open space.

Wonder what day he's reading?

On an average day, Nathan was at least two weeks behind on his newspapers.

"If it's important, they'll print it," Nathan had once explained when asked about his collection. On Robert's second day of employment, he attempted to organize the stacks of papers but was swiftly scolded and told to stay away from them if he wanted to keep his job and his hands. Robert was happy to comply and let his boss cling to his expired newspapers like a goblin and their shiny trinkets.

Robert leaned, reading the date on Nathan's current selection.

Last Tuesday.

Robert considered ruining Nathan's read by telling him the "storm of the decade" ended up being a light dusting of rain. A clearer mind warned Robert not to press his luck—especially being already two hours late. Yet, it didn't stop him from making one smart-ass comment about the empty establishment.

"Glad I got here before the rush." Robert looked around the empty bar. "I don't know what you would have done without me."

Nathan gave him the finger.

Robert returned the gesture and started his 'morning' assessment.

He started with the counters and the glasses and then moved to the tables and the trash cans. The bar had twelve tables, two booths, four barstools, and twenty-one chairs, in reality, twenty, since nobody could touch Nathan's chair. Robert wiped down the few bottles of liquor lining the shelves, though not enough time had passed from the night before for dust to settle. Very little had changed, but he still gave it a once over, content to burn at least an hour of the long day before him. The register contained fifteen dollars more than the night before, giving him little hope of any tips in the coming shift.

It astonished Robert that the bar could pay its monthly bills and somehow afford Robert full-time. Rarely were two seats occupied at a time; any more than that, and it would be considered a *crazy* night. Tourists occasionally stumbled far enough into Naked City and found their way to the Rusty Nail. Usually searching for something 'special,' but that was not something Nathan allowed. Robert calmly escorted those tourists out, knowing Nathan had a bat next to this table that he wasn't afraid to use.

This meant that the bar was relatively empty ninety-eight percent of the time, and Robert had concerns about affording rent one hundred percent of the time.

Robert waited behind the register, staring at the occasional person who walked past the windows. He could tell the difference between locals and tourists by how they walked. Tourists constantly explored their surroundings, while locals ignored them. An hour into his shift, Robert gave up luring any potential customers with a wave through the front windows and retrieved a pen and a stack of napkins.

Between the periods without customers, Nathan grunted and snorted at his paper, and Robert returned to an old hobby. During

Robert's first day of employment, Nathan complained Robert needed to be productive if he was on the clock. So, Robert replaced his doodling with something far worse: small talk. Nathan lasted thirty minutes before he ordered Robert to return to his "little doodles and leave him alone."

In a weirdly therapeutic way, Robert felt calmed by the sketching. It was a way to scratch the empty spot in his memory. He let the pen move across the napkin while his mind flitted from one thought to another. He couldn't tell if the sketches were imaginary, real, or just some twisted combination. But he continued to sketch every day, hoping one of his images would return his memory.

Yet, not a single image brought more than a headache and frustrated grumbling.

By the end of the day, Robert collected a pile of faceless doodles and $4.52 in tips. Nathan vanished into his upstairs apartment just before eleven o'clock, leaving Robert alone with an empty bar and his thoughts. He considered closing early, but the idea of sitting alone at home was decidedly worse than sitting at work.

"Another day. Another four dollars." Robert sighed. He checked his phone. "And no call."

Robert gathered his sketches and tossed them into the trash, finding no reason to add them to the collection underneath the bar, and cleaned the underside.

"You open?" a female voice asked as the front door creaked open.

"Yes, ma'am," Robert answered, slapping on his best customer service smile before standing.

"Perfect!" The woman opened the door and glided inward. Her long legs did quick work, crossing the space in four rapid strides. The theme of the woman's outfit was unmissable; her heels, top, and makeup were all the same shade of purple. Her mass of black curls bounced in time with her steps before she slid into the stool in front of Robert. She collapsed onto the counter, stretching her arms to the side. "It has been such a looooooong night, and I just need a place to relax. I'm not keeping you open, am I?" The customer lifted herself from the counter, noticing the space.

"Not at all."

"Oh, good." She smiled. Her deep purple lips formed dimples on her cheeks as her lips stretched to her purple shadowed eyes. A slight sheen of sweat covered the woman's dark skin. She raised a hand and searched within her curls for a particular one to twist while she thought.

"And what can I get you tonight?"

The customer looped her curl around her finger, twisting it rapidly and releasing it. "What's the house specialty?" Robert looked over his shoulder at the pathetic display. Nathan pushed back the most recent alcohol shipment, which meant that Robert barely had the means to make the simplest drinks.

"Well, we have vodka, vodka on the rocks, and then vodka with ice. I prefer the vodka with ice, but that's just my opinion." Robert leaned down and lifted a large bottle from beneath the counter, turning the label away so she would not see the generic brand. She tapped her chin in a playful yet quizzical manner as she thought. The corner of Robert's lips twitched.

"I think I'll have the vodka with ice, but can you hold the ice?" she asked, winking an overly shadowed eye. Their eyes connected, and Robert couldn't look away.

She's cute.

The thought felt wrong, but Robert couldn't help but notice it, especially as she continued to smile. She had a magnificent smile. Her dark skin and purple lips framed her perfect rows of teeth.

"One vodka, hold the ice." Robert pulled a glass from underneath, poured it a little heavier than usual, and slid it to the customer. She leaned into the glass and took the tiniest of sips before releasing a horrific gasp and cough. She shook her hands in the air as her throat burned from the taste. The tugs at Robert's lips grew too strong to deny, and he smiled. And it wasn't his fake one. "Not a drinker?"

"Trying."

Robert scoffed. "But why?"

"Everyone says life's more fun with it."

"Who cares what others think?"

"Me, I guess." The woman took another careful sip and shook her head. Her large curls bounced and slapped the sides of her face. The thimble worth of alcohol showed its effects as a rosiness flooded her cheeks. "This is your favorite?"

Robert nodded.

"God, I can only imagine what else you enjoy." The sentence ended with a sexual purr that ran up Robert's spine. He could feel a part of himself waking—a part that had been dormant for months and enjoyed how she looked at him. He waited for the tensing of his stomach, but his anxiety seemed to slumber in her presence.

She nursed another sip, shaking as the alcohol burned down her throat. Robert chuckled as she shook longer than the first time.

"I don't know how people drink that shit." She pushed the drink away and stretched her arms towards the ceiling. Robert couldn't look away as her purple blouse tightened around her breasts. She stretched further. Her blouse pulled tighter, and Robert's pants followed suit.

Fuck . . .

She caught Robert looking. He turned quickly, returning the bottle to the shelf as the pink flush turned red. "You here all alone all night?"

"Oh no, you just missed a whole crowd of people. I'm surprised you didn't see them when you came in," Robert joked before turning back around.

"Oh really? A whole crowd of people? The street looked pretty empty to me."

"Really?" Robert asked with a feigned look of shock. "That's so weird."

Seeing the water ring on the bartop, Robert squatted to retrieve a napkin. From below the bar top, Robert innocently watched as the woman took the glass, swallowing half its contents and sighing into the glass.

What in the world?

Robert rose slowly, his brows knitted in confusion. Awareness flashed in her eyes, realizing Robert noticed her lack of response and reacted speedily.

"Ewww!" Her squeal of disgust seemed off. She flapped her hands and shook her head like before, but now it seemed less endearing and more forced. "Wasn't expecting that."

"Yeah." Robert paused, unsure of how to act now. "Hits you when you least expect it," Robert said as he turned back to the till. "Is that all you are going to need—"

"So, are you from around here?" She asked, interrupting Robert's attempt to move the evening to a close.

"Is anyone really from here?" Robert answered, feeling suddenly uncomfortable with how she stared at him. Where once Robert saw the gleam in her eye as enticing, now it looked dishonest. "What about you?" he asked, turning his attention back toward his single customer.

"I'm from," she twirled her fingers in the air, "around." Before Robert could ask once more if she needed anything else, she asked him another question. "So, what brought you here?"

Robert remained silent, choosing not to answer the question.

"Business? Love? Family?" She offered. Robert's eyebrow twitched at the word family, and she proceeded. "Family it is—"

"Is there something I can help you with, ma'am?"

The customer sucked on her teeth.

"Dez," she corrected. Disdain replaced the light tone in her voice.

"Excuse me?"

"My name is Dez. Ma'am sounds just so . . . *old*," she said, wrinkling her nose at the word.

"Well, Dez, is there something I can help you with? You seem more interested in asking questions than drinking." Robert motioned to the room. "This is a bar, not a therapy session."

Dez tilted her head to the side and reexamined Robert. Without speaking, she took hold of her drink and swallowed every droplet.

No shakes. No waving. No wincing.

So it was just for show?

"Just trying to make conversation. Are you always so prickly?" Dez questioned as she dragged the empty glass back and forth on the bar top.

"Only when I'm asked questions I don't want to answer."

"How about you fill up my glass, grab one for yourself, and we can really get to know one another?" Innuendo filled Dez's every syllable. Her words wrapped around Robert, dragging him like a fish towards the fisherman.

When once Robert had felt relaxed in her presence, now he felt stiff. His nerves returned with a vengeance, knotting his initial interest with his nerves. Why was she playing with him?

Robert tightened his grip on the bar top and steeled his eyes.

She's just another liar.

Dez waved the glass in front of him. "So why don't you—"

Robert snatched the glass and threw it into the sink, shattering it. Shards flew into the air.

Dez blinked once. Then twice as she stared at him.

"A little dramatic, don't you think?"

"I think it's time for the bar to close up, *Dez*." Robert spat her name like a curse.

"Don't you want me to pay?" Dez asked, teasing him with the potential of money. "I would hate to leave without giving you a tip for your *superb* service."

"I'll manage." Robert met Dez's gaze.

"Very well." Dez nodded, slid from her chair, and walked towards the door. Midway, she laughed. Her condescending chuckle tightened Robert's back and, honestly, pissed him off.

"What the hell is so funny?"

Dez paused at the door and turned back to Robert, throwing her curls over her shoulder. Her once large flirtatious eyes were now cold and manipulative, amused by Robert's anger.

"Nothing," Dez taunted. "I just thought for someone with so many questions; you would have been open to answering a few."

Shock absorbed Robert's anger. "What did you just say?"

Dez gripped the handle and opened the door, acting as if she had not just dropped a bomb on Robert's life.

"Wait!" Robert rushed from behind the counter, running toward Dez. "Please!"

"Too late," Dez mocked, stepping outside. "Good luck finding your sister, Robert."

"I said wait!" Robert stretched for Dez, grabbing hold of her wrist as she stepped out into the street. The air turned chilly as she twisted back into the bar. Dez moved quickly, outmaneuvering Robert's attempt to stop her. She spun around him, extending her leg and hitting right behind his knees. Robert slammed into the ground before he even realized he was falling.

"Do. Not. Touch. Me."

Robert gasped for air. His body tingled pins and needles.

"If you want answers, my card is on the bar." The door slammed behind her.

Robert stood and hobbled to the front and opened the door. His back tightened with every movement. The cool night air blew past him, bringing the stench of smoke and trash. Robert searched both directions for Dez; she had vanished.

With shoulders slumped and body aching, Robert returned to the bar and locked the door behind him. The pain of the impact somehow settled around the empty spot in his memory. He touched the back of his head and felt the beginning of a lump.

Dez's black business card sat on the bar top like a beacon in the night. His fingers itched as he lifted the card and ran his thumb over the embossed lettering.

"Queen of Hearts Dance Club," Robert read, falling into the empty barstool. It wasn't a lot, but it was the first genuine lead, and he would take it seriously. "Who are you, Dez?"

He then realized Dez knew his name and Robert had never given it.

Chapter 6

"Fuck. Fuck. Fuck. Fuck," Robert cursed, running down the sidewalk. He clutched a paper bag of Nathan's favorite tacos in one hand and a single cup of coffee in the other. His stomach growled at their smell, but the tacos weren't lunch; they were a bargaining chip Robert would use to satisfy his boss and keep him from getting fired, or at the very least, reamed out.

Since Robert started working at the bar, there was an unspoken understanding between Robert and Nathan about his repeated lateness. An hour or two was potentially forgivable with the proper offering of coffee and pastries. On the other hand, three hours pushed beyond even Robert's negotiating abilities.

Just outside the bar, Robert brushed a hand through his curly hair, setting it into place. His short hair would be more unmanageable. Some days, he considered taking the bar's scissors and chopping off the length, but he had liked it—even if it annoyed him most days.

"Just act casual. You can do casual."

Nathan would react faster if Robert acted like he was late. There was a chance that Nathan would overlook the time, a slight, minuscule chance, but a chance. Robert barely crossed the threshold when his boss shot daggers at him from behind the bar.

"You're late." A wet rag smacked Robert's chest and fell into his open hand. Silently, Robert dropped his offerings off at Nathan's table and stepped behind the bar.

"I know," Robert responded as he popped open the till and counted the cash. There wasn't a single new bill within the register, but that didn't stop him from counting a second time to keep himself busy while Nathan found the food. Robert listened for the taco's crinkling wrapper, and when he did, Robert calmed. Nathan took several large bites and sipped on the coffee, studying Robert as he worked. Robert kept his eyes on any available surface, not wanting to start a conversation surrounding his lateness.

"One day, you're not gonna be able to save yourself with a bear claw or a taco, Robert," Nathan said.

"I know," Robert repeated.

"I am patient, Robert, but even I have my limits."

Doesn't mean I won't keep testing them.

Robert was beyond thankful for Nathan, and his patience, being far more understanding than Robert deserved with the time he missed or took off. Robert knew his boss's grace and patience— already in short supply—would run out one day. And when it did, Robert wouldn't be able to blame anyone but himself.

In a sense, one hour was forgivable, but three hours was disrespectful. Robert hadn't realized how late he stayed up, researching the Queen of Hearts Dance Club. From its *lengthy* public record, he found several failed health inspections, multiple attempts to condemn the building, and more than a handful of assault charges from dancers at the club. It didn't seem like anything out of the ordinary— just a run-of-the-mill dirty dance club. But the internet could only tell Robert so much. A local could offer the insight that Robert wanted. He just needed *his local* to be in a mood to be conversational.

The afternoon proceeded as usual, with few words exchanged. Robert silently swept the floors and cleaned the bar while Nathan leisurely ate through his tacos and drank his coffee. Robert anxiously waited for the right moment when Nathan would crumble the paper bag and toss away the empty coffee cup. The two-minute window when Nathan was at his 'happiest,' which was still grumpy at best.

"Have you ever heard of the Queen of Hearts Dance Club?" Robert asked with the most neutral tone he could muster.

"Why?" Nathan grunted.

"Just had a customer last night leave her card, telling me to come and visit." Robert paused, waiting for Nathan to jump in with a comment, and when he didn't, Robert pressed with another question. "Is it worth going?"

"It's a titty bar. You wanna see titties and don't mind getting an infection, then have at it." Nathan looked over his newspaper, noticing how Robert repeatedly wrung the towel. "Why so curious?"

Nathan placed his paper on the table and directed his full attention toward Robert.

Lord, help me.

Nathan Rachofsky loved three things: his bar, his coffee, and his newspaper. If he were to put any of the three aside and give his full attention, there was definitely something about the bar that Nathan knew and was not telling Robert.

Robert weighed his thoughts and considered telling Nathan about his strange encounter with Dez, how she knew about his sister, and how she alluded to knowing what had happened to her.

Though Robert felt his secret was best kept by one.

"No reason. She came in. We chatted a bit, and she left her card. I just wanted to know what I was getting myself into if I followed through with meeting her." Robert shrugged, attempting to sound aloof. It wasn't exactly a lie, but it wasn't exactly the truth. Nathan scowled at him as he silently judged Robert's answer before picking up his paper.

"Don't say I didn't warn you. And don't think you get any days off if you catch anything," Nathan warned before he returned to his newspaper, and their agreeable silence resumed.

The slow pace of the day allowed Robert's mind to drift. The single customer and the lack of conversation did little to keep Robert's mind busy as he washed and rewashed the counter. When nighttime arrived, Robert was confident that he had taken at least two layers off the bar top with his overenthusiastic approach to cleaning.

"I'm going to bed," Nathan announced near midnight. He collected two more papers from his stack, the previous week's Monday and Wednesday, and went up the back stairs to his apartment.

Robert listened to his boss's feet shuffle in the upstairs' apartment, anxiously waiting for them to cease. The sounds ended an hour and a half later, and Robert closed the bar.

"It's not like anyone was going to come in anyway," Robert said, justifying his choices as he locked the front door and turned off the lights. He searched the location online and groaned at the distance. The Rusty Nail was off the beaten path, but the Queen of Hearts tucked itself much further into Naked City than most would deem safe to walk—Robert included.

Which meant that Robert had only had one option—he had to order a freaking taxi.

Chapter 7

Robert had $27.43, and the taxi cost $23.00.

The driver sneered at the lack of tip before Robert exited the cab. He wished he could have given something to the driver, but he couldn't walk into a club without a single dollar. Robert waved goodbye to the driver before he turned to the large concrete building.

"Homey." Robert joked, trying to calm his nerves.

A large red neon sign flashed along the rooftop, reading the Queen of Hearts Dance Club. Flickers of scarlet lit the empty parking lot. The building had no windows and a single metal door. Spray-painted graffiti images of dancing men and women decorated the gray concrete. The club honestly looked equally abandoned as the surrounding structures, but a man stationed at the front door proved otherwise. The bouncer sat on a barstool beside the front door. He cut his tiny eyes toward Robert and rose from his chair, moving in front of the door. He inflated his chest and flexed his biceps as he crossed his arms.

Just pretend you belong.

As Robert's father had told him, act as if you belong, and people will believe it.

"Hey, how's it going?" Robert asked, slightly too cheerfully, as he stopped near the bouncer. He had hoped the man would step aside if Robert walked close enough, but he stood resolute in his stance. The bouncer was an unsettling sight from far away, but was damn near frightening up close. When paired with the dozens of scars scattered around his face, his sloped forehead, bald head, and prominent underbite created an appearance that few would consider testing. The bouncer scowled at Robert, pushing out his bulbous chest. His black shirt stretched across his pectorals and looked ready to rip.

"Invitation only," the bouncer growled.

"Oh . . . um . . . I got an invitation ." Robert stuttered. The bouncer raised an eyebrow in jest. "It was from Dez. About this tall. Lots of curls. Can take a man out at the knees" Robert hoped her name or description would sound familiar.

Instead, the man laughed at Robert.

"Doubtful." The bouncer snickered. He looked Robert over and let out another huff of disbelief. "You're too scrawny for her. Come back when you get a real invite." Robert remained in his spot as the bouncer stared and laughed. His laugh quickly died when Robert didn't immediately obey him. The guard's forehead creased as he stepped toward Robert, intimidating Robert with his size. "Are we going to have a problem?"

"No, no problem," Robert said as he pushed his hands into his pockets and searched for the card that Dez had left. "Hold on, I know it's—aha! Here she left me this the other night," Robert said as he produced the small black card and watched the bouncer's aggressive face turn a deep shade of green. If he hadn't already looked like an ogre, the green-tinted skin made it undeniable.

"I'm so sorry, sir!" The bouncer scrambled to the side of the door. His domineering appearance dissolved, transforming him into an oversized puppy in a blink. "Here, let me get that for you." The fearful bouncer firmly gripped the handle and opened the door. Robert swore he heard the handle crunch beneath the man's grip, but the thought was ridiculous. The bouncer looked strong, but couldn't be *that* strong.

Robert gazed down the entryway. Lights from the main room shot down the hallway, illuminating the discarded bottles and trash gathered at the walls' base. The hallway looked just about as welcoming as the bouncer. With raised eyebrows and a forced smile, Robert stepped through the entrance. The carpet squished beneath Robert's feet.

Let that be beer.

"Please don't tell Ms. Dez I gave you any problems."

Fear filled the bouncer's eyes. Robert nodded. Relief fell over the muscular man. Robert knew firsthand what Dez could do, but seeing the man quiver in his boots proved there was even more to the Dez than sturdy legs and a love of purple.

But why were people so afraid of her? That was the question.

The smell of beer and cigarettes grew heavier as the door closed, sealing off Vegas's 'fresh air.' Robert followed the music, walking into the main room.

The number of people inside surprised Robert. Dozens were scattered around the room, occupying the stage, the tables, and the couches. A bar dominated the main wall, and the stage took the corresponding one. Customers sat atop the stained, ripped furniture that lined two small walls. Scantily clad men and women paraded and danced around the room. Employees took their position on the laps of the men and women, grinding or taking orders. Robert searched the club, expecting to see Dez among the dancers or servers, but could not find her bouncing curls or cutting voice.

Robert wandered further, continuing his search. He motioned to a server, but they gave his plain shirt and ripped jeans a once-over and continued walking. Robert tried two other servers, both responded in the same manner. It wasn't until Robert set his eyes on the young, overly tanned bartender did someone willingly make eye contact with him. The bartender lifted himself from the counter and beckoned Robert toward him with a single finger. The bartender coyly played with his short, bleached blond hair as Robert sat on a nearby stool.

"What can I get you, handsome?" The bartender asked as he leaned on the bar top. Blue and pink gems covered the man's chest like a beautiful coral, growing around his pectorals and the angles of his face. The man's cologne swaddled Robert, hiding him from the stench of cheap perfume and spilled beer. It was woodsy and flowery, wild and enticing. The bartender reached out and stroked the underside of Robert's jaw. "Maybe something off the menu?" The bartender's fingers were like live wires, sending an electric current through Robert with every touch. His fingers flourished down Robert's chest and went to his bicep. He squeezed it tightly. "Firm."

A redness traveled from Robert's neck and up to his ears, and his pants tightened. The compliment embarrassed him, but Robert wanted to hear another. Robert flexed his bicep within the bartender's grasp and received a gasp of excitement.

"Oh," he purred, "Even better."

The bartender, who smiled so sweetly at him, leaned even closer. His breath hit Robert's face, and even that smelled intoxicating. His decorated face was perfectly shaped: round cheeks sat high on his square jaw, extra full lips that pouted permanently, and a pair of blue eyes like an imp. A single earring hung from his right ear, with a blue gemstone that matched his eyes. Though Robert was straight, he couldn't deny that the bartender was attractive and that he enjoyed how the bartender touched him.

"So, what can I get you? Drink? Dance?" The bartender leaned toward Robert and whispered, "I'll give you one free of charge." He winked an eye surrounded with pink eyeshadow. "Maybe something a little better for the body?" The bartender gave Robert a once over and bit his plump bottom lip. He was hungry, and Robert was aching to be touched.

"Dez?" The words slipped from Robert's lips before he could stop them.

The bartender pulled away and released Robert's arm. The connection they had snapped as quickly as it formed, taking the attraction Robert felt for the bartender with it.

Robert shook his head, throwing away the thoughts of kissing another man, confused by them.

What the fuck was that?

Robert adjusted the tightness in his pants. "How did you—"

The illusion of the sultry bartender evaporated as he let out a moan of annoyance.

"Why would you want to talk to her?" The bartender whined, interrupting Robert's question. Robert tried to figure out how to respond, but the bartender spoke again. "Please tell me she didn't set another car on fire? I swear she's going to bankrupt this place with claims." The bartender turned and bent low into a cabinet behind him, revealing a shiny pink thong buried between a pair of pert, round butt cheeks. The bartender peeked over his shoulder, catching Robert's stare, and gave him a wink in appreciation.

Robert's cheeks returned to their shade of red. Robert couldn't explain it. Why couldn't he stop looking at this man?

"How much was the car worth?" the bartender asked as he flipped open a binder full of blank checks. Torn edges of previously cut checks filled the spine; this was not the first time the bar paid for damages caused by Dez.

"Oh, she didn't set my car on fire," Robert stammered, realizing that he had never corrected the male when he offered to pay.

"What did she do then? Sink your boat? Medical bills?" The bartender listed several other rather expensive options, and Robert declined each. But after an excessive amount of no's, a gleam formed in the bartender's eye. "Ohhhh." He slammed the checkbook shut, grinning a knowing smile. "So you're the guy who comes to make sure everything still works down there." He darted his eyes toward Robert's crotch.

Robert shook his head vigorously. "No! You got the wrong idea! I was—"

"Well then, what is it? It's not like she has friends."

"She told me to meet her here so we can . . . talk," Robert said, selecting his words carefully. The bartender's lips twitched as he smirked at Robert.

"Oh, 'to talk,' huh?" He air quoted. "Well, I'll be right back." The bartender laughed as he walked behind a swinging door.

"What the hell am I getting myself into?" Robert leaned his back into the bar, staring at the patrons and the employees. He smiled at a passing server. She almost stopped to speak with him, but was quickly rushed away by a dancer. They whispered at each other and gave him a look that made him feel like a dead man walking.

Is she really that scary?

A finger tapped Robert's shoulder; he turned and found the bartender. "She said she's ready to see you. I just told her she had a visitor; I didn't wanna ruin the surprise. Just walk through that door and down the hallway. Her office is the only door on the right, and don't worry." The bartender winked. "She doesn't bite . . . hard."

"Thanks." Robert dug a hand in his pocket, withdrawing a few singles. "I don't have much, but—"

The bartender waved away Robert's tip. "On the house. Honestly, I'm damning you more than helping you here."

"Thanks," Robert said again before walking through the backroom door.

The back hallway was the cleanest part of the building. The walls were still messy. Old flyers and fraying pictures sat atop each other like a chaotic wallpaper. The decades of stains covered the carpet, but it at least did not squish. At the sound of crying, Robert stopped walking.

Is Dez crying?

Robert's answer came in the form of a woman with straight brown hair in pink lingerie. She ran from the office with hands covering her weeping face. She bumped into Robert and didn't stop, rushing through the door into the main room.

"And if I find you sleeping on the couches again, you won't have to worry about keeping those extensions clean cause I'll rip them from your head!" Dez screamed.

Ah. She's the one causing the crying.

That tracks.

Peering around the corner, Robert found Dez seated in the most lavish purple chair he had ever seen. It was overly plush and lined with silver accents. It looked more like a throne than an office chair.

Dez's familiar long curls were straightened and slicked back into a high ponytail that laid heavily on her chest. She stroked it with one hand while she thumbed through a stack of papers with the other, already moving on from the crying employee. A purple suit jacket and clean white blouse replaced her bra-like shirt. Her lips and eyes remained the same shade of purple, styled less playfully than before. Harsh lines and aggressive angles spread from her eyes, making her already fierce gaze seem more intimidating. Dez's sharp brows tilted as she lifted another paper and scowled.

Perfect time to interrupt.

With a breath of confidence, Robert walked forward and rapped on the doorframe.

"What now?" Dez snapped, cutting her eyes from the paper. Her eyes widened at the sight of Robert. The look of annoyance dissolved into shock and then settled somewhere near self-satisfaction. She knew she would see Robert; it was just a matter of time. She crumpled the topmost paper on her desk and tossed it aside, missing the trash can entirely and adding to the pile surrounding the bin.

"Hello, Dez." Robert walked into her office, observing the cluttered space around them.

Folders and files littered the floor and covered most table space. The walls were layers of invoices and overdue bills. However, the most peculiar piece of the office was the shelf lined with Beanie Babies, each arranged carefully and posed. A layer of dust covered most items, but the Beanie Babies were pristine.

She doesn't look like the cuddly type.

"Well, well, well, that didn't take long." Dez fell back into her plush purple armchair. "Please take a seat." She motioned toward the folding chair opposite her. "Couldn't stay away now, could you?" Her sensual smile curved upward, turning from taunting to straight malicious.

"Were you lying about my sister? Do you know what happened to her?" Robert asked as he settled into his chair.

Dez laughed.

The sound was a mixture of soft wind chimes and nails as they scraped across a chalkboard—a mix of amusement and malice.

"Well, I *know* what happened to her, and I *know* a few things about her, but I am most curious about *you*," Dez said, emphasizing her selection of words.

"Me?" Robert asked in disbelief. "What about me?" Dez examined her nails before returning them to her desk. They rapped against its surface as she thought of her answer.

"Well, you are quite the peculiar one, Robert. You remember what happened the night your sister was taken?"

Robert nodded.

"Tell me about it."

Robert rolled his eyes at her request, feeling as though she already knew the answer to her question. Obediently, Robert spoke of the night, recounting every detail he had scribbled down on that pad of paper. Dez sank into her cushioned chair and listened silently, tapping her nails throughout Robert's story as she patiently waited for him to end. Robert watched her as he spoke, looking for some hint of compassion or surprise, but she gave neither.

"And now, I live here and hope the detective I hired finds something. Honestly, when you said something about her the other night—that was the real first lead I've had. The first one that gave me some hope that she was still out there. Somewhere." His face fell. "For all I know, she's not even here anymore. Maybe she's dead."

Robert couldn't believe he had finally said the word: dead.

The word that sat on the tip of his tongue during every moment of every day. Every time he thought of his sister, the word moved soundlessly through his mind, tempting him to speak it into reality. Robert denied its existence—of the possibility. Yet, no matter how often Robert fought the thought, it always resurfaced when he was at his darkest. And now, after saying it, he knew there was a possibility—a strong possibility—that his sister could be dead.

Releasing the word into the air took what life Robert had within him. For the first time, Robert did not feel heavy with emotion. He felt empty.

She could be dead.

Silence settled between them while Robert fell deep into his thoughts. Dez gave him the time to think and sulk, embracing the quiet. After several minutes passed, Dez spoke.

"What about the morning after they attacked you?"

"Huh?"

"The morning after the attack. When you woke up in the hospital, what happened then?"

"I don't understand."

"When you met with the captain—it seems like everything didn't go smoothly. Did something happen? Was there a reason you aren't seeking help from the police?"

"What does it matter?"

"Well, it seems interesting that you would care so deeply for your sister but not use a legion of people willing to help. That is . . . unless you thought they wouldn't be helpful." Dez pursed her lips. "But why would you think that?"

Robert hardened his gaze. "Why are you so invested in knowing what happened?"

Dez paid no attention to Robert as he asked his question; instead, she examined her nails and flicked an invisible piece of dirt from beneath her claws.

"I'm not."

"Liar," Robert accused. Anger quickly filled the hollow space in his chest as he stared at Dez. She lifted her gaze, and emotion finally showed. Robert's remark amused her, while her smirk infuriated him. "You clearly have some interest in it. Why else would you find me, cryptically tell me you can find my sister, and then ask me these questions? Why else would you do all that unless you are interested?"

"Did I say I know how to find your sister?" Dez faked a look of surprise. "That is news to me. I know I was drinking, but I think I would remember saying something so *outlandish*."

"I'm tired of these games!" Robert's voice raised. "Tell me what you know, and leave me the hell alone!" Robert's anger fueled his outburst, but the anger simmered quickly, and he felt empty once more. "Please. Just tell me."

Dez leaned into her chair, examining Robert. Her look was not that of a hunter studying its food but one that had met a challenger and was intrigued by what it offered.

"You have some bite to you, Robert. It is unexpected and enjoyable."

"Why did you come to my bar last night?" Robert asked. "You sought me out. Was it just to play with me? Break me even more? Taunt me?"

Dez made a show of blinking her purple shadowed eyes, slowly and knowingly. "My *business partner* has his reasons for needing to meet with you and find your sister. I was instructed to ensure you were real and not some red herring."

"Your business partner? Who the fuck is that?"

"Me," a boyish voice answered.

Robert looked over his shoulder and found the young bartender leaning against the door's threshold, extending one overly tanned leg seductively.

"You?"

The bartender dropped his leg and slapped his face. "Le gasp!"

Dez made a hurling noise from her desk. Evidently, she wasn't a fan of his games.

"Who doesn't love a good plot twist?" He pointed his foot at Robert's face. "I had a feeling it was you when you walked into my club and asked about Dez—I was sure of it! I have been dying to talk."

The bartender pulled himself from the doorframe and entered the office, moving his attention toward Dez. "You may want to go ready the girls. Kitty's on her way over, and we have little time to prepare the place."

Dez's calm exterior shifted to annoyance as she stood. Robert noted the visible lines between her brows as she walked around the desk.

"Infernal fires burn me," she cursed before focusing on Robert. "I leave you in the capable hands of Luke." Dez's lips parted as she had something else to say, but a loud crash stole her attention, and she marched towards it. "Nadia! If I come out there and find one more table broken, I will hang you by your big toes and make. . ." the blaring music on the opposite side of the door overpowered Dez's threat as she entered the main room.

Robert didn't know Nadia but hoped she knew to run for her life.

The bartender entered the office and plopped down in the oversized purple chair. The chair overwhelmed his body, looking more like a boy playing in his father's office than a business owner. He crossed his legs atop a stack of papers and grinned like the Cheshire Cat.

"So, what do you know about the Bible?" Luke asked.

Chapter 8

"The Bible?" Robert asked, perplexed at such a random question. "Like Old Testament, Noah on the ark, Jesus Bible?"

"The one and only. But less fire and brimstone and more creation. What do you know about the Garden of Eden?"

"What does the Bible have to do with anything?"

"Humor me."

Robert racked his brain and spouted a combination of what he learned from Sunday school and Hollywood.

"Um, Adam and Eve are in a garden made by God. Eve gets tricked into eating an apple. Gets her and Adam kicked out, and then they have kids, and a few hundred years later, Jesus shows up."

Luke laughed at Robert's shortened tale.

"Yes, that's the Sunday school version." Luke gave a friendly grin before pulling his legs into the chair and resting his chin on his knees. "What if I was to tell you there was a little more than that?"

"Okay. . . I'm still not seeing how this relates to me."

"As I said, humor me."

Robert sighed.

Luke coughed a few times as if he were preparing for a monologue. "Let me give you a less than friendlier version of the story. Eve wasn't tricked into eating the apple. She willingly ate the tree. She—"

"Why does this matter?"

"No, no, no, no questions or interruptions." Luke pressed a finger to his lips and began his story once again. "Now, where was I?" Luke's eyes glossed over as he stared through Robert. His irises moved from side to side, as if reading something unseen.

"The apple?" Robert suggested.

"Ah, yes!" Luke's eyes focused. "Thank you, the apple. Yes, Eve willingly ate the apple," Luke began again. "With a single bite, she gained the world's knowledge and the freedom and independence she longed for."

"But I thought the Devil tricked her?"

"Yes, some people believe Lucifer persuaded her to eat from the tree—and I said no questions—but it wasn't persuasion that made her eat it. It was love." The blues in Luke's enormous eyes became like the ocean at the word love, shimmering with the intensity of the word, lit as if a sun hid behind the crystal blue irises.

"It was an emotion that Eve had never experienced before. Love. Passion. Fulfillment. To be treated like an equal. She did not know what love was before Lucifer showed it to her. God and Adam taught her to obey, to listen, to serve, while Lucifer showed her how to live. Eve found something in Lucifer that made her feel wanted. They spent hundreds of years discussing their love and future beneath that tree. A life outside of the Garden. Freedom. Children." The air around Luke warmed as if their love radiated from him. "He offered her freedom from an eternity of servitude to *Adam* and *God*." He spat the words as if they soured on his tongue. "Do you know what they called the tree in the Garden of Eden?"

"The Tree of Good and Evil."

Luke wobbled his head back and forth, weighing Robert's answer.

"Some translations, yes. But the proper title is the Tree of Knowledge. One bite would give someone the ability to choose. To see the good and the bad within the world and make a choice. So she took it, and the world became clear to her." He flashed his hands beside his face. "She was Judy Garland going from black and white to technicolor. She was ready to run away with Lucifer and escape the Garden's prison, but Adam followed her. Being the pathetic sheep of a man, he ate the core of her apple and drew the eye of the Almighty." Luke's disposition quickly changed, and the glow of his eyes dimmed. His shining blue eyes darkened like a storm swallowed the peaceful ocean.

"He ruined it. He ruined . . . everything!" Luke shouted, surprising Robert with his emotion. "It was his stupidity that caused Eve to be caught. It was his fault that she and Lucifer were torn from one another. It was his fault that Eve was banished to the Wasteland!"

His eyes darkened. Robert couldn't tell if it was a trick of the light or if they were special contacts, but Luke's light blue eyes transformed, becoming a whirlpool of spinning blues around his pupils. "She was forced to wander with Adam for the rest of her life. Living with only a memory and a wish of what her life could have been. Forced to be forever bound to a man who saw her as nothing but his property."

Luke turned away from Robert as tears formed in the corner of his eyes. He took a deep breath, reaffirming his control over his emotions. Luke blinked; two heavy tears rolled down his cheeks, streaking Luke's makeup.

Why was he so emotional about a bible story?

Robert felt awkward speaking, but he needed to know. "I'm still not seeing the point of the story."

A smile broke through the sorrow on Luke's face.

It was a hollow grin, a trait that Robert knew well. A smile that stretched too far and swallowed a person's lips. Most probably wouldn't notice a difference, but Robert could see it. He saw the same smile in the mirror most mornings.

"I'm getting to that part. Sheesh, some guys just don't understand flair," Luke said as he waved his fingers in the air, trying to bring joy back to his voice. "So, what do you think happened to them when they were set free from Paradise?"

"If we are talking straight from the Bible, I assume they had a bazillion kids and died."

"Points for effort. Yes. Technically, that happened. They fucked and had a few kids. Even though Eve hated Adam with the heat

93

of a thousand suns, she still threw him a pity fuck. But I'm talking about right after they were kicked out. What do you think happened after they were thrown from the Garden and out into the Wasteland? How do you think they *felt* after being set free?" Luke asked, searching for an answer.

"I don't know. Hungry? Confused? Angry?" At Robert's last guess, Luke snapped his fingers at his correct answer.

"Exactly! They finally felt something: anger at God, greed for something more, lust for the Garden's pleasures." Luke wrapped his arms around his bare waist and hugged himself with the last example.

"Are you talking about the Seven Deadly Sins?" Robert asked, picking up the breadcrumbs so heavily laid down for him. Luke's grin twisted. Robert finally found the deeper meaning behind his story.

"Right again, my handsome friend." Luke winked. "The Seven Deadly Sins sprouted from Eve and formed into the ideals we know today. Pride, gluttony, envy, wrath, greed, sloth, and lust. Being one of the first creations, Eve was endowed with what some would call godlike abilities. So much like how God created man, Eve created her Sins." Luke waved his hands up and down his body, insinuating something still unclear to Robert.

"What do any of those things have to do with you or me?"

Luke rose from the desk and extended a hand toward Robert. "I don't think I have introduced myself properly. My name is Lucas Jameson, but many call me Lust the Uncompromising."

Robert stared at the man in disbelief, the enormous grin, the big blue eyes, the deep dimples on either end of his pouty lips, and laughed.

Chapter 9

"You're kidding me," Robert scoffed, laughing at Luke's supposed 'title.' "You can't possibly expect me to believe that."

"Oh, I am quite serious." Luke threw himself back into the chair with ease, crossing his oversized sneakers on a pile of Dez's paperwork. "I'm a pretty big deal, in the right circles," Luke said in his best valley-girl accent.

"So, what, you're some sort of thing that sprouted from Adam and Eve some three thousand years ago?"

"Eve," he corrected. "Nothing good ever came from that idiot."

Robert expected Luke would reveal the *actual* reason after realizing Robert was not amused, but Luke just sat and smiled, waiting for Robert to believe him.

"You're serious? You think you're *Lust*?" Robert asked, and even the words seemed too bizarre for him to say. It was like someone trying to convince Robert they were Santa Claus or the Tooth Fairy.

"Did someone put you up to this?" Frustration infiltrated Robert's tone. "Was it my parents? Victoria? Well, you need to tell them, I am not leaving this fucking city until—"

Luke held up a hand, ending Robert's rampage. "No joke, Robert. Don't let the glittery and bedazzled tits fool you. I am very serious. I thought it helpful that we spoke before *Kitty* arrived," Luke explained.

Robert started to ask another question but stopped at the sound of heavy heels. They both turned, and Dez appeared at the door with an irritated scowl on her face—more so than usual.

"Time's up, boss. She's here." She glared at Luke's feet propped up on her desk. "Get your feet off," she snapped, knocking Luke's feet off with a swipe of her hand. She gave Luke a once-over as he stood from her desk. "Are you going to change?"

"Why? You don't think I look cute?" Luke gyrated his pelvis. "You don't think I look seeeeexy?" His heavy front pouch bounced at her as he danced closer; Dez stopped him with a backhand to his crotch. Luke clutched his privates, feigning pain before looking like a puppy whose master swatted them. "Why you gotta be so mean all the time, Dezzy?" Luke pushed out his bottom lip, forcing it to tremble.

Dez answered his question with a roll of her eyes and a flip of her hair. Her attention moved to Robert.

"Did he get to the juicy bits yet? Or do I need to jump to the end of his story?" Dez asked, having no time for games.

Robert still did not believe Luke's story or his reasoning, but Robert decided he would play their game, if only to end it.

97

"Um, he's Lust?" Robert asked again. Dez nodded a stern affirmative. "And what are you—anger? Wrath?"

Dez and Luke laughed at his ignorance.

"Oh no, she's much, much worse. Just make sure you're polite. She forgets how easily your kind break." A loud crash exploded from the front of the building. Dez released an annoyed grimace. "If they break one more freaking table, I'm ripping off heads tonight." Dez marched out, returning seconds after leaving the office. She looked at Robert and Luke, both still in their original position. "Well, are you coming or what? *Her Majesty* doesn't like to be kept waiting," Dez said with a distasteful look on her face.

Whoever Robert was about to meet, Dez was not a fan.

"Who's she referring to?" Robert asked as Luke dragged himself from around the desk and down the hallway with Robert. Luke's feet shuffled on the floor with every step.

"Let's just say she's the head of our little ragtag group. She's not that bad. Just very tense! And doesn't play well with others. But if you are looking for answers, she will be the one you want to talk to."

Answers to what exactly? The Bible questionnaire or Becca?

From behind the door, another table shattered. "Infernal burn me; they're gonna give me wrinkles." Luke held the door open and stepped to the side. "Ladies first." Luke nodded for Robert to enter.

Hesitantly, Robert followed the instruction.

The room was empty. In the fifteen minutes Robert had been in the back, the entire club emptied, and the furniture pushed to the side. The unfilled dance space stirred an eerie feeling inside Robert as he

98

stared at the remaining table, occupied by three. Two broad-shouldered men flanked a woman with fiery red hair, dressed in identical black suits. From what Robert could see, they were expensive. Crisp edges and a tailored midsection—definitely not something bought off the rack. Whoever they were, they had money.

So this must be the "she" Dez was complaining about?

An itch formed in his mind as he observed the woman across the room. Something about her scratched that empty spot in his memory, but he couldn't place it.

Had he met this woman the night of the attack?

"Kitty girl!" Luke squealed as he ran over to greet the woman. Both of the female's bodyguards reached out to intercept the hug, but froze with one quick glare from Luke. Robert could only imagine the look Luke gave that would freeze a man three times his size. "You just couldn't wait another hour before we closed, could you? Do you know how much money you cost me tonight?" Luke released the hug, and the woman adjusted her suit, smoothing out the creases until it was pristine once more.

"Time is of the essence, as you know, Lucas." She stepped away from the partially nude man. Her deep green eyes slid past him and stopped on Dez, who kept her distance as she lounged disinterestedly at the bar.

"Desdemona."

"Katherine."

They exchanged names like a scorpion's attack, calculated and lethal. Venom filled each syllable, a poison they hoped would kill the other. Their eyes were connected and tension shaped.

Robert glanced at the two, feeling the stiffness in the air. What kept the two at a distance? A rivalry? Hatred? Their eyes remained unblinking on the other, waiting for one to make the first move.

"Come, Desdemona," Katherine commanded, turning away from Dez and towards the table.

"I am content where I am."

"I wasn't asking."

"And I am not a pet to be called and sent away at your pleasure."

Katherine paused. One moment, she was standing with her back toward Dez, hand grasping the top of her chair, and the next, it was wrapped around Dez's throat, holding her aloft against a wall.

Robert jumped at Katherine's swiftness and aggression as she lifted Dez into the wall. Cracks splintered across the wall, growing larger as Katherine forced Dez into the wall a second time.

"Kitty the wall," Luke whined, more concerned about the damage than Dez's safety.

Dez's face was disinterested in Katherine's attack or the nails that sunk into the soft flesh under her chin. Blood trickled along Dez's throat as Katherine's claws dug deeper. Dez showed no pain or concern as blood flowed freely down her neck and into her purple jacket.

Robert gawked at Luke, who leaned against the table, watching the bout unfold, looking almost annoyed. "Luke!" Robert snapped. "Why isn't anyone doing anything? Someone help her! She's—"

Luke pressed a finger to his lips and shook his lips. The message was clear: Robert was not to get involved.

"I do not ask for obedience, Desdemona. I ask for respect."

"Respect is earned, Katherine. One would think that you would have learned such a simple rule after all these years." Dez's face remained apathetic as Katherine tightened her grip around her throat. She did not beg for her life or wince as the blood further drained. Her eyes did not register the threats that Katherine spewed. Dez raised her hand and took hold of Katherine's wrist, tightening her fingers slowly to show her intent. Her eyes narrowed into slits, and begged Katherine to make the first move so that she could only retaliate. "Do you think we will finally see who is the stronger of the two of us, Katherine? Tick Tock Katherine. Time is running out for one of us."

Katherine's anger flared. She lifted her other hand and pulled back.

"Katherine." Luke appeared at Katherine's side, moving with the same supernatural quickness as Katherine.

"How the fuck!" Robert cursed, snapping his neck to where Luke was not two seconds before. "Who the hell are you, people?" Robert backed away from the three. His slight movement drew the attention of the bodyguards, and Robert dared not to move again. If Robert wanted to leave, he would need to fight his way out. And against these people, he would surely lose.

"Let her go. We have guests here." Luke nuzzled his face into the crook of Katherine's neck. His once cheerful pitch had dropped into a seductive growl as he whispered into Katherine's ear. "We talked about behaving at my bar, Kitty Kat." He pressed his lips into her neck, leaving an imprint of lipstick on her ivory skin. "We behave ourselves here unless . . . you are interested in punishment."

Robert shook as something dragged across his body. He warmed as the sensation kissed and touched his most sensitive places. His cheeks tinged with pink as he grew firm.

"You know how much I love our time together," Luke growled, speaking only to Katherine and every individual simultaneously. Robert could feel Luke's embrace, his warm breath on his neck. Luke and his words caressed every part of him, arousing Robert, stroking Robert.

"Fuck . . ." Robert gasped as he throbbed. The room exhaled collectively. Katherine released a soft moan as she rubbed her head into Luke's, bathing him in her red mane.

"For you, darling," Katherine eyed Dez and then Luke, weighing her options, "anything."

Luke kissed Katherine one more time before he stepped away from her. As they broke, the sexual energy in the room faded. Everyone was left flushed and desperate for a smoke.

Katherine freed Dez, who fell to the ground with two soft *taps*. Katherine returned to the table, unconcerned with Dez and the blood that dripped down her neck. She swiped a handful from her neck and threw it to the ground.

Robert prepared to help Dez, but with another swipe of her hand, Dez erased the puncture marks. The bruised skin and bloody holes knitted together, healing instantaneously. Dez pressed her hand into her chin, cracking her neck once, twice, three times before looking back at Robert. She shook her head.

Robert's concern was unnecessary. Her wounds were already healed.

How could . . . but she was . . . what are they?

No plausible explanation came to mind. Robert gawked at the three as they positioned themselves in front of him. Luke couldn't have been telling the truth. They couldn't be devils or whatever he called themselves. This can't be real.

"Is this him?" Katherine motioned to Robert before she settled into her chair. Luke wormed his way between her guards, hovering behind Katherine like a living shadow.

"Yup, that's the brother." Luke cheered, slipping back into his playful nature. "Briefed him, well sort of briefed him on the matter. Even though I am more used to debriefing my men." Luke raised a hand for a high five, but neither guard responded. "What? That was funny!"

The group let out a collective sigh—even the two silent bodyguards.

Katherine beckoned Robert toward the table. He swallowed whatever uncertainty he felt about Katherine and approached her. The idea of escaping crossed his mind, but there was no way Robert could outrun them. He took the seat across from her, and she smiled. A shallow, pleasant grin meant to welcome Robert, but only made him uneasy. She extended a set of long, elegant fingers toward him.

"Katherine O'Donnell."

Robert took her hand, squeezing it slightly to show he was not as weak as he appeared. The corner of her lips tweaked. She squeezed tightly. Robert squeezed back. She squeezed harder.

"I wouldn't play that game if I were you," she warned, before tensing her hand and tightening her grip. Robert winced in pain. His bones bowed under his skin as Katherine's handshake became iron—a shrinking cuff meant to crush his hands. She released just before Robert's finger snapped.

He flexed his hand, feeling the pain in his bones.

"Drink?" Katherine offered, holding up her overflowing glass of dark alcohol. This high-class woman looked to be in her early thirties. Robert recognized the expensive tailoring of Katherine's suit, reminiscent of clothes worn by his mother's friends. No skin showed beyond her hands and below her neck—a curious choice for a woman her age—but the areas Robert saw glowed a pale radiance under the bad lighting of the dance club. She had no makeup on her eyes. Her bright green irises shined with enough vibrance that eyeshadow was unnecessary. A deep red lipstick painted her lips, matching the curls pinned away from her face.

"No, thank you."

"Pity." She swirled the dark liquid. "I once thought like you, deciding not to mix business with pleasure. But you learn some meetings need just a splash to get through them." She tipped the drink back, swallowed a large amount, and placed it back on the table. "We have much to discuss, Robert."

"Like what?" The two locked eyes. Flecks of red floated to the surface of her green irises. Small bursts of ruby red set fire to the emerald-green forest hidden within her eyes.

"Well, for one thing, Rebecca."

Becca.

It had been long since he had heard her name—since someone else had said it. Robert lived in a world where she did not exist. People did not know her. Robert could not see her. Her whole person was confined to the space in Robert's mind. Hearing her name confirmed Robert was not crazy.

His sister existed.

"So, Robert, what do you—"

"No," Robert interrupted.

Katherine raised her brows. "No?" she said, tasting the word.

"No more questions," Robert said firmly. "What do you know about my sister?"

A snort of laughter came from behind Robert. Without looking, he knew Dez was the perpetrator. He hoped it would not cause Katherine to attack her again, but Dez made it abundantly clear—she could handle herself. Katherine gave a subtle smile to Robert as she drummed her French manicure against the table. Robert was testing her patience.

"I wouldn't do that again." Dark intent dripped from the words, bitter and toxic. Her scowl and threat meant nothing to Robert as he held his bearing. He had nothing left to lose.

"What do you know? No more riddles." And with an even more desperate tone, Robert begged, "Just please, is she alive?" Robert hated the question and the quiver in his voice, but he needed to know.

"Yes. She is alive."

Robert relaxed for the first time in six months. Those words weakened the knot of self-hate that encircled his heart.

She's alive.

"We have good reason to believe that your sister is still in the city and being held captive."

"By you?" Robert accused.

Katherine waved a hand, dismissing the accusation. "The last thing I wish to do is cause any harm to your sister."

"Then why do you care?"

"Let's just say that I am a concerned citizen, and the . . . people who have her are colleagues of mine."

"You mean enemies," Robert said, correcting her word choice.

"I don't have enemies, Robert."

"I doubt that."

Katherine laughed and took another sip of her drink.

"You're quick, Robert. Let me rephrase. I have enemies, but not ones I deem dangerous enough that I worry. It is my friends that concern me."

"I doubt even more that you have friends."

Dez snorted again and received a glare from Katherine.

"Friends are just a label for people who I found useful. I do not keep you when you are no longer useful to me. Let me ask you, do you think you can be useful?" Katherine leaned forward, waiting for Robert's answer. "Do you think we could be friends?"

"Will you find my sister?"

Katherine didn't take a second to consider the question. "Yes, Robert, I believe I can find her."

"Then I'm in," Robert said finitely. He didn't one hundred percent believe her, but it was better to put his faith in them instead of a detective who no longer returned his phone calls. But Robert's doubt shifted to anger as he observed Katherine's air of self-satisfaction. This was a game to her, one she thought she had won. But for Robert, this was his life—his sister's life—and he couldn't stop speaking. "I'm warning you." Robert's voice dropped. "If anything happens to my sister in whatever game you play, I'll make you regret it."

A deep, mocking snicker slipped through Katherine's lips. "Oh, you're warning me?" She threw her head back in a wave of red hair and amusement. Her howl of enjoyment shook the room and the people within it.

Katherine leveled her head and examined Robert with now scarlet eyes. The fiery shards scattered among the green of her irises expanded and swelled, overwhelming the greenery like a fire tearing through the countryside.

Robert's body tightened, frozen by the fear brought on by her changing eyes. He thought to Luke's tempest-filled gaze. It wasn't just the light that made them appear to change, but something far more inhuman.

Something about the way Katherine studied him seemed familiar. He twitched as a dull pain of remembrance surfaced. Robert held Katherine's gaze, and pain exploded behind his eyes—a sharp, clean strike driven into the space. Robert doubled over, hands grasping his skull. An incomplete memory formed, and then the pain disappeared as quickly as it appeared.

"What fills you with rage?" Katherine asked.

Robert's eyes opened for a second. "What?"

A second nail was hammered into his mind. He shrieked as nails were struck again and again and again.

Each nail pierced a hole in the walls Robert built around his memories, containing the emotions he did not want. The openings created allowed the remembrances he tucked away to leak through. Memories he had locked away for months emerged, ones of his cheating ex-girlfriend, his uncaring parents, and the obese officer who somehow stole away his memories.

"Oh, that is unexpected," Katherine said, her voice raising in interest. "Lucas, did you know Robert had a run-in with the captain?"

The pain paused, and fury simmered as Robert registered Katherine's words.

Can she see what I'm seeing?

"I had a feeling, Kitty Kat, but wasn't sure since he didn't walk away a brainless potato."

"I guess his residence will be my next stop. I need to chat with him about pertinent matters' proper chain of command." Katherine turned away from Luke and focused her eyes back on Robert. Her gaze pulled him back into her painful thrall, and the striking began again.

That look.

He knew the look—the impression surrounding the empty spot in his memory held the same intensity.

Her eyes were different, so vastly dissimilar, but somehow, they held the same might as Captain Russo's. Robert remembered the sleepy, forgetful touch of the captain's gaze. The way his brain moved at a lethargic pace. But under Katherine's scrutiny, Robert's mind was set aflame with pain and rage. It whirled from one awful thought to another, unable to escape them. Robert's breathing sped up as he tried to focus, calm himself, and bury those memories, but there were too many.

A strange voice whispered to him, feeding his fury. The voice slithered through his consciousness, adding to his rage, warping his vision and grip on reality.

You hate them.

You hate yourself.

Punish them.

Punish all of them.

It's their fault.

It's your fault.

Your fault.

Your fault.

A pounding filled Robert's ears as the words empowered every nerve in his body. The anger grew and became tears that drowned his cheeks. Ghostly apparitions appeared around Katherine's shoulders, his parent's mocking smiles, his ex-girlfriend's cruel face, and his sister's troubled gaze. Robert's nails dug deep into his palms as he swayed—his body felt ready to explode. Blood filled his palms and trickled onto the floor. The pain grounded him as the ghostly vestiges pulled him away.

Becca would never have been taken if you weren't so weak.

Victoria would have never cheated on you if you were more of a man.

Your parents wouldn't have deserted you if you weren't so pathetic.

I shouldn't have stopped you.

The holes in his mind widened, drawing out Robert's darkest thoughts—feelings he had buried years ago. Things he had forced himself to forget.

"No. No. No. No." Robert rocked in his chair, sensing other emotions swim to the surface. Helplessness. Anxiety. Loneliness.

Pain flared along his wrist. A memory flashed within Robert's mind.

It's not real.

Robert felt something inside him grin at the dark treasure and drew the agony surrounding it.

It's not real. It's not real. It's not real.

His bloody palms made the nightmare real. The pain. The emotions. Everything felt just like that night.

IT'S NOT REAL. IT'S NOT REAL. IT'S NOT REAL!

Robert internally screamed the words, wishing he could deny the reality, but it was happening again. Anger and terror saturated every molecule of his body.

His vision went dark. The world around him vanished and became an endless void of black. Only the apparitions of his family remained. Their detestable gazes condemned Robert, burning holes in his mind as they pushed him further to the edge. Their anger fueled his despair.

Worthless.

Stupid.

Weak.

"ARGGHHHHHHHHHH!" Robert slammed his body onto the table. "GET OUT!"

Something snapped in the void. A thread snipped. A levy broke. The dark world around Robert and the memory of his family withdrew. The shadows dissipated like a fog, taking the emotions with them. The bar refocused, and two very dazed faces came into view.

Katherine's stunned expression broke through her shell of collected confidence. Even the strange glow of her face seemed to flicker. A shaking hand raised and touched her lips, slightly tapping as she weighed what had just occurred. The red glimmer in her eyes dimmed and retreated beneath the blanket of green. Luke leaned toward her with a concerned look, but Katherine quickly pushed him away.

"What are you?" Katherine breathed as she collected herself.

I don't know.

"Who are you?"

I don't know.

Robert staggered from the seat, backing away from the questioning eyes surrounding him.

Dez slid from her corner of the room and leaned toward Luke. They exchanged hushed words. Katherine's guards' hands disappeared within their jackets, ready to attack whenever their boss commanded.

"Robert, take a seat." Katherine motioned for him to return to his chair. Though his heart slowed and anger died, fear still raged through his body. "We have things to discuss."

Run, Robert.

The voice inside of him was frightened.

Robert couldn't sit. He couldn't endure that again. His eyes saw the door, and he ran.

He slammed through the front entrance and gasped at the fresh air. The cool night kissed Robert's scorching skin as he raced from the bar. Distance meant nothing as he moved through the empty late-night streets. The broken streetlights covered him in shadows as he ran as far as his feet could carry him. A moment came when Robert fell into a wall and slid to the ground. He knew he should keep going, but Robert couldn't get up—he didn't want to get up.

Robert curled into himself and wept. His bloody hands gripped his legs as his jeans absorbed his tears, and the empty air took his screams. On several occasions, Robert tried to regain control of himself, but was not strong enough to do so. His emotional dam had collapsed. Now, Robert endured his past until he could bottle it once again.

Chapter 10

Robert cried on the ground for hours, petrified by his emotions. Feeling so fiery, Robert burned himself every time he tried to contain them.

Seeing the sunrise, Robert felt his dark edges pull away, hiding back to where they belonged. He staggered home, walking blocks without realizing. His body found his bed, and his eyes found the ceiling. He begged for sleep, but it never came. His thumb rubbed along the tender side of his forearm, missing Victoria's gifted watch for the first time since he pawned it.

He stroked his wrist for hours, feeling the small scars—forever reminding him of what he owed Rebecca.

By eight, the idea of sleep seemed far beyond Robert's reach, and he prepared for work. The walk to the bar was a flash as he continued to think of the night before: the memories, the pain, the look of surprise in Katherine's eyes, and the question constantly asked of him.

"What are you?"

Robert let himself into the bar at a quarter to nine and started his list of menial tasks. Nathan came downstairs closer to ten, surprised by Robert's appearance so early in the morning. Robert's earliness did not bother Nathan. Robert arriving without a coffee or pastry annoyed him.

To their surprise, when the bar opened, several customers were already waiting. The Rusty Nail offered nothing that resembled breakfast, but Robert knew how to make a Bloody Mary, and every customer was eager for a 'Vegas Style Breakfast.' Robert was thankful for the unprecedented line of customers. His hands were kept busy with the mundane task of making drinks, which quieted his thoughts.

The morning quickly moved easily into the afternoon. Robert persisted in a constant state of movement while Nathan grumbled in his corner of the bar, muttering about the lack of quiet and inability to read. At two o'clock, Nathan gave up and left with three of his papers and a bowl of pretzels. Robert was happy to see him go, especially when a party of six entered and Nathan's chair was needed. Robert hoped Nathan wouldn't care, or at least not notice someone else had sat in his chair.

The bell over the front door jingled.

"Welcome to the Rusty Nail!" With a glass of ice, Robert turned to the front door to greet the customer. The icy glass slipped from his hand—but was caught—when Robert saw Luke walk through the front door.

"Nice place." Luke smiled, looking around at the building and the bustling clientele. His sleeveless crop top and exceedingly short pair of denim cut-offs drew the interested eye of several women and one man. Simultaneously, his bedazzled fanny pack and Walkman received looks of confusion from the rest. Luke looked as if he walked right off the page of a '90s fashion magazine—backward snap cap included. A deep bronze highlighter splashed against his cheeks, accentuating their roundness. He strutted across the bar, bouncing to the beat of the make-believe music that played in his head.

Settling into the seat closest to Robert, Luke plopped his hands onto the bar top and smiled. "Busy day?"

"Uh . . . yeah." Robert faced the back shelf, finished making the drink, and slid it down the bar top toward a tall, thin lady. She fluttered her long eyelashes in appreciation, and Robert responded with a smile.

"Do you work here most days?" Luke asked, trying to make conversation. Robert gave him a slight nod and quickly returned to his job, ignoring Luke's first attempt and the subsequent attempts at starting a dialog.

While Robert openly ignored Luke, the man happily sat at the bar and kept himself busy; he munched through two bowls of pretzels, chatted with an older lady about her yellow pumps, and flirted with an older gentleman who nearly dropped dead at the sight of Luke.

Luke forcibly ended the silent treatment when he slid from his chair and collected dirty glasses from a recently emptied table.

"You didn't have to do that," Robert said, thanking him in a way of sorts as he accepted the dirty glasses.

"Oh, he speaks! Call the press!" Luke said, feigning excitement as he settled back onto his stool. Robert, however, did not crack a smile.

"Do you always make bad jokes when you're uncomfortable?" Robert asked. Luke went rigid. Robert had poked a clear, sore spot.

"Okay, I'm gonna level with you here. I'm trying, and I would appreciate some effort from your side of the table . . . metaphorically and physically." Luke shook an empty glass, beaming at his joke.

Robert rolled his eyes, refilled it with water, and placed it back on the counter. Robert leaned forward and looked at the people surrounding them. All his customers were deep in conversation, or their drinks, to be concerned with what the barkeep was doing.

Robert leaned closer to Luke and whispered, "Is it true?"

"Santa Claus or the Easter Bunny? My money's on the Easter Bunny, but I can always hope for a sexy older man to come down my chimney at Christmas?" Luke smirked and waited for a laugh, but Robert again responded stoically. "Lord, you are a buzzkill, aren't you?" Luke collapsed onto the bar top in submission, drained by Robert's unwillingness to play. "There are a lot of questions in the air right now; if you have one, I'm gonna need you to be a little more specific."

"I felt something in my head last night. What was that? It was like I couldn't control myself. Like every feeling I had, wanted to explode." Robert tried to find the words to explain his experience, but it was indescribable. It was both real and fictitious at the same time.

"Ms. Kitty Kat doesn't always have the softest touch when prowling around in another's brain," Luke explained casually. "Do you remember what you saw last night? The feelings you felt?"

Robert shivered at the thought. "Vividly."

"And do you remember who you thought my little purple monster was?"

"Wrath."

"Bingo! Wrath the Vengeful if you want to be formal or Kitty Kat if you feel particularly dangerous. I wouldn't recommend it," he said with a shrug. "Though I'm not too big on titles."

"And the captain?" Robert questioned. "Who was that?"

Luke let out a grunt of revulsion. "Sloth the Corrupt, disgusting pile of filth. I can love just about anyone, but he's an acquired taste and does what we typically ask of him. Helps with the cleanup for when things get a little too out of control."

"What's his um—power?" Robert felt ridiculous asking, interested in his power as if he were some sort of supervillain. But Luke did not bat an eye.

"He can bury you deep down. Make your mind go lethargic. Make you care less about yourself, the world, your family. You won't ever come out if he pushes you too far into his mud, as he likes to call it. He could turn you into a certified vegetable."

Mud was the perfect word to explain what Robert felt when gazing into the eyes of Captain Russo.

"Then, it's true. It's all true. So, what are all of you? Demons? Devils? Angels?"

Luke's face turned at the word *angel*.

"What's wrong with angels? Aren't they supposed to be the good guys and all?"

"Stop thinking of everything as good and bad. The real world isn't as black and white as the good, pious Christians like to think." He placed his hands together in prayer. "And a veritable angel isn't as friendly as the Bible makes them out to be."

"Are they really that bad?"

"Again, stop thinking about good or bad. It's all about perspective when it comes to good and bad. Bad is subjective. I'm bad to them. They're bad to us. Lust the Unquenchable, the evil sin of perversion. Running rampant around the city, causing unheard-of proclivity." Luke placed a finger on either side of his head and pretended they were horns. "Converting the good men and women of Las Vegas one piece of ass at a time."

A smile peeked through Robert's tight lips, and Luke grinned larger

"See, I knew I could get you to smile!" Luke beamed. "It only took, like, sixteen jokes, but I have a—whatever sticks approach to my comedy. But to answer your original question, I would stay away from angels at all costs. If you think Ms. Red Hair Ferocious is bad, you wouldn't want to get caught up with them. And no, I am not a demon or the Devil. I'm just a normal guy with a few gifts up his sleeve and a few excellent friends in rather low places." Luke faked a look of shock and pointed down. "If you get my drift."

Another set of questions for another time.

"So, do you have any powers?" Robert couldn't help but ask, but Luke moved with the same supernatural quickness as Katherine. Surely, he could do something.

"What? Do you want to see me spin my head around and spit pea soup all over the bar?"

"Please don't."

"I'm kidding!" Luke teased. "You really need to lighten up. I know your sister was taken, but you can't let it steal your life?"

But what kind of life would it be without Becca?

Robert wasn't sure if he could ever stop looking for her. He knew Rebecca wouldn't stop. She would turn the universe upside down and shake it until Robert was tossed loose from whatever trap had caught him.

Luke saw the pensive, depressing look swamp Robert's face; his question landed deeper than expected. With a hesitant hand, Luke reached out to Robert, brushing his fingertips just along the outside of his forearm.

A candle of peace lit inside Robert's chest. A pleasant, calming fluttering washed away the depression, and the despair summoned by Luke's questions. Robert looked at the hand that stroked his arm, the friendly gesture. And looking at Luke, Robert couldn't help but smile. It was like love at first sight.

"That was you."

"What was me?"

"That feeling." Robert didn't pull away from Luke's touch, enjoying the false feeling of love filling his chest.

"What feeling?" Luke drew out the questioning, enjoying how Robert stared at him, how pink flushed Robert's cheeks, how his eyes crinkled at the corner as his smile deepened.

"When Katherine attacked Dez. I felt you. I felt this." Robert lifted his arm, breaking their connection. But unlike before, the heavy sadness did not come back. "You just did it again. I felt it."

Luke laughed. "You caught me."

"But what exactly are you doing?"

"Lust isn't all about fucking and sucking. It can also be sweet. Lust is at the heart of the first look shared across a room. It is what fuels courage to make someone introduce themselves. Lust can calm a troubled heart."

Robert needed to know. "What else can you do?"

Luke's eyes danced with excitement as he began his explanation. "Let me tell you a little something about lust. Lust is a companion to many other sins—gluttony, wrath, envy—and is still a sin on its own. I am the other side of the coin—the small droplet of the yin in the yang. Go too far, and it can be disastrous—a little too much lust—and it becomes an obsession." Luke nodded to the older couple sitting together. "Look at Mr. and Ms. Beige over there. Just one push and that friendly look can become something more." Warmth radiated from Luke as if he had become the bar's personal sun.

Luke's energy was soft and reassuring, unlike the fiery nailed driven through Robert's brain by Katherine. The phantom fingers brushed Robert's body. Each touch gentler, softer, and more encouraging than the last. The blues of Luke's eyes became sapphires, glittering gems that shined with thoughts of first love, passionate kisses, and lustful experiences. His irises soon expanded, swallowing the blacks of his pupils.

Luke nodded toward the two in the corner, and his warmth—his power—was flung towards the couple.

It took seconds for Luke's influence to affect the couple. The man was the first to move, sliding towards the woman. He pressed their bodies together. Her hand found the back of his head and pulled him close. Their lips smashed together in a messy kiss. The loud sound of their lips smacking drew the surrounding people's attention.

"And even the most chaste kiss can kindle passion."

The aura of warmth around Luke increased, changing from a tender touch to a blazing heat. Luke motioned toward the couple. Their kiss broke, and the woman licked her lips, looking underneath the table. The man smirked and leaned away, allowing space for the woman to work her hands. His moans were loud and unbothered. Other patrons voiced snarls of disgust at the public nature of the actions of the two, but those noises of distaste became sounds of intrigue and pleasure.

Slowly, Luke's influence took hold of each person. Grunts and moans grew and resonated within the area as people paired off. Desire traveled like a plague through the room, staining everyone with lustful thoughts—even Robert felt the draw.

He turned to the friendly woman who sat alone at the bar. She eyed Robert, unbuttoning the top of her blouse, revealing her lacy bra and heavy, milky breasts. Robert groaned. He wanted to touch her. Feel her. He wanted to bite the soft peaks of her chest and rip the rest of her clothes from her body. He licked his lips, imagining her taste.

How had he gone so long without sex?

"And just a little more." Luke's hands explored his body, releasing the room's sexual awakening. His fingers found his pert nipples poking through his thin shirt. He grabbed both and twisted. He howled in enjoyment. The noise vibrated through the building, mixing his pleasure into everyone within range. Moans joined in a chorus of passion as Luke touched himself. Luke became a living voodoo doll, where his victims felt his every twist, caress, and squeeze. His motions drew Robert's eyes from the woman, and he lost himself in Luke's soft features.

What would it be like to hold Luke's face?

What would it feel like to kiss Luke's lips?

What would Luke taste like if Robert were to worship him?

Luke smirked, somehow reading the words on Robert's face. A gentle voice whispered within Robert's mind, nudging him to find answers to the questions.

Give in to those feelings.

Robert's cock bulged as he fantasized about the two of them together. He recalled how Luke looked shirtless and the roundness of his ass. He remembered how it bounced when he walked and swayed, tantalizing back and forth as if he knew everyone was watching his every movement. Robert leaned into the counter, grinding against a wooden beam.

I want you . . .

"But with too much lust," Luke said, interrupting Robert's thought, "comes mania."

The sensual touch that coerced Robert to daydream became hostile. The gentle warmth in his stomach turned wild, increasing his hunger and desperation to be touched. Robert stared at the woman and watched her lustful smile twist and grow into a maddening grin. She extended her arms. Her nails drew deep lines into the wood as she dragged them back, like a lion readying itself to pounce. If not for the man who bumped into her, Robert would have been the target of her zealous aggression. With the mania tingling through Robert, he wanted to be the target.

"Lust and madness are sisters that cannot live without one another." Luke swayed as he spoke, dancing to the sounds of lust and obsession.

"That's enough, Luke." Robert swallowed his moans. He fought the urge to seek companionship or pleasure himself. "Stop," Robert softly begged a second time.

Luke twisted to Robert; he had descended into insanity with his captives. Robert felt Luke's deep blue eyes pull him into the seascape of irrationality and lust that filled them.

"Let me quench your thirst, Robert?" Luke lulled. "You are so hungry to be touched. Why not give in to those feelings, Robert? Enjoy yourself. Let loose. Give in to lust."

Robert felt something rustling through his mind, searching for an idea, a wish, a fantasy—something it could use to bring Robert further under Luke's control. Purple flashed, and Luke's eyes glimmered.

"I knew it." Luke clapped, and the world rearranged itself. The customers vanished. The sky became dark. And Luke became Dez.

"Any other plans tonight?" Robert asked as he stared at Dez. His eyes moved across her body, imagining what hid beneath her blouse. Robert inhaled the flowery scent that drifted off her skin and wanted more.

"I don't know . . . do you have any plans for the evening?" Dez asked, playing Robert's game. She smiled a coy grin and arched her back, knowing why Robert had asked.

"Now that I have you here, I sure do." Robert leaned over the counter and kissed her. Her large lips were softer than he could have imagined. She played coy, but her tongue was aggressive. Her hands moved across Robert's chest, grabbing onto his shoulders, deepening their kiss. Her teeth dragged against Robert's bottom lip as she broke the kiss. Dez smiled mercilessly, and Robert desired more.

"Want to go somewhere else?" Dez downed her drink, gathered herself, and stood from the stool. She reached out a hand and smiled at Robert. "My place is just around the corner." Robert stared

at her alluring smile. A twinge of pain came from the back of his head and words to his lips.

"Don't touch me," Robert whispered, remembering Dez's words.

"But why?" Dez asked; sadness tinged her voice.

"You told me, do not touch you." Robert looked around the space. "You knocked me out at the knees, and I hit the floor. I have the bruise to show for it." Robert shook his head. "None of this is real."

"It can be." She said, hopeful.

"It's not.

"But don't you like me, Robert?" Dez asked as she drifted a hand along the collarbone and onto her breasts. Her fingertips trailed along the soft spots of her skin. "Don't you . . . want me?" Robert stepped back, fighting the magnetism that drew them together. He backed away, knowing that he should have bumped into the back shelf, but nothing stopped him.

"Luke!" Robert shouted as the tingling of Luke's influence pulled him to obey. "Let me out!" Robert yelled at the illusion. "God damn it, Luke! Let me out!" The world splintered at its edges, unraveling as Robert fought Luke's hold. Dez called out to him to return, but—Robert turned away, and the fake world shattered.

Robert jolted back to reality, awakening as if from a dream. Luke's maddening gaze inches from his face. He held Robert's face in his hands and lowered himself, pursing his lips.

"Don't you want a taste?"

"Let me go, Luke." Robert slapped away Luke's hands, having broken free of Luke's spell. "Listen to me. You need to stop."

Robert stepped back as Luke reached out to touch him again; his lustful influence pleaded to invade his body once more.

"But . . ." Luke's voice trailed off as he faced the orgy he had unleashed. Confusion glazed his eyes. "Why would anyone want this to stop? So much chaos. So much lust. Do you not want a taste of freedom, Robert?" Luke sounded so far away, so unlike himself as he spoke. "Kiss me, Robert. Have a taste of freedom. I promise you I can make you happy. Much happier than Victoria ever did."

At the sound of her name, Robert ground his teeth. "I want you to stop, Luke."

Luke's eyes flickered like a dying light.

"Luke," Robert began, his voice strained as he fought the pull of Luke's promised happiness. "End this immediately."

A force empowered Robert's words and pulled Luke from beneath the craze. His glowing blue eyes dimmed and died, returning his eyes and the bar to normal.

Luke repeatedly blinked; eyes dry from the relentless watching of his puppets. His influence left no space untouched.

Silence arose as the participants of Luke's orgy broke from his control. Before anyone could speak, Robert took command.

"Everyone out! NOW!"

Customers fled, leaving behind their destruction, wads of cash, and Robert and Luke to clean up the mess. The former locked the front door and closed the blinds. Robert felt himself about to burst, but Luke had already reprimanded himself. He remained seated in the same chair, bent over, staring at his hands as they fidgeted, unable to even look at Robert.

"What just happened there?" Robert kept his voice soft in an attempt not to sound angry.

Luke kept his eyes downward. "I'm sorry," Luke whispered. "Sometimes, I get a little too excited. I'm still new to this whole thing." Shame slowed his hand motion, replacing his usual laissez-faire attitude.

"What do you mean?" Robert picked up a fallen chair and righted a table. Luke took a deep breath and exhaled an even deeper one.

"How old are you, Robert? Twenty-two? Twenty-three?"

"I'm twenty-three," he answered.

"And how old do you think I am?"

Robert started at Luke's face. "Maybe twenty-one?"

Luke gave a half-smile.

"Older?" Robert asked, somewhat surprised.

"I turned fifty-three last August," Luke said with disdain at the word *fifty*. From Robert's shocked expression, Luke knew his answer needed further explanation. "I wasn't always like this." He put his fingers next to his ear, halfheartedly pretending them to be horns once more. "I was like you once—normal. I was born in 1976."

"So, when did you . . . I mean, how did . . ?"

"I become this? It's a long story. But I will hold the Sin of Lust until the next Lust comes along."

"So, you were twenty-something when you—I guess—turned is the right word?" Robert asked.

"Yeah, it was the mid-'90s when I changed. I had just become a production assistant at an adult film studio and—"

"You worked in porn?"

"Adult films," Luke corrected. "Anyways, that was where I met the previous Lust. He was the lead actor in the film, and something about him pulled me towards him. I just had to know him. And when he saw me, I knew he felt it, too. It was like my entire life had snapped into place at that moment. Everything just made sense. Come to find out. He already knew who I was and who I was meant to become." Luke laughed at the memory. "He was actually the person who hired me. Then when the day came, I became Lust the Uncompromising in all my glory." Luke halfheartedly fluttered his fingers up his body.

"But how did you—"

Luke placed a finger to his lips, stopping Robert's question. "I can't go spilling all our nasty little secrets on a first date," Luke advised before he hopped off his seat with a gentle push. "I'm sorry that I messed up your bar. Sometimes, it's a little harder to control. It's like cracking a hole in a dam and letting out a little trickle and keeping the rest of the water barricaded inside."

"It's okay." Robert looked around the space. There were a few broken pieces of furniture and glasses, but nothing that couldn't be fixed or replaced. "I asked for you to show me. So, I can only put so much blame on you," Robert said, accepting his portion of the responsibility.

"But enough about me. What are you doing this Sunday?"

Chapter 11

As they cleaned, Luke revealed the purpose of coming to Robert's bar, to invite him to a meeting with Katherine and the people they assumed had abducted Rebecca.

"Really?" Robert inhaled. "You know who actually took her?"

"Did you think we were lying?" Luke cleared the last bits of broken glass and tossed them into the trash can. "We may be 'bad' guys, but we aren't bad people. We have standards," Luke teased before tying up the trash bag. "I will say Katherine is very confident. You'll be surprised to know that Katherine has been searching for Rebecca just as long as you have."

"She has?"

"Yes, Sir. Tirelessly, I might add. So say thank you next time you see her." Luke winked.

"So," Robert paused, "why haven't you done anything about it until now?"

Luke bit the inside of his cheek.

"There are complications. It's a very delicate situation—our relationship with them is a sensitive matter, so we needed to be sure before we requested a meeting," Luke said as he turned away and tossed the smaller trash bag into an even larger bin.

"What are they? Angels or something?"

Luke's shoulders pinched together at the word but quickly laughed away the question before Robert could press further.

"This is for you." Luke dug into his fanny pack and withdrew a small book. As Robert accepted the object, the smell of mold followed it. The front cover was faded, practically illegible, as Robert squinted to read the words. The broken spine groaned as Robert opened the book. "I thought you should know a little about what really happened after Eden. If you are going to be working with us, you might want to learn about our history." Robert thumbed through the first collection of pages. Luke visibly flinched at Robert's careless approach to the book.

"Please, just be careful with it. If you damage it, Kitty Kat will have my head." Luke choked himself slightly to instill his warning further. He looked toward the clock and *tsk'd*. "I gotta get going. I have my own bar to get ready for tonight. So, I will see you on Sunday?"

Robert nodded, and Luke grinned.

"Fabulous." Luke grabbed his Walkman, slipped his fanny pack back around his waist, and paused. He gave Robert a once over. His lips went to the side as he thought. "The look is business casual, by the way. So, try to wear something—nice," he said with a half-smile, choosing the least offensive word he could muster.

"Uh, sure," Robert answered in a rather unconvincing manner as he paged through the antique book, trying to read the faded lettering.

"Well, it's been fun, darling. Please let me know if the blood doesn't come out of the upholstery. I have a guy who has saved my ass more times than I could count for blood removal."

Robert chose not to ask why he needed such a guy, but he had an inkling it had to do with Dez's short temper.

With an unexpected peck on the cheek, Luke said his goodbyes and left Robert with the recently restored Rusty Nail. The bar looked nearly identical, save for a few blood stains and broken glasses. With the book in hand, Robert flipped the sign back to open and returned to his spot behind the bar.

"I'm so close," Robert said, feeling hope swell in his heart. He looked at the old book, and, for the first time in a long time, Robert was hopeful.

*   *   *

Robert arrived home slightly after two in the morning with a pocketful of desperately needed cash—not as much as he wanted—but enough to get him through the month. The double shot of espresso he got on the way home didn't give him the late-night burst of energy he had needed. Yet, as Robert settled into his bed after washing away the day's grime and the dried blood, he felt more awake than ever.

Placing the book on his lap, Robert plugged in his phone and stared at the black screen. He realized that today was the first day he hadn't spent waiting for his phone to ring. He couldn't remember when waiting for a message did not consume his day. His time with Luke was unexpected, but overall, the day stood out in the sea of numbness.

"Seems like someone got to this before me." Robert examined the book and its broken appearance; it was at least a hundred years old, if not older. He opened the cover—gentler than before—and turned the first page. His fingers ran along the inner spine, feeling the torn edges of missing pages. There had to be at least forty pages missing—if not more. "An odd place to start a story," Robert commented before he started to read.

For eternity you shall walk, he commanded to Eve and Adam
Forced to wander The Wasteland
Never shall you know my kingdom or the prison of The Void
Never shall you learn the release of death
Never shall you be free from the freedom you craved

And so, Adam and Eve were cast from Paradise
Exiled from Eden and eternity within the Holy Gates
They wandered The Wasteland
Forced into the unmade world
Their food became ash
Their water turned to acid

Hope died, and promises withered
Eve waited for her savior, but Lucifer never appeared
She had been forgotten

The Morningstar watched as his Eve floated away
His gaze stretched far
His need stretched further
Lucifer's pain formed fiends of darkness
They followed her closely, seeking to rescue her
But God saw his efforts
And ceased Lucifer's attempts
By his command, God banished the creatures

The Lord then looked unto Lucifer and exiled him to The Void
A world of darkness
A world of un-creation

Infinity shall be your companion, God decreed
Your skin shall never touch, your will shall never reach,
An eternity, you shall wallow and ponder what you have lost
And so, Lucifer was cast below and watched as Eve suffered

Why have you forsaken me? She cried
Where have you gone, my beloved?
Her spirit called darkness into The Wasteland
Betrayal, abandonment, fury

From her emotions, she created the first of her children
Go forth, Wrath, and bring change to the world, she declared
Set the world aflame with my agony

Seven Sins formed within Eve, finding purpose from her pain
From her passion, she grew lust
From her arrogance, she founded pride
From her need, she produced greed
From her idleness, she built sloth
From her resentment, she shaped envy
From her hunger, she forged gluttony

Robert read the entire book, all 122 pages, three times.

The book went on, telling the story of Adam and Eve. Their trials, their misfortunes, their children, and the creations Eve unleashed on the world. Adam's contempt toward Eve was unlike anything Robert had ever read before. Everything he knew about them seemed twisted through this lens.

Eve rejoiced in her freedom, growing wilder with each new creation, and Adam resented her. While God and Lucifer fought above and below, Eve and Adam pledged an unending war within the Wasteland—a desert that would one day become humanity's home.

The book answered the questions of the origins of the Seven Deadly Sins, but not how Luke or Katherine became them. But the book stirred more questions.

What happened to Adam and Eve?

Were they still alive?

Robert sighed, turned the book over in his hand, and turned the first page once more. With nothing else to do, Robert read the book for the fourth time.

Chapter 12

BANG. BANG. BANG.

The apartment shook as the unknown—and unwelcomed—visitor assaulted the front door. The sound startled Robert awake. He pawed for his phone, moving it just enough to push it off the table and onto the floor. Robert groaned, slapping his phone until it lit, and the single digits stared back at him.

"Ugh."

He had been asleep for barely three hours.

BANG. BANG. BANG.

The front door shook again. Whoever it was, they were not giving up.

Groggily, Robert stumbled toward the front door as another quick succession of bangs shook it. "I'm coming!" Robert mumbled, more to himself than to the knocker. The list of people who would visit him was small, and the people he wanted to see him were even fewer, especially at the ungodly hour of nine AM.

Worst-case scenario, it's the landlord, best case—well, there are no best-case options.

Blinking a few times to right his eyesight. Robert looked through the peephole and shirked in surprise. It was Dez.

She stood in the narrow hallway with arms crossed and lips tight. Her foot repeatedly tapped on the carpet as she glared at the door. For a second, Robert thought she could see through the door, but that was crazy . . . wasn't it?

"I can hear you breathing, " she said matter-of-factly.

Robert jerked back at her statement.

Seeing through doors is crazy. But apparently, supernatural hearing was well within the realm of possibility.

Robert returned to the peephole as her tapping increased in speed and intensity. Robert watched her, unsure if he should let her in or not. Annoyed by the silence, Dez unfolded her arms and stepped forward with an audible rolling of her eyes.

"You have two choices, Robbie. You can either open the door, or I can open it for you. I don't think your landlord will be happy about a door being ripped off its hinges, but if you ask me"—she looked to her left and right—"it would be an upgrade."

Robbie.

The name pulled him back into his dreamscape. To the horrible sounds of his sister calling his name. The name that only she used.

The sound of Dez's cracking knuckles pulled Robert back.

"Fine." Dez pulled back an arm, rearing to punch a hole through the door.

Robert decided and hastily undid the locks on the door. Dez's face curved into a look of smugness as she advanced, but Robert braced the door in his hand, denying her entry.

"Two things, don't call me Robbie, and second, what the hell are you doing at my house at nine in the fucking morning?"

Dez scoffed, pushing the door open and Robert backward. "I wouldn't exactly call this place a home, but I guess beggars can't be choosers." Dez studied the apartment. It wasn't much, and Robert knew that—but how much did one guy need? He had a bed, a table he had never used, and a few mismatched furniture pieces. The space was small, but Robert was content with the less-than lavish lifestyle. "Coffee?" Dez asked, wandering into the kitchenette.

"Eight blocks down the street. I take mine with three packets of sugar. Thanks." Robert slumped into one of the two chairs surrounding his small table. "If you can grab me a bear claw, I promise I'm good for the money."

"I don't get coffee for Luke. What makes you think I would get it for you?" Dez searched through the cabinets, making a triumphant squeal as she pulled a coffee machine from the cabinet beneath the sink. "Knew it!" She exclaimed. "No self-respecting man wouldn't have at least a coffeemaker," she said before continuing her search. "And . . . where . . . are . . . aha! Grounds!" Dez shook the half-empty bag of coffee grounds. She opened the bag, sniffed, begrudgingly poured it into the coffee machine, and pressed start.

"Not that I don't appreciate you barging into my house like the Kool-Aid man, waking me up, and making yourself coffee, but why are you here?" Robert chuckled at an unspoken thought, drawing Dez's interest.

"What? Something amusing?"

"With the amount of purple you wear, I should have called you Barney."

Dez's neck turned with a slowness that made Robert regret his comment. Her jaw was tight and her brow raised.

Silently, Robert made his peace with God.

She stalked across the floor, moving like a jungle cat approaching its recent capture.

She slid into the opposing chair and smiled. Robert blinked, and Dez transformed. Contempt burned through him as her eyes darkened with vengeful thoughts.

Her face was ready to kill.

"I'll give you one." Dez lifted one razor-sharp nail. "But if you think there will ever be a second, I will gouge out your eyes and feed them to you." Her threat sent tremors through Robert's body. The icy disdain that filled her eyes made him realize why Luke did not interrupt her and Katherine; she was just as formidable. "Do we have an understanding?" She asked, needing Robert's confirmation. Robert's throat bobbed as he swallowed a mouthful of air and nodded. "Perfect," she said with an oddly human smile.

She blinked, and her icy stare vanished, reverting to her more humane visage. Though nothing physically changed, the shift in her gaze made Robert feel less on edge, but the switch made Robert wonder what else hid beneath her human mask.

The two sat, content with not talking, until the machine dinged.

"Thank, Lucifer," she moaned as she sailed to the machine, poured herself a cup, and returned to the table, leaving Robert coffee-less. She swallowed a mouthful of the piping hot drink and winced.

"Too hot?" Robert teased. The coffee had to be scalding.

"Hell is hot," she lifted the cup, "this is just disgusting. I can't believe you drink this trash." She regretfully swallowed another mouthful, scrunched her face in distaste, and settled back into her chair. "But I guess it goes with your whole"—she waved a hand lazily in the air—"starving artist vibe you have going here."

Oooookay. I'm done.

"Not that this hasn't been a *lovely* visit and a *fantastic* surprise," Robert said through an overly toothy grin. "But why are you here, Desdemona?"

Dez's eyebrow twitched at the full name.

Kill me. I don't care. Then at least, I could sleep.

Dez clicked her tongue. She weighed the options of torture versus having a productive conversation. Luckily for Robert, she chose the less messy of the two.

"I suppose Luke has already invited you to the meeting on Sunday?"

Robert nodded.

"And fully explained to you . . . what we are?"

Robert motioned his hand in a back-and-forth manner. "Sort of, but not really."

"Sounds about right. This Sunday is best dress required, and Katherine assumed you would not have the appropriate wardrobe and was concerned about walking in with someone who looked homeless." Dez's lips lifted in a half smile. "Is she wrong?"

Robert turned to the pile of clothes in the corner of his bedroom. The closet door sat open and showed his less-than-average selection. Months back, Robert had more clothes than he could ever wear; each held a designer label and a price tag that could pay most people's car notes.

For the first time, Robert regretted not saving something that would be 'best dress.'

"She would be correct," Robert grumbled.

"Then I'm glad I came." Dez withdrew a black credit card from her front pocket, smiling like a lunatic. "We're going shopping today, and Mother's paying."

"Dez, I'm not letting you pay."

"Oh no, this is that redheaded bitch's card." Dez twisted the card between her fingers. "I wonder how high her limit is? Think we can max it out in a single day?"

She was a terror with a potentially limitless credit card; if anyone could max it out—Dez could.

*   *   *

Over the next hour, Robert dressed and showered while Dez criticized every step of his routine. His hair was stupid, his clothes were tasteless, and his deodorant smelled like the back end of a donkey. Robert landed a few quips at Dez and received an empty coffee cup thrown at his head. She missed, and it shattered, but her annoyance was worth the broken dishware.

At a quarter to ten, the two exited the building, and Dez announced she was driving—not that Robert owned a vehicle.

Robert expected to find a sleek motorcycle or something like Christine, but to his surprise, it was a very sensible, bright purple sedan. The vehicle looked to be something from the early 2000s, if not older. Dents and scratches covered the front of the car, ranging from small quarter-sized indentations to one that seemed rather human-shaped on the bumper. Chips decorated the sides and the rear of the vehicle. The vehicle had lived a life of danger. Dez must have seen how Robert smirked at the sight of her purple dinosaur. She danced her fingers across the top, daring him to comment.

For once, Robert did the sensible thing and kept his mouth shut.

Robert barely had time to shut the door before the engine roared, and Dez threw the car into drive. Pedestrians lunged out of her car's path as Dez blew through the first stop sign and took a sharp turn left. Robert frantically grabbed for his seatbelt, snapping it into place right as Dez took a quick—and dangerous—U-turn.

"Jesus Christ!" Robert shouted as his body slid into the door.

"Not even close." Dez laughed, pressing her foot heavily onto the accelerator.

Robert swayed back and forth in the passenger seat as Dez wove through traffic. It wasn't until he saw an enormous clock on the side of a building that he realized he had forgotten something important.

"Fuck!" Robert cursed.

"Lucifer!" Dez shouted, swerving within her lane abruptly in surprise. "Did I hit someone again?" She searched the hood and then her mirrors.

"I gotta get out. I'm supposed to be at work at eleven." Robert read the passing signs. "You can just drop me off at the next corner. I think I can walk from here."

"Oh, you won't need to go to work today."

"What do you mean?" A sinking feeling formed in Robert's stomach. Dez seemed a little too excited when she said the word *today*.

"I took care of it."

Robert frowned at her answer, feeling even less comfortable with her second, vague answer.

"What do you mean, you took care of it?" Robert questioned. Luke's earlier suggestions when Robert first arrived at The Queen of Hearts came to mind. "Please tell me you didn't burn the place down?"

"Of course not!" Dez responded quickly. "I don't just carry around jugs of gasoline. What kind of woman do you think I am?"

Robert relaxed slightly into his seat.

"I called in a bomb threat."

"You what!?" Robert's shriek surprised Dez, and she swerved slightly in the road.

145

"Can you calm down?! It was just a threat. I didn't actually put a bomb anywhere . . . this time," Dez said with a smirk.

"You haven't," Robert couldn't formulate the words.

"You and the police cannot prove a thing," Dez said confidently. Fond memories flashed behind her eyes, and she smirked. There were probably several things the police could not prove.

A beat of silence followed Dez's 'admission' when Robert remembered something else.

"Wait. Wouldn't you notice if you hit someone?" Robert asked, recognizing the casual way she threw out that question earlier.

"Sometimes I do." She shrugged. "Sometimes I don't." Dez sounded nearly giddy at the admission, almost like she was bragging. "But if they get out of the way quickly enough, I don't have to worry about that."

Chapter 13

"Come on! I wanna see!" Dez cried from the opposite side of the dressing room door. "You've been in there for literally ten minutes. I've seen the view; you don't need that much time to stare at yourself in the mirror." She dragged her fingernails against the door, scraping it like a cat that wanted to be inside the room.

Robert stood immobile, frowning at his reflection. He adjusted the too-tight collar and pulled at his wedgie.

Sure have grown.

"I'm not sure if these fit properly." Robert rubbed the back of his neck, unable to look away from his reflection—it wasn't changing, no matter how long he looked. Reluctantly, he showed the results.

Robert pushed the door open, and Dez stepped back. Her face pinched as she tried to form an opinion. If it was so horrible that Dez couldn't think of an immediate response, then it was definitely *not* the look. Robert stepped back into the dressing room, not wanting another minute spent feeling like a sausage about to burst.

"I didn't say anything," Dez said defensively.

"Your face said volumes," Robert called back to her.

"You're the one who said you *knew* your sizes." Dez taunted. "Claudia! We'll need a size up on the trousers and shirt." Dez barked her orders to the sales associate assigned to them.

"You really know how to command a room," Robert said before unbuttoning his shirt and peeling off the trousers. Robert caught Dez's eyes in the reflection, peaking through a crack. Her gaze moved over Robert's bare skin. Her gaze slightly focused as Robert turned to the side, and she glimpsed his full front pouch. Playfully, Robert raised an eyebrow in the mirror. A subtle pink bloomed in her cheeks before she slammed the door and shouted for the sales associate again.

"Claudia!"

A soft yelp squeaked in response to Dez's call, followed by the hurried tapping of the woman's heels as she rushed around the store.

"I'm almost done, miss!"

Robert hoped the commission outweighed any emotional trauma heaped on her by Dez.

Robert's attention turned from Dez commandeering the sales staff and back to his appearance. There was no truer critic than one's reflection. It had been months since Robert faced a full-body reflection, and it seemed even longer since he purchased new clothes. Robert turned to the side and sucked in his stomach, and then released.

There was, in fact, a bulge.

"I guess I can't deny it," he said as he slapped his slight belly.

After months of late-night binging, drinking on the job, and little exercise, it surprised Robert he wasn't bigger. He knew his clothes felt tighter in certain areas, but it was a thought that he buried under the monotony of the day and worries of the future. His midsection and hips had taken the brunt of the weight gain. Robert's upper body was not unscathed. His once muscular, trim pectorals had formed a layer of fat and looked heavier. It erased the definition he spent years achieving, but they looked fuller. Robert had laughed at how tightly the first pair of trousers spread across his buttocks. The middle seam looked ready to burst if he even contemplated sitting down.

"So, Ms. Dez, may I ask you a question?" Robert added an extra bit of sweetness to her name, making her verbally gag on the other side of the door.

"As long as you don't call me Ms. Dez again." She gagged once more. "You sound like some sort of perverted student. What do you want to know?" The dressing room door opened, and Dez offered a stack of clothes to Robert, which he placed on a bench and peeked his head outside.

Dez settled into the cushioned chair she dragged from the opposite side of the store. One employee tried to stop her but was quickly sent away with a verbal lashing.

"To stay politically correct—what exactly are you?"

Dez clicked her tongue at the question.

"What do you think I am?" Dez asked. Her words took physical form, wrapping themselves around Robert. The sensation was chilly—almost ticklish. He shook the impression away, but the sense returned more potent than before. Ideas fluttered in his mind, nothing fully formed, but he could feel something try to take root.

"Stop doing that," Robert snapped. Dez laughed, and the sensation vanished.

"Doing what?" she teased, feigning innocence.

"So, are you one of them?" Robert asked, and Dez scoffed.

"Do you think I am one of them?"

"Do you always answer every question with a question?"

Dez laughed again. "They wish I were, but no, I am not a part of their secret club," she said flatly. "I am just another side character in their endless story." She made an aloof motion.

"You seem less like a side character and more like the villain, if you ask me." Robert shut the dressing room door, content with her answer.

"I'll take that as a compliment." The smile in Dez's voice was unmistakable. She was pleased to be a villain.

It was meant to be one.

"So, how did you become wrapped up in all of this?" Robert asked, pressing Dez's good graces with another question. Maybe if he layered his questions with compliments, they could get through an entire conversation without someone ending up hurt or broken.

"Do you want the long story or the short story?" Dez requested. Robert looked at the stack of clothes, seeing several more selections than before.

"Long story," Robert grunted as he stepped into the first pair of pants. They reached halfway up his thighs and stopped. Robert gave a gentle tug; they weren't going any further.

Another pass.

"I work for Luke's boss." Dez did not go into further explanation.

Robert tossed the pants and slid on a pair of jeans. Luckily, they fit, but the polo was a different story.

"And?" Robert asked as he exited the dressing room. Dez gave him a once-over.

"And you look fat in that shirt. Try a size up." She rotated her fingers, and Robert turned, giving her a full 360 view. "Pants are good. Your butt looks nice. Next."

Robert closed the door and moved to the next outfit, but continued the same conversation. "So, you work for Luke's boss and?" Robert asked, trying to bait her into continuing her story.

"And that is the end of the story." And the end of Robert's question.

Robert worked through the stack of clothes, receiving a thumbs up from Dez on some while she gagged at others. By the end of his impromptu fashion show, Dez approved five dress shirts, two pairs of trousers, two pairs of jeans, several pairs of underwear, and a black pair of dress shoes. Claudia happily rang up their purchases, eager to be rid of the two of them.

Robert choked on his tongue at the total.

"Two thousand five hundred and forty-three dollars and fifty-two cents," Claudia said with a smile. Her commission did, in fact, outweigh Dez's torture.

Happily, Dez handed over Katherine's credit card while Robert wandered away. He browsed through a rack of forgotten pieces and unsold accessories from prior collections. Most of the items were unsold for a reason, but one thing stood out among the gaudy bracelets and glitzy jewelry.

I have the extra money, was the lie he told himself as he paid for it with the tips he made the day prior. *It wasn't too expensive,* was the second one, he repeated as he accepted the small, black bag and went out searching for Dez.

Robert found her seated on the edge of a water fountain, watching a group of children play in the water. He hung back, interested in the way she watched them. She observed them silently as they tossed handfuls at one another, following them with a peculiar glint in her eye. A small wave struck Dez's thigh, and the children paused. Dez looked at her wet jeans and then toward the children. Robert prepared to run toward the children's rescue, but Dez splashed them back. They squealed in delight at the water's assault and returned to their battle in the fountain.

So, she isn't all fire and brimstone.

Her usual stoic features relaxed as she smiled at the children. The tension that Robert usually saw in her straight back seemed to loosen the longer she watched. A glint formed in her eyes, one that warmed Robert in a way that made him fear her less and admire her just a little more.

Robert imagined what Dez was like as a child—if she were one. He laughed at the image of a ten-year-old Dez. He didn't see her as a bully type, but more the child who fought the bully when they became too mean—just like Rebecca. Robert was usually the one that needed the saving.

"Having fun?" Robert asked as he came to stand beside Dez. The pleasant look evaporated, as if she were afraid to show her softer side. Her mask of calm ferocity slipped back into place as she stood.

"What did you get?"

"None of your business."

Dez glanced toward the tiny bag he held in his hands but shrugged. "Wanna do some more damage on Kitty Kat's card?"

Robert surrendered to Dez's need for more obnoxious spending. Most of the purchases were for him, but Robert caught Dez's signature purple hidden among the stacks. The morning slid into the afternoon, and the bags on Robert's arms grew. At the high points, Robert forgot his troubles and felt almost normal. Robert didn't know if it was foolish to admit, but he enjoyed his morning with Dez and felt insane to say, but it looked like Dez enjoyed herself as well.

Chapter 14

Midday approached quickly, and the rumbling in Robert's stomach became harder to ignore, despite Dez's best efforts. The scent of cinnamon buns and pretzels presented Robert's suggestion, while Dez requested a place without plastic silverware, specifically an upscale sushi bar attached to the mall.

So, they compromised—and got sushi.

*   *   *

"You have to try this." Dez plopped a piece of sashimi onto Robert's plate.

He frowned at the raw slice of tuna, seeing his singular culinary enemy. Robert liked most foods, but there was just something about uncooked food that he could not stomach. The pink, squishy surface agitated Robert's stomach, and the thought of the slimy texture made it even worse. With the tips of his chopsticks, Robert pushed away the tuna and returned to his third plate of crispy dumplings.

"I'll just stick with the gyoza." He raised one golden brown pot sticker and grinned as he swallowed it. A dumpling caught in his throat, ruining his smooth move, and causing him to choke for just a moment. Dez laughed between her fingers as Robert gasped for air.

"No. It's Okay. Just let me die. It would be the humane thing to do," Robert said as he gulped down water and coughed again, clearing his airway.

"If you were eating one of these, you wouldn't have to worry about choking. Just slides right down." Dez opened her mouth, placed a large piece of fish on her tongue, and swallowed with ease. The chopsticks dragged down her throat, following the food before ending at her sternum. Robert's eyes lowered slightly, and he stared at the slit in her shirt, the small keyhole that offered just a glimpse of her skin. The sight was enough to tease Robert with the idea of more.

Robert could not shake the vision created by Luke's influence or the thoughts it brought. He could still feel her lips against him as if the illusion were real.

She is beautiful.

It was undeniable that Dez was gorgeous. She slicked back her baby hairs while two buns held the rest of her curls. Her purple smokey eyes closed as she enjoyed another bite. Her glossy purple lips pushed out, holding the flavor in her mouth before she swallowed.

What would it feel like to kiss her?

Robert was unsure if the idea was his own, or something placed there by Luke. He hadn't had a romantic thought in months, and now he couldn't stop. It was like Luke awoke a part of him that Robert had buried, and now it demanded to be acknowledged.

A tap on his forehead broke Robert's concentration. Two chopsticks floated in front of him, tapping him a second time.

"Not used to being in front of someone so breathtaking?" Dez asked as she leaned back. "Am I just sooooo irresistible?" she teased.

Robert chuckled. "I was just wondering if Katherine will be at my door tomorrow morning with a mile-long receipt, asking how I expected to repay her." As if conjured by the thought of their already obnoxiously expensive lunch, a waiter placed a large bottle of sake on the table and two cups. Dez tapped her fingers together in slight applause, eager for a taste of the alcohol.

"How much was that?" Robert asked as Dez poured two heavy glasses.

"You don't wanna know," she warned. "Drink?"

"I assumed at least one was for me." Robert accepted a full glass.

"Wouldn't be the first time I got plastered here."

"I can't tell if you're lying or not."

Dez ignored his question, tipping the cup and dumping the shot into her mouth. She happily exhaled and placed the glass on the table.

"Just let me know if the manager walks this way or not," she laughed as she poured herself another round as Robert sipped from his. "For someone who works at a bar, you know how to milk a drink." She tipped her second glass into her mouth and swallowed. Dez wiggled her brows, challenging Robert to keep pace.

Robert looked at his glass. It was pretty full, and Robert wasn't the biggest fan of sake, but he wasn't a bitch, either. Robert took it like a shot, one mouthful, and swallowed quickly. The drink burned as it went down his throat. Robert coughed as his stomach accepted the unwanted liquor.

Okay, maybe he was a bitch . . . when it came to sake at least.

Dez's face shone with laughter as she poured them both another drink.

"Not a drinker?" Dez asked, replaying their first conversation.

"Trying." A deep smile appeared on Robert's face, almost matching Dez's and a connection formed for just a moment. One where they both saw how much the other was enjoying their time together. It was undeniable.

Dez looked away first, and Robert moved quickly after.

Robert's attention returned to his food while Dez stared into her glass. A weird tension filled the now joyless space. He scolded himself, wondering how he had changed so drastically. Robert was never the popular wild one—that was Rebecca—but he was well-liked. He didn't have many close friends, but he had a list of acquaintances that enjoyed his company. But now, Robert couldn't string a sentence together without becoming anxious.

You can do this. Just ask a question.

Ask one question.

Robert looked up at Dez. She kept her face low, angled towards her food, but Robert saw her brown eyes examining him through her lashes. Her head lifted marginally, and his gaze returned to his cooling dish.

Just one question.

You don't need to be so worried. Just relax.

Maybe he was overthinking everything? Maybe Dez was only here because she had to be? Or maybe she did like him, and Robert was ruining it all? Robert's anxiety battled the confidence he attempted to build, but it was Dez who broke the silence.

"So, tell me about yourself, Rob-bert," she said, over-articulating his name. Her question lifted Robert's head and his spirits. He caught her face and felt the anxiety-induced depression pull away.

"Well, I like long walks on the beach, white chocolate, and I have a deep love for romantic—"

"Never mind. I take it back. I don't care," Dez said, interrupting Robert's response. She held up her hands. "Please, Lucifer below, tell me you're lying."

Robert grinned.

"Cause if that's true, I *will* stab these chopsticks into my neck." Deftly, Dez maneuvered the chopsticks around her fingers and pointed them toward her jugular.

"Well, only one of the three is a lie. Your guess which." Robert laughed before he lifted his drink. "I wrote to you every day for a year." Robert recited the famous line, ending it with a sip of his sake and another pot sticker. Dez playfully stabbed herself in the neck with the chopsticks, and Robert chuckled.

He looked at Dez with playful disgust on her face, and he felt it again as their eyes met. A connection? A friendship? He didn't know how to label it, but Robert liked it. It made him feel something that he was not afraid to experience.

"Your turn," he said, nodding toward Dez.

"My turn, what?"

"Well, during a proper date, the guy talks, and then the lady talks. It's called a conversation. But I haven't been on a date in a while. So, as far as I know, the rules could have changed," Robert said, thinking back to the last date he went on with Victoria. He couldn't remember much of it, but Robert assumed he spent most of the date talking while Victoria spent her time looking at her phone or flat-out ignoring Robert's attempts at conversation.

"I bet mine is longer." Dez plucked another piece of tuna.

"Really?" Robert said, faking a sense of surprise. "But you are so approachable. I would think you had suitors lined up to ask for your hand."

Dez flicked one of her chopsticks at Robert. He ducked. But it still hit his shoulder.

"My hand?" Dez quoted. "How old do you think I am?"

Robert laughed nervously. "I fell for this trap with Luke already. I know he's somewhere getting the early bird special."

Dez's brow arched. "Don't even wanna try?"

"No, thank you."

"Not even a guess."

"Nope."

"What if I gave you a range?"

"Not interested." Robert raised his hands. "Never guess a lady's age or her weight. No answer will ever be correct."

"Smart man. But it has been . . . somewhere in the ballpark of thirty years since my last date. I think we went to Pup'n Taco."

"What the hell is Pup'n Taco?"

"Joint that closed in the late '80s or early '90s. Can't remember. It was a shit place. So honestly, not surprised. Most things don't last over thirty or forty years, so I try not to get too attached." Dez's playful aura dimmed at her admission.

For a moment, Robert had forgotten that Dez was not playing a game, making him guess between twenty-five and twenty-eight, but between decades, maybe even hundreds of years.

In a roundabout way, Dez confirmed she was not a Sin, but that still left a laundry list of options. And that was a list of things that Robert could name. There was a possibility that she was something beyond his knowledge.

How did Dez fit into the grand scheme of things?

Robert studied Dez's face, how her posture shifted as he thought. She pushed the last piece of sushi with the tips of her chopsticks. Her snarky façade had gone pensive. She was lost somewhere in thought.

A dark question floated to the forefront of Robert's mind as he watched Dez.

How much had she lost in her extended life?

"You, okay?" Robert asked, knowing she wouldn't answer the question, but he knew he had to ask.

Dez threw away the thought with a blink of her eyes.

"Just wondering if you're gonna braid my hair first or if I get to do yours," Dez countered. "I bet it would look gorgeous with a French braid." Her words were sarcastic, but they lacked the usual bite Robert expected. Robert smiled halfheartedly as he turned back to his food, and the silence returned.

He didn't press the issue, but he could have sworn he saw her brush away a tear as they silently finished their food. Robert wanted to say something, but he couldn't find the words to console someone who had probably lived through lifetimes of tragedy.

*   *   *

Twelve stores, three energy drinks, and an extra-large cinnamon bun later, Robert and Dez ended their day how it started, outside Robert's apartment building. Robert tensely waited for the moment. Dez turned off the engine and began their goodbyes. They were short and unsentimental, as Robert expected, but he felt the courage to do something unexpected.

"I actually wanted to give you something." Robert confessed. Dez gave a blank look as Robert dug through the bags at his feet.

"What could you possibly have for me?"

Robert lifted the small bag from the first store.

"I'll say it's a thank-you for today. It was fun. I haven't taken a day for myself since I moved here." He passed the small bag to Dez and awkwardly smiled. "I bought it with my own cash, so don't think I sneaked it in on one of the purchases. But I saw them and thought it went with your overall aesthetic."

Dez furrowed her brows. She tilted the bag on its side and dumped a pair of deep purple cat-eye sunglasses into her hand. She lifted them and turned them in her hand, examining them.

"Do you like them?"

She turned her attention to Robert and dissolved his confidence with just a look. The friendly sparkle cultivated was gone. Her mask of stoicism had once again been placed over her features, hiding away whatever she felt. Empty eyes stared at him. No snark. No friendship. Just empty.

"What do you think this was, Robert?"

"Huh?" Color drained from his face.

"Do you think this was some fun day out? Two friends enjoying each other's company? A date? "

"Well, I thought—" His throat tightened, unable to answer.

"Make no mistake, Robert," Dez interrupted. Her voice was even-toned and absolute. "Today was a job. You are a job. We are not friends. I am here because I was told to do this." She held out the glasses for Robert. "Take them back."

"What? No," Robert said firmly, even as his voice shook.

"Robert, take them back. I don't want them."

"Dez, can you please just listen—"

"I am not here to listen, Robert. I am here to—"

"Can you stop being heartless for two seconds and let someone be nice to you?" Robert snapped. His chin trembled as he formed words. "I wanted to thank you for making me feel like a person for the first time in a long time. But apparently, you don't know what it's like to feel alone in the world." Robert expected Dez to push further, but she was frozen. He opened the passenger side door. "Do what you want with them? Break them. Return them. I don't care."

He grabbed his shopping bags and rushed outside with one sweeping motion. He caught Dez's eyes as he turned to slam the door. Her mask had cracked just slightly, and emotion leaked through. Pity. She looked like she wanted to speak but didn't know how to form the words. Robert slammed the door before Dez could speak.

Halfway up the stairs of the building, Dez called out to Robert. His steps were uneven, and he stumbled at the top of the stoop, but he kept moving. Robert did not stop until he was behind his locked apartment door.

"So fucking stupid!" Robert threw his shopping bags. His purchases spilled across the floor. "How could I be so stupid? " Robert stepped atop his new clothes, wandering towards his bed as every emotion rushed to the surface. Why did Luke have to do that to him, awaken parts that Robert was much happier to leave dormant? Why did Luke have to put those thoughts of love in his head?

You're so stupid. Why would someone actually want you?

"Just a job."

Chapter 15

The days following Robert's excursion blurred together as he sank back into himself, rebuilding the emotional blockade that fell to pieces in just one afternoon with Dez. He said little to Nathan, though Nathan held a conversation of one quite effectively as he complained about the 'bomb threat.' His annoyance was a constant stream of grumbles, grunts, and side comments about how he was 'forced' from his home and onto the streets. Robert kept his thoughts to himself and silently prayed that Dez's bomb threat was indeed a false alarm. The day after, a notice advised that the threat was a prank. Robert relaxed just slightly, happy to know that even Dez had her limits. Or at least he hoped she did.

Late Saturday evening, Robert received a message from Dez. It was a brief text telling him to be ready by eight in the morning and that he would ride with Luke, Katherine, and her. He responded with a simple "K," ending any potential conversation, not that he thought Dez was interested in small talk. But, to his disbelief, Dez followed up with a request to wear the blue trousers and white button-down with the pink floral pattern. Robert did not answer.

For the rest of the night, Robert paced, organized his now bursting closet, cleaned his kitchenette twice, and when he ran out of chores, he counted the popcorn ceiling and wondered what he would find the following day.

By six AM, Robert gave up on the idea of sleep and occupied himself with an activity he had not done in months. He slid on his running shoes, shorts, and a somewhat clean shirt and greeted the morning.

The sun had not yet risen, but the traffic and people were already flooding the streets. Robert jogged for the first few blocks, feeling pain in his joints. Immediately regretting that he did not have the foresight to stretch, but the aches were not wholly unwelcomed. The pain forced his brain to contemplate his bad knees and tightening muscles instead of the day to come.

With every stomp, a few seconds passed, and Robert traveled further. He counted out his steps, timing them with each inhale and exhale.

The sun peaked in the spaces between buildings as six became seven. The first light summoned the masses from their hotels. As the streets filled, running became difficult, and Robert could no longer keep pace as cars and pedestrians filled his pathways; for the first time in over an hour, Robert stopped at an intersection.

Two men materialized at Robert's sides as he waited for the light to change: one a fresh-faced tourist and the other an emotionally dead capitalist. Neither paid attention to the other, but Robert felt drawn to both.

Robert had been both men in his life. He was the overly excited tourist, ready for an adventurous weekend. Though Captain Russo stole his final night, he recalled the fun he and Rebecca had as they ran through the city. And before that, Robert had been the emotionally exhausted businessman for several years. He couldn't help but gape at the businessman. The tailored suit. The smooth face. The overly gelled hair. Once upon a time, Robert looked nearly identical to this man; down to the empty look in his eyes—a gaze that said the man would ride the rest of his life in neutral.

It was a look that Robert remembered vividly.

Wake up at six for a day of uninspired work, be home by five for a lackluster dinner in silence, and sleep by nine. Some nights Rebecca would come over, or he and Victoria would visit her parents. They filled their weekends with mundane activities: parties at the country club, forced business dinners, unsatisfying sex. His life was once a dull routine—a road he would have marched to the grave if not for Victoria.

Fucking Victoria.

But as Robert thought back to the endless cycle he walked, he wondered, was his life any better today?

Robert worked all night and slept all day. His days were full of meaningless conversations with customers. Meals he ate alone—if a gas station hotdog and a bag of chips were considered a meal. What money Robert earned was spent on finding Rebecca. Robert never realized it, but he found himself in another cycle.

Suppose his recent acquaintances hadn't found him. Would Robert have spent the rest of his life searching for Rebecca? Could he ever have forgiven himself if he gave up his search? Could he have ever moved on? Thankfully, those were not questions he ever considered, or at least—Robert hoped he wouldn't. If the day went as he expected, he would have Rebecca back before the day's end, or at least a way forward.

"Do you need something?" The businessman snapped, noticing Robert's unblinking focus on the stranger's face.

"Oh-um-sorry," Robert stuttered as the light changed and ran off, thinking of his current predicament.

What would Becca think if she saw me?

She would be disappointed.

Rebecca always pushed Robert to take more risks and open himself up to people.

He chuckled

Wonder what she'll think of my new friends if I could call them friends. Definitely Luke, at the very least.

Maybe it was time for him to take his sister's advice finally.

He added the thought to the hundreds that plagued his mind as he turned down a long stretch of sidewalk that led back to his apartment. Robert looked at his watch. He would be late if he didn't pick up the pace. An image of Dez standing at his front door, arms crossed, and a sour look on her face appeared in his mind. His lips curved into a smile.

It's not like they'll leave without me.

It was ten minutes past eight when Robert was showered, dressed, and shaved. He wouldn't admit it, but he was a little disappointed when Dez hadn't barged into his apartment at precisely eight o'clock and ordered him to get his ass into her purple dinosaur. By eight-thirty, Robert grew slightly concerned that they had left without him, but Robert's phone rang shortly after.

"We're downstairs," Dez said.

"Hello to you, too," Robert responded. "What happened to being on time?" Robert collected his wallet and keys and walked out his front door.

"I said eight, knowing you would be running behind. Just be happy that I didn't say half past seven." Her voice practically vibrated with enjoyment. Robert rolled his eyes and ended the call. He went into his bathroom and checked his appearance. He adjusted the neck of the blue floral shirt, ensured his shirt was still tucked, and smoothed his fly-away hairs.

He grinned at his reflection. Robert hadn't seen this man in months, and it felt nice to look good for once.

"Make one mistake today that you'll be grateful for tomorrow." Robert took a deep breath, parroting his sister's 'wise' words. Robert nodded to his reflection. He could make at least one mistake today. Whether he'll appreciate it is another question, but that was the price of risk-taking.

Stepping back into the street, Robert expected to see Dez's purple sedan crookedly parked on the road but found a stretch town car idling in front of the building. The vehicle was a shiny black, waxed and polished so much that it reflected the sun. Robert squinted at the overly blacked-out windows but could see no passengers.

The front driver's door opened, and a well-dressed man stepped out. He silently circled the vehicle and opened the back door for Robert, motioning him forward.

"This way, sir," the impeccably dressed man requested. Robert stepped closer to the town car and saw only the dark inside of the back half of the vehicle.

A vision flashed in his mind's eye—hands stretching out of the darkness, reaching towards . . . something. Robert backed away, seeing the hands so clearly in the morning light. But they did not stretch for him. They reached for . . . something else. And before he could examine further, the vision was gone.

The driver gave a pointed cough as Robert hesitated on the sidewalk. "If you would, sir. We have a—"

"Get in the fucking car, Robert!"

Dez's voice sliced through Robert's concerns and the driver's request.

Yup, it's the right car.

Robert shook his head, banishing the thoughts of hands, as he stepped into the vehicle and slid across the warm, black leather seating. The door hadn't even closed before a blur of baby blue launched at him.

"Robert!" Luke squealed as his arms wrapped around Robert's body and pressed his face into Robert's chest. "You smell soooooo good." Luke inhaled deeply, sniffing the cologne Dez chose for him. "Practically delectable."

Robert laughed and patted Luke's tan thigh.

"You are looking nice as well, Luke. I see you have on your fancy short shorts," Robert said, nodding toward Luke's legs. The baby blue shorts ended just a few inches below his hips. A pair of white knee-high socks covered most of Luke's lower legs, but a few inches of bare skin were shown between them. A white dress shirt with a baby blue bowtie covered his chest. His face was pristine and highlighted, with speckles of blue underneath his eyes. His hair was gelled and combed into a perfect side part. Robert would say that Luke looked practically angelic but deemed the compliment inappropriate for his current company.

"Why would I ever wanna hide these legs from the public?" Luke said as he pointed his shiny brown leather shoes toward the two women who sat at the opposite end of the vehicle. "These two sourpusses wanted me to wear pants. COULD YOU IMAGINE! Like I'm some sort of virgin." Luke collapsed on Robert's lap and waved in his face. "Oh, the humanity." Robert looked toward Dez and Katherine. They rolled their eyes in tandem.

At least they agree on something.

"Hello, Robert," Katherine said in her unnaturally cool tone. Her deep red dress changed in the filtered light of the tinted windows. With every movement, the color shifted from red to black, as if the

170

threads could simultaneously be both colors and something more. The dress seemed like cocktail attire with the draped sleeves, the sweetheart neckline, and the abundance of chest she showed. "Glad to see you again." Katherine's face held a similar appearance as the first time Robert met her, minimal makeup, bright red lips, and hair pulled away from her face in an artful yet causal way. "You look very nice."

"And same to you, Katherine." Their hands met, and her aura wrapped around his hand. It was a soft, testing flicker of power, teasing him to play her games. Robert knew better than to test her again, and he broke their grasp before she forced him. His eyes rolled from Katherine over to Dez, who lounged in the corner. Just seeing Dez struck against the wall Robert had built back.

Fuck. Why did she have to be so beautiful?

Dez replicated her signature deep purple from the shade of her eyeshadow to the tips of her pointed heels. Her outfit was modest compared to her everyday ensembles—a tight-fitting corseted blouse with flowing sleeves and tapered high-waisted trousers. Dez's curly locks were straightened and pulled into another high ponytail. One arm lay along the back of the seats while her other held a to-go cup of coffee. Robert smiled at the sight of her drink, remembering her dire need for coffee the other day. She gave a slight nod, acknowledging his arrival. Robert's eyes glossed over her and her smile before moving his attention toward Luke. A dismissal Dez did not miss.

"So, where are we going all dressed up? Party? Virgin sacrifice? Both?" The vehicle lurched forward, and the four swayed.

"No, silly! Virgin sacrifices are Friday. On Sundays, we go to church!" Luke said with a fake Southern accent. Cheerfully, he bounced from the seat next to Robert and onto the center cushion. "I do declare. I hope I remembered my hymnal," Luke teased as he clutched an invisible string of pearls around his neck.

"Jesus Christ," Katherine grumbled, openly regretting her choice of company.

"Exactly." Luke's eyes glowed with an excitable intensity that pulsed through the backseat. Phantom strokes moved across their skin as Luke's influence filled the car; it caressed their faces, pressed against their lips, and grazed every inch of exposed flesh. Robert mentally pushed away whatever touched him, feeling it shove back like an overly excited dog wanting its owner. Luke's influence became aggressive, squeezing a moan from Robert's tight lips. "What better people to play with than those who seek salvation? Looking for someone who they can serve," Luke growled. "I can practically feel their repressed desires from here." Luke rubbed his hands along his chest and up toward his lips. He kissed his fingers and threw the taste into the air. "So delicious is their repression."

A small purple purse flew from the corner of the town car and landed squarely on Luke's privates. The impact jolted him from his lust and pulled him back into reality.

"Cool it, or I'll throw you out of the car," Dez threatened. Luke stuck out his tongue and folded his hands in his lap, covering his erection as it bulged in his skintight shorts.

"So, this meeting is at a church?" Robert asked. "Who are we meeting exactly?"

"Friends." Katherine turned her gaze out the window, ending the conversation. Her hand searched through her curls, moving toward the one that twisted along the curve of her face. The silver vein that shined against the red backdrop of Katherine's hair was hard to miss. Her finger looped around the coil and pulled it from within the clump, turning more around her finger as she thought.

Did she have gray hair before?

Robert could not remember seeing any grays during their previous meeting.

Katherine's eyes moved from the window and found Robert's quizzical gaze and furrowed brow. She tucked the hair within her curls, hiding the gray. The action seemed intentional, but Robert couldn't help but examine her further. Yes, her skin was still perfect and alabaster smooth, but it lacked her unnatural glow and seemed only pale. Katherine kept her face emotionless, but Robert could see lines—tiny wrinkles forming around the edge of her eyes and lips with every slight facial tick.

Those definitely weren't there before.

Something was happening to Katherine, but Robert chose silence instead of asking a question he knew she would not answer.

*   *   *

The silence of the vehicle gave way to the sound of tolling bells and singing people. The driver slowed as pedestrians crossed in front of the car and swarmed the streets. Robert looked out the window and saw hundreds flocking toward the white-spired cathedral. People marched up its stone staircase and through the two-story-tall doorway. The white marble shone under the cloudless sky. The stained glass windows on the front and the sides of the building scattered colored light on the pavement. Children danced on the colored ground while parents greeted one another before they walked up the main stairway. The antique architecture looked almost out of place, with fast-food joints across the street.

Robert was in slight shock; they weren't lying.

The door opened, and the full impact of the white building nearly blinded Robert. It was a radiant beacon of salvation in a city of devils.

"Sir, if you would," the driver asked, motioning for Robert to exit the vehicle. He stepped onto the sidewalk, followed by Luke, Dez, and Katherine. The driver closed the door, and Katherine leaned toward him, whispering. "Of course, Mistress." He responded with a bow before returning to the vehicle and driving away.

"What did you tell him?" Robert questioned.

"To stay close. I appreciate a quick getaway when necessary."

Dez raised her eyebrows in fake excitement before she threw her gaze around the parishioners. She wrinkled her face at their ugly outfits and opened her purse.

A smile tweaked at Robert's lips.

She kept them.

She withdrew the purple sunglasses and placed them on her nose, not realizing the cracks that formed in Robert. Hope seeped through his emotional boundaries.

Make one mistake . . .

Robert sighed a happy breath. Although it hurt, he was thrilled that he took the risk of giving her the glasses. He made a mental note to tell Rebecca that she was not wholly wrong about her motto.

Seeing Dez wear her gift made the fluttering return. It wasn't that Robert wanted a girlfriend. He just wanted a relationship that meant something; maybe if Dez wasn't so stubborn, he could form that with her. Robert knew she enjoyed their time together almost as much as he did; who knows? Maybe something could happen in the future, but for now, Robert was happy calling her a friend, even if she didn't want to admit it.

Not friends, my ass.

Dez looked up from her purse and found Robert's grinning face. He tapped his temple. *I see you,* his smile said.

Though he couldn't see it, Robert knew Dez rolled her eyes behind the dark frames before she walked toward the church while the three trailed behind her.

"So, how bad can a meeting be if it's happening at a church?"

"When you are, what we are—a church is the last place you want to go." Luke placed an arm around Robert. "But I would rather be us than one of *them.*"

Dez hmphed in agreement. "They're like sheep going to slaughter. One mindlessly following the other." Dez pulled a cigarette from her purse, lit it, and blew smoke upward.

"Those will kill you, Dezzy," Luke teased.

"Not quick enough." Dez blew upward again.

"Love the glasses," Luke said. "Serving very sexy librarian. Where did you get them?"

Dez ignored Luke's question and how largely Robert smiled beside him, and continued to smoke.

"Excuse me, ma'am, there are children here," an older Southern lady said, tapping Dez on the shoulder. "Ma'am. Excuse me." She stabbed her crooked nails into Dez's shoulder several more times. "You need to put that out."

As Dez faced the short, round social justice warrior, Robert's eyes became saucers. Dez wouldn't fight this woman, would she?

Dez took another drag of her cigarette, leaned towards the woman, and blew her smoke into their face. She responded with an overly dramatic coughing fit that drew the surrounding people's attention.

"I can't-I can't breathe!" The woman wheezed.

"And?" Dez stepped away from the woman. Her gaze went up and down, sizing up the woman. She nodded.

God, she is actually considering fighting her.

Fearing the worse, Robert snatched the cigarette from Dez's hand and crushed it under his foot.

"We don't smoke at church here." Thinking quickly, Robert leaned toward the woman. "I'm so sorry, Miss. My cousin isn't from here. She is . . . uh . . . European."

The older woman scowled at Dez and gave a half-smile to Robert, happy that she had earned an apology.

"Clearly, they don't teach manners over there." The woman turned up her nose and marched off.

"Can we keep a low profile? They already know we are here. We do not need to cause a scene," Katherine instructed.

Dez waved away Katherine's words.

Katherine's hand snapped like a whip, snatching Dez's wrist mid-movement.

"Do we understand?" Red ignited around the rim of her green irises, like fire encircling a forest. Her aura pulsed around the group, warming the area as her power spiked.

"Understood?" Dez said the word as a question. "Do not forget, *Katherine*. I do not work for you. I work *with* you. So next time you think about telling me what to do, remember who I answer to." Dez flexed her fingers, breaking free from Katherine's grip.

Before the tension escalated, Luke slid between the two, acting as a physical and spiritual barrier.

"I hate breaking up this love fest, ladies, but he's here." Luke nodded toward the top of the steps. The group's attention climbed the stairs until the four stared at a man who stood at the entrance of the church.

He created a picturesque scene with arms outstretched, a gentle smile, and long, wavy hair. His white button-down and black pants were simple and appropriate. He greeted every person who approached him, hugging them and shaking their hands with the same intensity one would exude when meeting a lifelong friend. His honey brown eyes focused in a way that made every person he met seem important—special enough for him to devote just a fraction of his day to their arrival. He looked at them with a gentleness that Robert felt at the base of the stairs. The smiling man's attention swept through the crowd and found Robert.

A burst of compassion swelled inside Robert as the two men's eyes met. A tingling sensation moved along his body, soft and gentle.

The smiling man beckoned Robert forward, and the distance between them melted away. The steps, the people, and his companions all vanished. And in this world, only the two of them existed. The man beckoned Robert to approach, and Robert floated forward.

His voice called to Robert. *Come into the light. Come to salvation.*

He shone like a saint resurrected, like God in human form.

"Yes." Robert felt lighter and happier than he had ever felt before. He felt like he could accomplish anything with this man by his side. Robert reached out a hand toward the man. "Please."

The stranger nodded, hearing Robert's plea. Robert stretched out his hand, and the stranger mirrored his movement.

Just reach for me, Robert, the gentle voice urged. *Let me help you, Robert.*

A hand took hold of Robert's shoulder, and the benevolent sentiments inside him were set aflame. Rage flooded his body, burning away the kindness and kindness until only fury filled him. Sweat dotted his forehead. Robert's reaching hand became a clenched fist.

A growl started in the back of Robert's throat.

Him.

Robert leered at the man. His sympathetic face seemed patronizing. He didn't want to help Robert; he was taunting him.

Allow me to wash away your fury, the voice offered.

The softness reached out toward Robert once more but retreated, burned by the anger that Robert fumed. The voice withdrew, and the world became real once more.

And just as soon as the fury appeared, it was smothered, returned to its bottle like the genie forced back into his lamp. The hand on his shoulder squeezed. A minor act of reassurance. Robert expected to see Luke but found Katherine.

Her green eyes faced the man at the top of the stairs. Blood red rubies and jaspers floated atop her emerald eyes, begging to be freed and be allowed to consume.

"Be on your guard, Robert." Katherine released his shoulder, taking her remaining influence from his body. "Though he appears to be a shepherd, it does not mean he will not slaughter his flock to accomplish his desires."

Is he truly that dangerous?

The man atop the steps withdrew into the church, taking the welcoming sight with him. An organ blared to life, announcing the beginning of service. The sound summoned the few stragglers, leaving the four alone at the base of the stairs.

"Everyone ready?" Katherine asked.

The three nodded and stepped forward.

Into the Devil's den, we go.

Chapter 16

"Please, somebody, anybody, kill me." Luke threw himself into the wooden pew, neck laying limply against the back. "I'm so booooooored. How do people handle this every week?"

Katherine and Dez sighed, silently wishing Luke could act like an adult for five seconds of his life. The group sat in the back of the sanctuary, comfortably distanced from the overflowing front rows of screaming and crying worshipers. A few latecomers attempted to sit with them, but—thanks to Katherine's continual glare—they found someplace more suitable. But the worshipers, three rows in front of them, were close enough to fall victim to Luke's constant whining.

"Where are all the sexy churchmen?" Luke commented in a somewhat hushed tone. "Could I at least have some sexy daddies to gawk at?"

"Hush." Dez slapped Luke's thigh with her purse before turning back to the preacher, mirroring Katherine, who sat respectfully silent as the service progressed.

The preacher stood atop a raised stage. His heavy white robes restricted his movements. Every raise of his hand or gesture seemed to be a struggle as he ranted and motioned to the congregation. White curtains stretched behind him, reaching from the rafters of the sanctuary to the floor. A wooden cross the size of a minivan floated between the folds with an altar directly below.

Frequently, a crowd member would respond with an amen or a hallelujah, but the preacher was a pale imitation of the man who drew Robert's attention.

Robert didn't listen to what the preacher said, instead finding interest in the overly white sanctuary; how they kept everything so spotless in such a dirty city amazed him. A long cream carpet started at the entrance to the sanctuary and ended at the stage, and not a single stain showed. Dark wooden pews lined either side of the runner, each seemingly crafted by hand. White and light blue fabrics draped along the wall's lower portion with unlit sconces stationed between the drapes. The stained glass windows lined the upper half, portraying stories, characters, settings from the bible, and one somber depiction of Jesus.

"How much longer can this go on?" Luke complained.

Dez cut him a threatening glance. He went silent once more.

"You would think you never had to sit through service as a child," Dez hissed at Luke as the surrounding people became less forgiving of Luke's insistent sounds.

Luke lasted all of five minutes before he looked for ways to entertain himself. A tap on the leg brought Robert's attention to a game tic-tac-toe Luke drew on the back of a pamphlet.

Robert declined.

Luke's bottom lip quivered, but Robert held fast to his decision, so Luke turned to Dez, who shut him down with a less than church-appropriate response. Luke decided not even to consider Katherine.

So instead, Luke folded, unfolded, and refolded his pamphlet into an airplane, a flower, a crane. After several creations, the paper became too creased to continue his art and was discarded on the floor. Luke contemplated causing a scene by feeling 'the Spirit' but found interest in the tall Hispanic man across the aisle.

"Hello," Luke growled softly. The married man turned to Luke, somehow hearing his breathy introduction. Luke fluttered his fingers at the man. The stranger smiled, crinkling the area around his mouth and eyes. Luke sat straighter, presenting himself to the man. He pursed his lips and sent a kiss across the room. The man's face flushed with sexual thoughts. Luke followed his kiss with a not-so-subtle wink and nodded toward the back door. The man looked at the thin woman next to him and then at Luke. The stranger eagerly nodded, abandoning the idea of subtlety.

Swiftly, Luke rose from the pew and moved around Robert.

"'Scuse me . . . oh, sorry," Luke apologized as he brushed his ass against Robert's lap, moving toward the end of the pew.

"Lucas," Dez hissed as she reached for Luke's hand.

Luke slid out of her reach and squeezed down the narrow aisle walkway.

"I'm doing some reconnaissance," Luke said before power-walking away and out the main entrance. The man across the aisle excused himself seconds later, rushing out of the sanctuary to search for Luke.

"I'm going to kill him," Dez said, coming to terms with her reality. "I am going to kill. I will hang him upside down by his toes and keep him there until his head explodes." Dez tapped her purse against her thigh. "I can't believe this is how he acts."

"Desdemona, calm yourself." Katherine's voice was low and powerful. "Lucas knows what he is doing." Dez clenched her jaw at the sound of her full name. She muttered in a language that Robert could not understand as her tapping became a slapping.

Robert slid closer, filling Luke's gap, and held her tapping purse in place. Dez's body tensed at his touch, but the tapping stopped. Robert half expected her to swat him away, but Dez allowed his hand to remain.

"Is he always this . . ." Robert asked, remembering how he acted in the town car and at the Rusty Nail.

"Reckless? Uncontrollable?" Dez said, offering suggestions to Robert's unfinished sentence. Robert nodded, accepting both options.

Dez exhaled, blowing out her frustration. "Usually, but he's not as bad as Frank. Now, he was a constant ball of annoyance and humping." Dez slightly grinned, laughing at a memory.

"Frank?"

"The former Lust," Katherine said, interjecting into their conversation. She must have felt Robert readying to ask another follow-up question, as was his typical fashion, so she spoke again. "Someone we are not supposed to be talking about, Desdemona." Katherine's tone was warning enough for Robert not to ask about the former Lust, at least until he and Dez were outside of hearing distance.

Robert hadn't considered that there had to be a long line of former sins before Luke and Katherine. Hundreds of them, if not thousands, depending on how far back Eden stretched and how long a Sin lived. Robert looked at Katherine. He knew Luke was in his fifties, and Dez had to be well beyond that. But how old was Katherine? The way Katherine talked, she seemed much older than Luke. Seventy, possibly? Maybe older? But there was no way of knowing without asking, and Robert wasn't planning on doing that anytime soon.

Robert repositioned himself, pulling his attention from his questions and the pain in his lower back, and looked toward the preacher. The older man stood hunched over the podium. His arms waved frantically in the air as he spoke. His enthusiastic words of temptation held the attention of the men and women of the congregation. The preacher told the parable of Jesus's trials through the desert and the Devil's temptation.

Did the Devil tempt God's son because he took away Eve?

Robert lifted the Bible from the back of the pew and followed the story. Dez sat disinterested, but Katherine listened with a stoic face.

The two-hour service ended with the preacher offering communion to his congregation. The priest blessed each person, gave them wine and bread, and returned them to their seats. As worshipers passed the three, it became clear they were not planning on taking communion. The congregation judged them with hushed words and knowing glances—especially the short woman Dez nearly fought on the church's steps. When the last person sat down, the preacher closed his Bible, and the room let out a ripple of relaxation.

It was over.

"And with that, ladies and gentlemen, I would like to thank you for coming today, and I hope you have a blessed week!" The preacher took the Bible and walked off the stage through a side door. The room erupted into sound the moment the door shut. People talked, bones popped, and pews creaked as people moved through the sanctuary.

"Thank Beelzebub!" Dez groaned as she lifted her arms toward the ceiling, popping her joints.

Katherine rose and smoothed the creases in her dress. "The office is beneath the stage." Katherine motioned for them to follow as she walked opposite the traffic flow. Robert searched for Luke in the masses but could not find his bright blond hair or baby blue clothes. Knowing Luke—the little Robert did—he assumed Luke occupied himself with another husband. Converting them to the Church of Lust.

The three walked around the stage, down a sliver of a hallway, and descended a staircase. The sparse lighting gave just enough light to travel the stairs safely. But Katherine walked without hesitation, even as the darkness stole the light.

"Katherine acts like she knows where she is going," Robert whispered to Dez as she brought up the rear.

"Because I know where I am going. I have been here before. Though it has been many years," Katherine answered, stopping at a wooden door. Under the dim light, Robert could make out the faces of angels etched into the stained wood. Inlays of gold and silver enhanced their features. Jewels were placed in their eyes and adorned their crowns. The top looked freshly stained with a honey oak varnish, while the bottom seemed torched, purposefully charred by fire, and left to rot.

The metaphor was clear and a little heavy-handed.

"Prepare yourself, Desdemona, Robert, Lucas."

Dez and Robert twisted around at Luke's name, finding him beaming in a slightly less pristine state. His hair was matted, and his suit was askew, but his face glowed with an after-orgasm bliss.

"Have fun?" Dez said with a huff. Annoyance was heavy in her tone.

Luke wiggled his brows. "Five-star reviews wherever I go."

"Focus," Katherine commanded, ending the fun banter that had just begun. She turned her attention back to the door. Katherine inhaled a deep, steadying breath before opening the door and stepping forward.

Robert half expected to find a dungeon with virgins hanging from the ceiling and lamb's blood spilled on a stone altar, but the room was rather—mundane. The office space was warm and welcoming. Eucalyptus and spearmint spiced the air, flowing from scented candles scattered throughout the area. The furniture was rigid and not made for comfort. Paper-thin cushions covered the seats, backs built to be uncomfortably straight. Shelves lined all the walls—crowded with objects ranging from porcelain angels to empty Chinese food boxes. The floor matched the shelves in their disarray.

Scattered across the maroon carpet were hundreds of books. Some were kept in precarious towers, while others were in piles. A desk occupied the center of the chaos. The desktop held its share of clutter while the man from the church steps scribbled away atop a stack of papers.

His long hair fell over his face, hiding his eyes and lips as he muttered. One hand-scribbled notes within a book while the other thumbed through the stack of paper, reading and writing at an impressive speed.

Three of the four silently stood at the door, waiting for the man to acknowledge their arrival. While Katherine—being Katherine—walked inside without an invitation. She selected the least uncomfortable-looking chair and brushed its contents onto the floor. The small *thuds* of books stopped the man's writing.

Katherine positioned herself in the chair, with one ankle tucked behind the other. A picture of elegance. With the back of her hand, she beckoned the three to follow inside. They hovered around the chair like an unnecessary guard and waited for the conversation to start.

"Must you always create a ruckus, Ms. O'Donnell?" The man resumed his writing; his gaze never lifted from his work.

"Must you be so rude to your guests?"

The man sighed. "Patience is a virtue that you would do well to learn."

"And diligence will be your downfall if you focus excessively on work and not your surroundings. "Katherine added, starting the back-and-forth game that Katherine played so well. The man wrote a few last words before placing down his pen. He lifted his head, running both hands through his hair before tucking the strands behind his ear. A pair of honey-brown eyes moved around the room as he examined all its inhabitants. He looked disinterested, almost disgusted, as he eyed the group, never focusing until he found Robert. A thick brow slightly raised as he smiled.

"Interesting," the man said.

Hands strummed along Robert's conscious, like fingers moving along the strings of a harp. Each pluck sent a shiver along Robert's back and brought forth a memory. Only three memories surfaced before Robert steeled himself against the intruder, hardening his gaze as he stared at the man. The strumming fingers vanished with no struggle.

"Where did you find this one?" he asked Katherine as he propped his head on his interlaced fingers. "I could tell you were special the moment I saw you enter my cathedral."

Robert readied himself to finally ask the question that had burned inside him since Captain Russo had so shockingly asked, "What are you?" But Katherine held up a hand for Robert to remain silent.

"He is not the reason we are here today, Charles," Katherine said smoothly. "We are in search of a missing woman."

Katherine snapped her fingers, and Dez opened her pocketbook and produced a picture of Rebecca. Robert's neck strained as he bent to see the image. Though the memory of their last night together was a black hole, he could feel it in his bones that the picture was from that evening. "Her name is Rebecca Monte. She was taken a few months back, and Robert has been tirelessly searching for her ever since." Katherine launched herself into a riveting tale of their last night together.

It shocked Robert to hear the genuine emotion that came with her words. He practically fell over when he saw a single tear fall over her cheeks. Crocodile tears, he was sure, but she sure did put on a convincing show. Luke even had a few sniffles by the end of the story.

"My heartstrings tug for you, Robert." Charles clutched his shirt, the place right above his heart. "I wish there were something that I could do to help you." The man's eyes became glossy, but he quickly absorbed the emotion. "But alas," he said, shrugging, "I have heard nothing about a missing woman." He handed the picture back to Katherine, but she did not accept.

"Keep it, Charles," she said shortly. "Circulate it around the church in case someone has"—she paused, strategically selecting her following words—"seen her. Make sure your entire flock knows we are helping Mr. Monte in his search and will do anything within our power to find her. " Robert could feel the intention drip from Katherine's words. *Anything* was a hefty word that Katherine was not afraid to fulfill. The man before them may be a wolf in sheep's clothing, but Katherine was a hunter, eager to down any animal in her path.

"Why, dear Katherine, are you insinuating something?" Charles asked, returning to his overly emotional tone. "We have been friends for decades, and I'm hurt that you would assume such a thing."

"Never, Charles. I just want to clarify that whoever had a hand in her abduction would feel the full weight of my influence. My hand stretches far, Charles, as you well know." Katherine dragged her sharpened nail along the arms of the chair. The tip pierced the upholstery, spilling the cotton insides outward.

Annoyance flashed across Charles's face, and he quickly closed his eyes, hiding his faltered exterior.

"I do not wish to fight Katherine," Charles said with eyes closed.

"Neither do I."

Silence settled between them, and like a vacuum, the air pulled from the room. Robert gasped at the change in pressure. His eardrums popped in rapid succession as if he was ascending the world's fastest elevator. Charles and Katherine stared blankly at each other as they spoke on another plane, where only the two mattered. The pressure in the room shifted. The vacuum slammed into an invisible wall in front of the four.

A whirlwind formed as the forces fought one another and swirled around them. Small objects were jostled and toppled over. The windstorm grew, and the toppled things raised. Books, ceramics, and trash were all thrown but never hit a person. Katherine and Charles remained uninterested in their surroundings and focused on their silent conversation.

"Now, Katherine, if we are going to play, my love. Then let us play." Charles closed his eyes, and Robert felt those invisible hands play within the strings of his mind once again. Instead of deftly strumming each memory, they tugged forcefully on each cord, pulling the pain of memories through Robert's body, jerking on the thoughts of his sister.

Protect him, a tender voice begged.

Robert strained to force the intruder from his mind, but the sensation grew too powerful to cast away. Unlike Luke or Katherine's attempts, neither meant Robert harm, but this one—wanted to make him bleed.

Protect Charles, the voice urged.

Adrenaline surged through Robert's body as he stared at Charles sitting peacefully in his chair. The need to protect spiked in Robert's blood. Every inch of Robert vibrated with the desire to shield Charles—to defend him from whatever Katherine threw. The thought of sacrificing himself for the sake of Charles sat at the forefront of Robert's mind, aggressively pressing for him to obey.

192

"I . . . I can't!" Robert said through gritted teeth. He gripped the chair, and as the internal battle raged within him. "Stop," he gasped as an image appeared to him. One where Katherine crushed Charles's face into his desk, her nails plunged into his neck, and Charles pleaded for help. The desperation in Charles's voice pulled Robert towards him, begging for Robert to make his sacrifice.

"No . . ." Robert gasped as the phantom fingers found the missing string—the memory taken—and the vision took root, drinking in the emotions that surrounded the hollow spot, making Robert falter in his rebellion against Charles's pull.

"Robert, help me!" Charles gasped before Katherine silenced him.

Save him, Robert, the voice urged.

Do for him what you could not do for Rebecca, it said.

"No," Robert bit back. "You're not real. It's not real."

Do it! Sacrifice yourself! The voice demanded.

Charles's tearful gaze paused and became a look of intrigue, interested in how Robert fought against the pull. The air around his body wavered like a mirage. His light brown hair darkened and curled. His features shifted, his cheeks rounded, and his voice became one that haunted Robert's dreams.

"Help me," Rebecca begged. "She's hurting me."

Robert's defiance broke at the sight of his sister. Shakily, Robert pulled himself away from the chair. Each step was forced and heavy, moving like an obedient doll.

"Must . . . protect her." Robert panted as he reached out for his sister. Rebecca's hand stretched as Katherine cackled, pushing her further into the desk. Blood spilled across the surface. "Must save Becca."

"Robert, help me!" she cried.

Robert paused. The puppeteer strings tugged him forward, but Robert did not move.

"Robert, save me. Please! Don't you love me anymore?!"

"You're not her."

Robert's words fragmented the illusion. His sister's face became a combination of Charles and hers, shifting to reform.

"Robert, please! You are the only one that can help me! Why are you letting this demon hurt me!?" Rebecca's tearful face reshaped *again.*

"You are not her," Robert repeated, furthering his resolve. "Take off my sister's face, you bastard!" The mirage of danger dissolved, leaving Charles sitting in his chair, as calm and safe as before. "Stay out of my head." Robert's voice held contempt.

The man's serene face faded just slightly as he saw Robert had broken through the charm. "Quite an interesting trump card you have, Katherine." Charles leaned back in his chair and stared at the ceiling. The gears behind his thoughtful eyes turned, dissecting the battle. "Work with me, Robert."

The room stopped as Charles's offer hung in the air.

"Come work for the good and get away from these— *heathens.*" He spat out his last word as if it hurt to even speak of their true nature. "Maybe we could help you find your lost . . . sister, was it? I assure you that my church has people from all over the city, and each would be more than happy to help you in your search. What do you say?"

Dez and Luke stepped to Robert's sides, ready to act if necessary. Katherine remained sitting, calm and collected, as always.

"The devil I know is far better than the devil I don't," Robert answered. Dez relaxed, and Luke sighed in relief. "Thank you for your offer, Charles. But I will stay where I am. I don't care for sides in whatever war you all have. All I care about is finding my sister and getting us the fuck out of this city."

Charles's eyebrow raised, and he looked at Katherine, who couldn't contain the slight lift in her lips. "Interesting. Exciting game, you are playing Katherine." Charles's face tilted as he examined Robert's face.

For a split second, Charles's kind features shifted as if the illusion wrapped around his face released. He had hollow cheeks. His chin pointed. His eyes lacked an iris or pupil, leaving only sockets of white, burning light. They radiated an emptiness that singed the edges of Robert's mind. The vacant look in Charles's eyes felt like an eternity of nothingness. Robert couldn't tear away from Charles's gaze, even as terror overloaded his body.

"A dangerous game of chess you play, Katherine," Charles said with an ancient, powerful voice. "Pieces are moving on the board, but who shall take the first pawn?"

"Thank you for your time, Charles." Katherine stood from her seat.

Charles nodded, slipping back to his human appearance.

"If you have questions, my door is always open."

Though Charles spoke to the group, Robert felt the man's eyes on him. Even as the door shut, Robert could feel his gaze on the back of his head. The emptiness was like an itch he could not scratch. The irritation was present, clawing for his attention, until he slid into the safety of Katherine's town car.

"God, this thing is getting harder and harder to hide." Katherine shifted in her seat, lifting her dress very high on her thigh.

"Ooh, Kitty, do I finally get a taste?" Luke launched himself from one side of the town car to the other. Katherine stopped him with a heel to a shoulder as she pulled a gun from between her legs. "I always knew you were packing heat down there, Kitty Kat," Luke said as he fell into a seat next to her.

"You know you couldn't handle what I'm packing, sweetheart." Katherine tapped Luke's nose with the tip of her gun. Katherine's fingers gripped the pearled handle. Her finger remained hooked around the trigger, though no danger was present.

"How do you even hide that thing up there?" Robert asked.

"Practice, Robert. Lots and lots of practice," Katherine answered. She knocked on the closed partition behind her head. It cracked. "I require a drink."

"Yes, ma'am," the driver said from the front seat before pulling a quick U-turn. Robert and Luke were thrown around the back while the ladies wobbled slightly.

"We are gonna need more than one," Dez groaned as she undid her high ponytail. With a quick shake of her head, her pin-straight hair coiled up and bounced around her face until it returned to her natural curls.

"So much better," said Dez, as she checked herself in her compact, and Robert felt his heart thump just a little quicker.

He agreed.

Chapter 17

"Come to Mama," Katherine cooed as the server placed her fourth martini on the table. Her squeals of excitement increased in volume as the number of drinks climbed. Her long fingers wrapped around the glass. Her usual devious eyes and stoic exterior melted away as Katherine sipped her drinks.

Robert smirked, enjoying the person who sat in front of him. This Katherine seemed fun. Not just some overly vengeful creature that had appeared in his life a week ago. It wasn't just her posture that changed, but how she spoke. An accent seeped through her alcoholic slur and worsened the more she drank.

"Mama?" Robert whispered to Dez, who sat equally amused to his left, drinking a beer while Luke sipped a Cosmo and eyed an extremely busty waitress across the restaurant.

"She grew up during Prohibition, so she drinks excessively when she unwinds. They tease her, calling her the real glutton at their family dinners," Dez whispered. Her voice was low but stayed loud enough, so Katherine heard.

"I can stop whenever I want," Katherine slurred, tapping her red fingernails against the martini glass stem. Her Irish and Chicago accent peaked at her vowels. "And as of right now, I *don't* want to."

Katherine plucked the olive from her drink and swallowed the garnish before taking another sip. She purred at the taste. "I have to admit. This is one of the best inventions in the last two hundred years, and somehow, it just keeps being improved!" She took another sip, exhaled, and leaned back in her chair, satisfied.

Robert looked at her drink, noticing that it was nearly already gone. Catching the eye of their waiter, he motioned for another.

"That's what all addicts say, Kitty Kat," Luke teased as he ran his finger around his glass. "We can just drop you off at the rehab facility on the way back home. I'm sure Ernest would gladly enjoy the next seventy-two hours off."

"You will do no such thing"—Katherine paused, taking a long sip of her drink—"again."

Robert's mouth dropped, eager for a story.

Luke playfully shrugged his shoulders.

"A psychiatric hold was so much easier to get on someone in the '90s. A fake name, a few tears, and bam! Kitty Kat's in a straitjacket for three days, and Ernest and I get a weekend in her penthouse." Luke coughed twice and called tears to his eyes. "Please,

Doctor. Please help her. She doesn't even know who she is anymore."
Luke dabbed the corner of his eyes. "And scene."

Robert stared with wide eyes and laughter at the back of his
throat. "He didn't."

Katherine's glare peeled paint from the walls.

"He did," Katherine growled. "The headache that is
compulsory therapy, four times a day. Apparently, I have 'deep-rooted
daddy and abandonment issues.'"

Luke nodded. "I concur with their professional opinion."

Laughter broke through Robert's lips. Katherine playfully
swatted at Luke. Dez chuckled into her beer as she took another swig
while Luke just held his nearly full drink in his tiny hands.

"I'm surprised you aren't drinking faster." Robert nodded at
Luke's nearly full Cosmo.

"Never really had a taste for it," Luke said. "I prefer to focus
on my . . . other vices." Robert followed Luke's eye line and found his
attention on the waitress across the room. He looked back to Luke and
saw a glimmer of power awaken within his eyes. The sensual
impression danced past Robert before it found its home in the waitress.
She paused mid-stride, immediately becoming flushed. Her knees
came together and rubbed back and forth as she looked around the
space, hoping nobody saw her shameful display. The waitress pressed
the notepad into her groin. Her eyelids fluttered. Her breathing became
brassier.

Robert's neck snapped back to Luke, whose eyes became two
shining gemstones that matched the one that hung from his ear. A soft

moaning brought Robert's attention back to the waitress. Sweat seeped through her blonde bangs, pasting them to her forehead. She attempted to walk, but her knees gave out, and she fell to the floor. Nearby diners shared concerned glances at the waitress. Her lips parted to reassure them.

"Luke, you aren't—"

A roar of ecstasy interrupted Robert's question, drawing his attention back to the quivering female. The waitress's face tilted to the ceiling as her hands roamed over her body. She cried several high-pitched moans as she rode the wave of orgasm.

Luke inhaled, ingesting the pheromones she released, and relished their taste.

"As I said, other vices." Luke's glow dimmed as he took a sip of his drink and turned to Katherine, who squealed as the waiter brought her a 'surprise' martini. "So, are we going to talk about the meeting, or am I going to have to call for Ernest to bring the car around before you *unleash* yourself on these people?"

Katherine dismissed his worries and drank instead. The more Katherine drank, the more Robert was fascinated by their relationship. From what Robert assessed, Katherine was the pragmatic parent, while Luke remained the hyperactive child. But a few drinks in, and the roles reversed.

"Always such a spoilsport with drinking. What, dear Lucas? Wasn't a fan of it when you were human?" Katherine swirled the drink with a finger and sucked it clean. Her eyes glistened a simmering red as she spoke. "Some guy force himself on a young, innocent Luke who couldn't handle his vodka cranberries?" Luke's eyes hardened as she stabbed at a painful memory—a secret shared between friends. Luke stared into his drink, seeing memories in his reflection before Katherine turned her attention to the shocked Robert.

"What are we but the embodiment of bad choices and freedom?" She raised her hands and slowly ran them through her red curls, showing the multiple streaks of gray in her hair. "So, what if I want to unwind every once in a while? Have a few drinks. Live what life I have left . . . tick tock, tick tock." Darkness fell over Katherine's eyes as an unspoken secret bubbled up.

"I don't understand?" Robert frowned. "What does she mean?"

The table went silent. Robert felt the magnitude of his question, realizing more secrets kept from him.

"Dez?" Robert turned to the person he thought would answer, but she remained tight-lipped.

"That is none of your concern, Robert," Katherine said as she pushed her empty glass toward the side. She worked her hands through her hair, tucking her mounds behind her ears. Katherine tilted her neck to the left and the right, cracking several areas before sitting straight. Her stance shifted back to her usual uptight, professional nature—with only a hint of a slur. "Lucas, what did you find out at the church?"

Luke shook away the haunted look in his eyes, returning his mask of cheer and excitement. Luke reminded Robert of his sister. No matter how horrible she felt, she could summon a smile. Robert thought Rebecca would love Luke if she got a chance to meet him.

When she meets him.

There would be no more *ifs* for Robert where Rebecca was concerned, only *when.*

"Well, Ryan is such a top. Which was perfect because I was hoping for a good fuc—"

"Fast forward, Lucas," Katherine interrupted.

"He didn't talk much before, but I could pull a few things out of him . . . while he pushed a few things in me." Luke turned to Robert with a raised hand, and much to Luke's glee, Robert met his hand with a high five. Dez made a show of rolling her eyes.

"What? It was funny," Robert defended.

"Continue, Lucas." Katherine placed her hand against her face, lifting her eye slightly with her finger as she fought the alcohol's attempt to take control.

"Anyhoo! He told me about a cellar. Nobody besides the heads of the church may enter—not that anyone wants to go in there."

"Why?" Robert asked.

"He said there are rumors that the overnight cleaners have heard screaming. Most wrote off the sounds as the building settling or gas escaping the old pipes. But I looked inside his mind the night they charged him with cleaning the sanctuary." Luke shook. "I can confirm it was not piping with one hundred percent certainty."

"Where is the cellar entrance?" Katherine inquired as her face dipped slightly, giving in to the sleepiness.

"Directly underneath the altar," Luke explained.

"Splendid job, Lucas," Katherine complimented. Luke beamed at her praise.

"Wait. Was all that planned?" Robert asked, and Luke nodded.

"What, you didn't think I was just after a good lay, did you?" Luke asked as he batted his long eyelashes. "In the house of the Lord? I would never!" Luke put on his terrible Southern accent. "I am a lady!"

Dez snorted. "Yeah, a lady of the evening."

A giggle escaped Katherine's tight lips, followed by Luke and Robert as they all laughed at Dez's unexpected and well-timed joke. To the surrounding onlookers, they all seemed so human—so mundane. A group of friends out for a drink on a Sunday afternoon. Not a collection of demonic entities and a somewhat 'normal' human.

"So that's that! We break in, find your sister, and get out before they even notice that we are there. Easy," Luke announced.

"You think she's actually in there?" Robert struggled to hide the hope in his voice. The fact that she was just a hair's length away from him. It just didn't seem real. "Didn't Charles say—"

"Charles was *lyyyying*," Katherine said, elongating her words. "Pathetic little, cupid-loving ass."

Cupid?

"So he's an angel or something? He felt like you two, but . . .I don't know, different?"

"Or *something*," Katherine snorted. "You read the book that Lucas lent you, correct? Well, if the Sins came from Eve, what do you think came from Adam?"

"Charles?" Robert asked, realizing that "*or something*" was probably the best description for Charles.

"Correct." Katherine crossed her forearms on the table and laid her head down. "Think of us as two sides of the same coin. One of us is free, while the other is . . . what's the word I am looking for, Lucas?"

"Bitter? Old-fashioned? Restricting?"

"Bitchy," she yawned; her eyes remained closed for extended periods. The other guests noted the impeccably dressed woman falling asleep. "They want everyone so prim and proper, while we just want people to be free and have some fun. To not worry about what happens next."

"Not good or evil; it just is," Robert said, remembering Luke's words about perspective.

"Exactly. We are two sides that cannot live without the other. What is the push without the pull? The dark without the light? Too much sin and less grace, the world will turn wild. Too much grace and not enough sin and progression will halt."

With her last statement, Katherine fell asleep.

The group paid their bills and loaded Katherine into her town car with Ernest's help. He offered to drive Robert and Dez home, but they both declined. The mischievous glint in Luke's eyes gave them concerns about being named accomplices in anything he had planned.

"If he cuts her hair again, Katherine will kill him. Last time, she looked like a ginger poodle for nearly six months." Dez laughed at the thought as she withdrew her sunglasses and placed them on her face. Robert smiled at their second appearance of the day.

She really does like them.

"I would pay to see that." The image of a short poodle-like haircut on a scowling Katherine made Robert chuckle.

A hush came after the laughter died. The two hovered at the entrance to the restaurant, awkwardly waiting for one to start the goodbye process. But Robert didn't want to say goodbye.

"Guess I'll be seeing you soon." Dez saluted Robert with two fingers and turned away.

Go after her dumbass, Robert heard his sister yell in his mind. *Go make that mistake!*

The cracks in his wall widened as Dez furthered herself. With his sister cursing in his mind and a chest full of alcohol-infused confidence, Robert jogged after Dez, ready to make a mistake.

"What, you aren't going to let me walk you home? There are a lot of scary things out here, angels, tourists—"

"Me?" Dez lowered her sunglasses so that her eyes peeked over the rim of the purple frames. Her eyes became a swirling vortex of black. Her eyes should have frightened Robert, but they were not the same cold, empty gaze of Charles or the furious scowl of Katherine. They were like the night sky, an endless universe of possibility.

"Woah," Robert gasped as Dez's power washed over him like a wave.

"I think I can take care of myself." Dez pushed the glasses back into place and took one long step forward. Robert felt a slight ache form in his chest.

Now go make another Robert! Rebecca's voice barked.

Robert rushed to Dez's side. Her lips tilted to one side, amused by Robert's attempts to keep up with her long strides. That smile was all Robert needed to keep trying—a smile that gave Robert hope.

"Well, what about me?" Robert said, placing his hand on his chest as he power-walked beside her. "Just look at me! Poor. Defenseless. Powerless. I couldn't think of an easier mark. Did I mention poor? You have seen my home."

"Apartment," Dez corrected with a playful raise of her eyebrows.

"Exactly. I don't have money for a ransom." He stopped walking and hoped Dez would stop with him.

She walked two more steps and paused. She turned to Robert with her hands on her hips, frowning, but a smile was pushing through.

Now hit it home, baby bro, Rebecca cheered.

"I guess I'll just walk . . . alone and get mugged, or knifed, or just maybe just fall into an open manhole." He looked down at his shoes, playing the role of the coy weakling. He was not ashamed to play the part if it lured Dez into spending the afternoon with him. "You know that actually happens to people all the time! I wouldn't—"

"FINE!" she surrendered. "Lucifer and the eternal fire below, you are incessant," Dez groaned.

Robert lifted his head. "Incessantly delightful?"

"Annoying would have been my word of choice, but sure— whatever helps you sleep well at night," Dez huffed at Robert's pathetic show. "So, which way to your *apartment*?"

Robert's face became a wide, toothy grin as he turned in the opposite direction. He led the way while Dez followed; she even shortened her strides, allowing Robert to walk at a more casual pace.

Chapter 18

Perfect. You get her to yourself, and you don't talk.

Great. Just great.

Robert berated himself as the two walked six blocks in total silence. His sister's voice did not make any further appearances in his head. If he wanted to talk, he would need to find the confidence himself.

"So, tell me about yourself?"

Robert hated the question the moment it left his lips.

Dez popped her lips, and Robert wished he had let the silence happen instead of asking the most pathetic question in the history of questions.

"What? Like, what TV shows do I watch? What do I do with the girls on the weekends?" Dez's remarks had her typical bite, but they seemed playful. He hadn't completely ruined his chances at a conversation.

Thank God . . . or Lucifer, whoever's looking out.

"Let's start with an easy one. How long have you been working for Luke?" They paused at a corner. Robert watched as Dez considered his question and weighed whether she wanted to answer or give another smartass comment. To his surprise, she replied with an actual answer.

"*With* Luke," Dez corrected. "I work for his boss. But it's nearly been thirty years." She stepped from the sidewalk and out into the street. Robert followed her, processing Luke's boss's identity.

Only one person seemed plausible.

"The Devil?" Robert asked, feeling funny about saying it out loud. It made sense, though. Wouldn't it make sense for the Devil to be real if angels and demons were real?

"Bingo."

Images of red skin, horns, pitchforks, and pointy tails appeared in Robert's head.

"But I would recommend sticking with Lucifer. Devil isn't particular to him. There are dozens of devils in hell, lowercase *d* of course."

"Does he have, ya' know …" Robert placed a finger on each ear and stuck out his tongue in an evil yet cartoonish way. Dez snickered.

"No. Well, at least not in the form he typically takes. Usually, he sticks to Italian suits and dark and brooding features. But he can look like anyone, your mom, the lady across the street, your childhood best friend. You never know when he's watching."

"Do you all have horns?"

"Only the important ones," she responded passively.

Robert searched Dez's scalp, wondering if she hid a pair within the mounds of curls or if she had some illusion wrapped around her as Charles did. Dez caught Robert's curious glance. She looked around, leaned toward Robert, and parted her hair. Hidden among the roots of her hair were two small growths. Both were small, almost missed within her forest of curly black hair, but there were indeed there.

She has horns.

"Holy shit." Robert wished he could think of a better reaction, but he was genuinely at a loss for words. Even after everything he had encountered, some part of Robert believed himself crazy. But seeing the horns verified—once again—he wasn't crazy; he was just in way over his head.

"As I said, the important ones," she said with a wink. Dez released another small surge of her aura, and the horns grew two inches and then instantly shrank back to their reduced size. Robert reached a hand to touch, but Dez shirked out of reach.

"Don't do that," she said, her tone slightly frantic. "Unless you want to get jumped." Dez released her hair and shook until her coils fell back into their proper position.

"It hurts if someone touches them?" Robert asked, feeling bad about his curiosity.

"The opposite. It's very . . . sensual," Dez said hesitantly.

Robert could feel the importance of the secret she had revealed. Dez turned away, looking for anything to hold her attention. Robert could see the instantaneous regret in the corner of her eyes. It was clear. She revealed something extremely personal. So, Robert decided to over-share, if only to level the playing field.

Make mistakes today . . .

"I once tried shaving my pubes with an old Bic razor and ended up cutting my balls so badly I had to be taken to the hospital and get stitches. Five." Robert's face comedically fell.

Dez stared blankly at Robert.

For a moment, Robert was concerned he had shared too much, but when she erupted into laughter, Robert's worries vanished, and another welcomed crack formed in the wall around his emotions. The laugh was unlike anything she had ever shared. It was joyous, unabridged delight. It was unlike any of her scoffs or chuckles. This laugh was pure Dez. It was a sound Robert wanted to hear again, and again, and again.

. . . that I'll be grateful for today.

"You're a truly curious human, Mr. Monte."

"I'll take that as a compliment."

Their walk continued with a constant back and forth of sharing. There was less bark to Dez's answers, but she ensured there was a little sass in many of her replies. And Robert made a mental note of each response.

Dez was a fan of pretzels, the hard kind given out for free at a bar, not the overly buttery doughy ones purchased at a mall. She did, in fact, like to drink, but her interest was in ciders and beers, not in hard liquors. She disliked the cold, though she was fond of fur—the faux kind.

"I'm a demon, not a monster," Dez made a point of saying.

Robert shared bits of information about himself, his hobbies, his life back home, and his last relationship. Robert even admitted to Dez that he had his childhood teddy bear back at his apartment.

After much back and forth between the two, Robert felt brave enough to ask the question that had been burning inside him since he met Dez: What was with her obsession with the color purple?

"It was the first color I saw when I crossed over."

"From Hell?" Dez asked, making sure he understood where she referred to when she said: "crossed over."

"No. Cleveland," Dez said with a roll of her eyes. "Yes, Robert. Hell." Robert stuck his tongue out at her. "Did you want me to tell you the story or not?"

"Proceed," he said, motioning for her to continue.

"It was a lavender plantation I tumbled into, or I think a better word would be: *appeared*." They stopped in front of Robert's apartment building. Dez leaned against the bricks as she looked toward the darkening clouds. "It was the most beautiful thing I had ever seen—miles and miles of life. I had never seen that color before. It was—peaceful. It was so beautiful. The light was so warm. After an eternity of fire and darkness, I could have spent the rest of eternity there."

"What's it like down there?"

"Dark. Hot. But also cold. Some fires burn so hotly that it somehow freezes everything it touches." Dez thought for a moment. "The smell of sulfur is everywhere."

"Sounds horrible."

"It is." Dez took another deep breath and returned to her story. "That was what I noticed first. Before I formed my eyes, I could smell the lavender—the sweet floral scent wrapped around me as I found my form. Even after I formed a body, I laid and stared at the sky and the acres of purple flowers surrounding me. I don't know if I was there for days or weeks. I didn't sleep. I didn't eat. I barely moved. I just let myself be."

Dez breathed out a soft sigh as she recalled the memory.

"It wasn't until the owner of the lavender fields found me. Well, technically, it was his dog that found me." Dez squinted her eyes as the memory grew hazy for a moment. "Peter, the dog's name was Peter. The farmer was so embarrassed!" A rosiness appeared on her cheeks as a soft smile caressed her face. "For me, not for him. Or maybe both." She laughed once more. "That day, he offered me my first piece of clothing: a purple dress and stockings . . . Henry," she gasped as if she had said a name she hadn't spoken in hundreds of years. A tear rolled beyond her sunglasses and along her cheek.

"What happened to him?" Robert asked. Dez turned her back to him, removed her sunglasses, and wiped away her tears.

"He died." She looked over her shoulder. "He died, as all humans are destined to do. Have a good night, Robert." Dez turned from Robert and walked away.

The soft patter of water matched Dez's steps as she walked to the end of the block and turned. He looked to the sky and watched as the clouds darkened and opened up. The sky acknowledged Dez's pain and cried with her.

Chapter 19

The next day, life for Robert seemed surreal.

It was like he peeked behind the curtain of the world and somehow was expected to continue an everyday life until he had another glance. Reality became a fantasy, and fantasy seemed to be around every corner for him. As Robert filled drinks, cleaned the countertop, and chatted with the customers, he couldn't help but question his life.

Did the homeless man outside know something?

Could the friendly barista be Lucifer in disguise?

How often had Robert unknowingly met a demon?

Nathan hadn't commented on Robert's change in demeanor when he arrived at work on Monday morning, hours before when he typically came. But he grumbled when Robert arrived without coffee or breakfast. Without either, Nathan had no reason to talk and stayed silent the rest of the morning.

It was nearly midday when Nathan excused himself from his chair and took the past week's earnings to the bank. He grunted a goodbye, and Robert returned to his thoughts and the pile of doodles he had created. Sketches of Dez replaced his usual collection of half-memories and nightmares. Different angles of her eyes, her smile, and one particular moment that he continued to recreate, her staring up at the sky, crying. Robert imagined what her eyes must have looked like beneath the sunglasses as she wept. What they must have looked like, as she remembered memories from so long ago.

Grabbing another small napkin, Robert began another sketch, drawing her as she thought of the lavender field. His pen quickly worked as he sketched every coil of her hair—each line bounced around her heart-shaped face, bringing life to his image. Beneath the waves of curls, Robert drew two slight bumps. Nobody would see them, but he would know they were there, hidden. Robert lost himself in his illustration and hadn't noticed the door open, or the woman who entered, or the harsh smell of Chanel Number 5 as it infiltrated the space.

"Still wasting your time doodling, Robert."

Robert's pen stumbled.

Robert knew the voice. He hated that voice.

No.

It was a voice that wrapped around him like a python, squeezing what little joy he had in his day. A voice he dreaded hearing more than any other. He looked up from this drawing and saw the condescending smirk of his ex-girlfriend.

"Victoria," Robert said in disbelief. "What-what are you doing here?"

She twisted to the left and right. Judgment exuded from her eyes as she observed her surroundings. Her overdrawn—and overfilled—lips pursed together. Her overly tanned hands rested on her hip as her attention returned to Robert. Victoria looked precisely as she did when Robert saw her. Fake blonde extensions. A knock-off designer bag with matching clothes. An overly plastic sheen on her face. A skin tone one shade away from employment at Willy Wonka's Chocolate factory.

"I could ask you the same thing." She pursed her plump lips together as her eyes swept up and down him. "You look fat." Her eyes settled on his midsection.

And here we go.

Robert crossed his arms in front of his stomach, knowing that Victoria's comment would be the first of many. Her eyes moved to his bare wrist. She squinted her eyes at the sight. Though it had been months since he had sold the watch, the pale band of flesh had not tanned and was another reminder of Victoria and her carelessness.

"And you look just as bitchy as ever."

Victoria laughed a forced high-pitched laugh—one that spoke of high-class fakery.

"I see you're still not over me breaking up with you." She produced a wipe from her purse and cleaned down a chair before sitting.

"And I see you remember what happened *very* differently." Robert backed away from Victoria.

She leaned closer.

"So, how did you find me?" He didn't wait for an answer; Robert already knew. "My mother told you, didn't she?"

Victoria nodded. "She's worried about you, Robert. We are all worried about you." She reached to touch him, but Robert kept his distance. Victoria's emotions flipped like a light switch. One moment she was rude and crass, and the next, she was sensitive and 'caring.'

"Really? Erik too? That's a surprise."

Victoria jumped at the mention of Robert's ex-best friend's name.

"Erik is gone."

"What?"

"I kicked him out." An attempt at sadness overcame her face, but her frozen forehead couldn't form the lines, and her thin eyebrows could not come together. Her show of sadness was pitiful. Robert, unfortunately, felt his heart tug. The knife in his heart was still there, even if he wished it would dislodge, and Victoria knew how to twist it. "I didn't love him as I loved you, Robert."

"Then why did you do it?"

"Did you ever stop to think he did it? That Erik was the perpetrator?"

And there it was, the twist in the story. The misdirection that Victoria did so well.

"You never stopped to ask my side of the story," Victoria continued. "You never asked how I felt about everything." She dabbed invisible tears from the corner of her eyes. "You left me, and I had nowhere else to go, so I went with Erik. You abandoned me, Robert."

"That not what—"

"Don't you still love me, Robert?" She reached again for Robert, but he kept his distance. "Remember when we talked about marriage and a family? Remember when we talked about a future together?"

Robert remembered; he remembered it all. He was the one who started those conversations and talked about getting married, having children, and creating a life with her.

"I would never hurt you, Robert, you know that. You know I . . . that I love you." Victoria choked on her words. It was a flawless performance. She looked away from Robert as he gawked at her. Her hair became a curtain, hiding her face as she wiped away more tears that had not fallen. She moved her hair behind an ear. Every action was planned, a performance of what she thought Robert needed. "Do you still love me, Robert?" Her voice hitched at the question. Her voice sounded so fearful, afraid of Robert's answer.

"I . . ." Robert stopped, rubbing the back of his neck as he thought. Looking back, Robert knew he loved Victoria . . . or at least he thought he loved her, yet he could not remember why he ever did. Victoria was arrogant. She was vain. She was everything Robert disliked about people, but somehow Robert had made himself love someone who he despised.

"I promise I won't ever let anyone tear us apart again. Not Erik. Not your sister. Not anybody."

"She didn't tear us apart, Victoria." Robert snapped, finding his voice.

"Didn't she?" Victoria asked, sliding around the puzzle pieces of their past. "She wouldn't let me talk to you after the incident. She forced you to leave our home. To me, that sounds like she was keeping us apart. You know she was always jealous of us, Robert, of how happy we were together."

Victoria painted a different version of their past, one where she and Robert were the victims, and Erik and Rebecca were the villains.

"Victoria, I—"

The bell above the front door jingled. Robert and Victoria turned to the entrance. Robert beamed. Victoria frowned.

Lavender spilled into the room as Dez entered. The floral scent battled the stench of spilled beer and Chanel.

Without speaking, Dez jumped onto the bartop and slid over to the bartender's side. Robert's lips parted, ready to offer an introduction, but stopped when Dez's lips pressed firmly onto his cheek. His words became a deep inhale. Redness flushed his cheeks.

"Missed you, babe," Dez loudly whispered before she pulled away and hooked a hand around Robert's waist. A sizeable purple imprint of Dez's lips was left on Robert's cheek and drew Victoria's attention. He could feel Victoria's ferocity as her eyes went between the lipstick, Robert, and Dez. She had not expected Robert to have a girlfriend. "And you are?" Dez asked as her hand traveled up Robert's side.

"Victoria Edgefield." She answered, lifting a limp wrist for a handshake. She expected Dez to mirror the action, but instead, Dez smiled, showing her pearly whites and unreasonably sharp canines. After moments passed, Victoria dropped her hand with only a slight embarrassment.

"Pleasure." Dez drifted her hand up Robert's torso, choosing to touch him instead of continuing the forced pleasantries. "I was wondering if we would ever meet. I have heard so much about you. So many *wonderful* stories." Dez's hand grasped firmly onto Robert's bicep. She claimed her territory. Robert knew this was all a game for Dez, but he enjoyed how it made Victoria seethe.

"And you are?"

"Dez," she answered Victoria's question, but Dez's eyes never left Robert.

"Dez." Victoria sucked on the Z as if she did not understand the name. "Well, Ms. Dez, I was talking privately with Robert here. So, if you wouldn't mind—"

"Oh, but I would . . . mind that is," Dez interrupted. "I mind very much, Victoria. But I do have some questions for you."

Dez's fingers tingled as they touched Robert's skin. Each finger became an icicle, sending shivers up and down Robert's body as Dez released her power. The icy tingling left her fingertips and filled the air, thickening it with force and chill. The sensation was unlike the intense heat of Katherine, the seductive warmth of Luke, or the blinding tug of Charles. It was cold, strategic, like a wolf within the tundra, waiting for its moment to pounce. The icy impression encircled Robert, nipping at him, eager to be released.

"Dez." Robert's voice was firm. He was fine with Dez being defensive, but drew the line at any show of *force*.

"What?" Dez acted innocent, smiling. "Woman to woman, I just want to chat with Victoria. I haven't met any of your friends before. And I know she has opinions she would love to share."

The chilling imprint of Dez's power leaped from Robert's body and descended quickly on Victoria. She shivered as the freezing power wrapped itself around her. She looked at the circling, looking for a source of the cold impression.

Dez released Robert and leaned onto the bar, placing her chin in her hands. "Why exactly did you come here, Victoria?" Dez's voice shifted as she asked her question. Her voice became something different. It was hypnotic, almost musical. Robert noticed the difference; Victoria remained oblivious.

"I knew Robert would get back with me if I pushed him hard enough. Especially if that bitch of a sister wasn't there to cock block me again." Her hands couldn't move fast enough to stop the hateful words that spewed from her lips. "Robert! That's not true!" Victoria's fingers parted. "I came 'cause your father said he would give you your job back at the law firm, and I knew I could continue cheating on you without you ever doing anything."

"So that wasn't the first time with Erik?" Dez questioned.

"No, we had been fucking for years."

"Did you ever feel bad that you cheated on Robert?"

"I felt bad when he caught me. No! I mean, I felt bad when you found out! No, that's not right!" She squinched her face as she tried to form the words—the well-practiced lines that she desperately needed to say. "I. Felt. Bad. For . . . for"—she ground her teeth, trying to process the next word, but the truth spilled free without restraint like a broken dam—"for myself cause of the easy life I fucked up. I knew you would never have the spine to leave. If it weren't for that bitch sister of yours ferrying you away, I would have gotten you back and continued to cheat. I would have happily spent the rest of my days enjoying the wealth you offered while also continuing to ruin yours." Victoria gasped at her own words as Robert stared at her, dumbfounded.

Dez was prepared to ask another question, but Robert stepped forward. "Is that true, Victoria?"

"Robert, I don't understand what's wrong." Visible tears flooded Victoria's face, not the crocodile ones she sold to Robert before Dez's arrival. "Please, believe me. I don't know what is happening."

"Do you love me?" Robert asked, remembering what Victoria had admitted just moments before. He was unsure what he wanted the answer to be.

"I loved . . ." she grumbled the next word. "I loved . . ."

"VICTORIA!" Robert shouted. "Did you ever love?"

Just say it. Just say it!

Robert needed the answer to the question. He needed her to tell the truth. Not some script that she had rehearsed.

"I loved . . . the idea of you. The safety, the luxury, the money, the life you could have given me." As she spoke, the truth was like a rock rolling down the hill. "I pitied you, Robert. I pity you now. How badly you wanted someone to love you. I knew I could live my life if I gave you the companionship you were so desperate for." She no longer restrained herself. Her eyes became cruel, enjoying how Robert cringed at every word. His eyes became glossy, but he held in his emotions.

Victoria saw the emotions in his eyes and sighed with disgust. "Be a man, Robert! For once in your life, stop being this sniveling bitch."

"Stop, Victoria!" Robert shouted.

"Everyone back home knows you're over here sleeping with whores, living in poverty, and working in this dump. I pity you, Robert. Your parents pity you. You know they wish you would just disappear just like your worthless—"

A slap silenced Victoria.

For a moment, Robert saw red. Rage painted his vision as if Katherine had again slipped him under her influence. A red handprint surfaced atop Victoria's cheek.

Had Robert finally snapped? He looked at the impression and watched as it took form. Five long fingers and a thin palm appeared. It was not Robert's hand.

"Get out." The temperature dropped as Dez growled an ungodly noise. She had struck Victoria.

Frost crept along the sides of the bottles nearest to them. The thin sheen of water within the sink froze into a layer of ice. The air turned crisp, almost like it could snap if only someone tried.

"Or what?" Victoria straightened herself and pushed her shoulders back, confidently standing against Dez's threat. Tension built as the two women glared at each other, waiting for a moment of weakness. One radiated unnatural confidence, while the other held only ruin. Dez's hands disappeared beneath the bartop, grasping on a beam to quench her need for destruction. Her grip became too great, and the wooden beam split with a loud *crack.* Victoria flinched at the unseen noise.

Dez had won.

"You have two choices. You can leave, or I can pull you out and figure out where the extensions start and your *real* hair begins. Then when I've scalped you bald, you can stumble back to whatever overpriced hotel—that you clearly can't afford—and tell Robert's father that you failed to entice his son." Dez smiled so sweet it sickened Robert but made Victoria swallow a mouth of fear.

Victoria's confidence reemerged one final time as she looked between Robert and Dez. With a simple nod, Victoria withdrew from the fight. She collected her purse and rose from the stool. She threw one last look at the pair and tilted her chin upward.

"I can see you are quite *comfortable* with your new life, Robert. I'll let your parents know you are the lost cause we all expected you to be." She glided out of the bar without another threat, word, or goodbye to Robert.

The door slammed, and Victoria was gone. Her chapter in Robert's life had finally closed. He leaned into the bar, releasing his held breath.

So it was all a lie.

Robert thought it would have hurt more, but he felt almost— relieved. Sure, it hurt like hell knowing that he wasted nearly seven years of his life, but her admission made letting Victoria go that much easier.

"Lucifer! She's a bitch." Dez let loose a snarl of disgust as she reached for a bottle of whiskey from the back shelf. She popped the top and drank deeply from the bottle. Her fingers brushed away the frost collected around the base of the bottle and sat atop the back bar. "You, okay?" She asked, her voice dropping just slightly.

Robert shrugged.

"Want me to go beat her up for you?"

A smile broke through his tired expression with a huff.

"As entertaining as that would be, thank you, but no."

"You sure?" Dez offered again. "I know a guy who can shave her head while sleeping."

The thought of a bald Victoria was amusing, but he declined.

"Well, you're no fun today," Dez joked. She took another swig of whiskey but kept her eyes trained on Robert, watching him closely as he remained pensive.

"So, what was that?" Robert asked, trying to change the subject.

"What was what?"

"What you did to Victoria."

Dez lowered the bottle, surprised by Robert's question.

"Hmm," was her response.

"What, hmm?"

"Most people have at least an inkling when pulled under infernal or angelic influence. Hence the whole devil and angel on people's shoulders. But I haven't heard of someone being able to feel when they influence someone else."

"What does that mean?"

Dez shrugged. "Beats me." She took one last drink of the bottle, finishing the last drops before placing the empty container back on the shelf. "Maybe you're just sensitive to it all."

Great. Sensitive. Exactly the descriptor I want.

Robert turned towards the empty bottle, seeing his reflection and the purple imprint of Dez's lipstick in the dark amber glass.

"So . . . the kiss?" Robert asked. She waved her hand and refused to answer the question. "Dez, do you like me?" Robert teased.

At the question, Dez gagged loudly.

"You do! Robert continued his teasing, "You *liiiiiike* me."

"You wanna *kiiiiiiiss* me. You wanna *touuuuch* me." Dez pointed a threatening finger at Robert.

"Say that again, and I'll take that bottle, smash you in the head with it, and leave you here to bleed out," Dez threatened, but her tone remained playful.

Worst-case scenario, she'll throw the bottle.

"Peace offering." Robert slid a small bowl of pretzels toward her and held his hands in surrender. She eyed the overflowing bowl of dried carbs and greedily grabbed a handful.

"So, what brings you to this side of town, oh, great defender of the weak and mild?"

"We have a plan to get your sister back," Dez said before she tossed a pretzel into her mouth and shared their plot.

Chapter 20

Twenty-four hours. Robert repeated the words. In less than twenty-four hours, Robert would have Rebecca back.

"Tuesday night," Dez had explained. "The cleaning crew has the night off. There is no choir practice. So it will be a quick in and out."

"What about the employees? Or Charles?"

"I'll handle that."

Robert had asked what Dez meant, but she, "didn't want to ruin the surprise."

The rest of Monday and most of Tuesday came and went without incident. Robert asked to leave work early Tuesday night, complaining of a stomach ache. Nathan begrudgingly permitted Robert to leave, accepting his place behind the bar with an annoyed huff. With his sparse tips, Robert hailed a taxi that dropped him across the street from the church.

"Good evening," Dez welcomed, stepping from the obscurity of the alley. She, much like Robert, dressed in head-to-toe black, but her sneakers, nails, and makeup remained her standard shade of purple.

"If we get caught because of my shoes, then we have much bigger problems," Dez mocked. Robert agreed.

"So, what is this big surprise?"

"Just you wait." Dez took out her phone, pressed a few keys, and slipped her phone back into her pocket. "We just need to wait on Luke."

Robert looked around the short alleyway. "He didn't come with you?"

"No, I enjoy making a statement when I arrive." Luke's voice echoed down the theoretically empty alley. From a darkened corner, Luke stepped forward. Darkness dripped off him like ink, reverting to the shadow's structured form the further Luke walked. "Tada!" He exclaimed, picking the last bit of shade from his body and throwing it into the wall.

Dez and Robert frowned.

Luke took the assignment to wear an inconspicuous black outfit and moved in the opposite direction. A shiny black leotard clung to his broad shoulders and tiny waist. Its plunging neckline exposed his chest, ending somewhere between his belly button and sternum. Luke replaced his usual colorful makeup with smokey blacks, grays, and heavy eyeliner. He strutted down the alley, furthering his modelesque appearance, stomping one shiny black, latex thigh-high boot in front of the other.

"This was your idea of an inconspicuous?" Robert asked.

"Who's a better burglar than Catwoman?" He pointed toward his head, showing the cat-ear headband holding back his bangs. "Circa Eartha Kitt."

"Could you have at least found a proper pair of shoes?" Robert asked. "Can you even move in—"

Luke became a blur of darkness as he flew at Robert with his supernatural speed. He stopped with just an inch separating the two. Their noses practically touched.

"Don't worry about me, Ms. Kitty; I can move as quickly as I need." Luke pecked Robert on the cheek. "Glad to see you." Dez huffed from her side of the alley. "What? Does my Dezzy want a kiss too?" he asked as he walked toward her like some deranged doll, with arms outstretched and lips pursed.

"Do it, and your stuffed animals end up in the shredder."

Luke froze mid-step, did a one-eighty, and marched back to Robert.

"You have stuffed animals?"

"No, I don't have stuffed animals. I have Beanie Babies, and they are collectors' items. Someday, they'll be worth a lot of money!"

"Someday, they're gonna find their way into a wood chipper," Dez grumbled under her breath. Robert thought back to the Queen of Hearts manager's office and remembered seeing a shelf overflowing with Beanie Babies.

Everything is coming full circle. Well, some things.

Luke walked towards the end of the alley and gazed at the white-spired building. "Is everything in place?" Luke asked, losing the playful tone in his voice.

Dez nodded. "Just say when."

Luke turned over his shoulder and winked. "When."

Dez lifted her phone, pressed a button, and the city plunged into darkness.

Screams exploded from all around them. Cars honked and then quickly collided. Dez laughed as police sirens sounded in the distance. Splashes of red and blue were seen down the road as cop cars sprang into action.

"How did you . . ?" Robert was at a loss for words. How could Dez cut the power to the entire city of Las Vegas?

She placed a finger to her finger lips. "A good magician never reveals her secrets."

You never cease to amaze me.

Robert hoped he would continue being surprised by her, even if just until he escaped with Rebecca.

An hour passed as they waited in the darkness. The sounds of the city quieted as people realized the blackout was not a momentary obstacle. The cars on the street lessened, and people returned to their hotels. When the city became unnaturally quiet and the last car left the cathedral's parking lot, the three stirred.

Stealthily, they crossed the street. Dez and Robert launched up the stairs, taking two or three at a time to reach the top hastily. Luke seemed to enjoy the drama of moving at a snail's pace.

He lunged. Paused. Lunged. Dipped. Spun. Then lunged again. He bounced from one step to another like a well-trained ballerina, taking a moment to enjoy every perfectly executed movement. Dez hissed at him to move quicker while Robert examined the door.

Robert jiggled the handle. "Of course, it's locked." The soft *pat* of Luke's feet on the landing took his attention from the door and toward his partners in crime. "Anyone know how to pick a lock?"

Dez gave a pointed cough and nudged Robert out of the way. She placed her hand around the handle and squeezed. The metal crunched beneath her grip, and she pushed open the door.

Robert and Dez gazed through the crack, one head atop the other. The room seemed much larger without the hundreds of parishioners. Shelves were organized, papers were aligned, and someone professionally placed the cushions on the couch. Every inch of the room was meticulous in its positioning. The perfection of the room made it appear uninhabitable, too flawless to be of any use.

"Spooky," Luke said as he poked his head underneath the two others.

Dez entered the atrium, sliding open the door, while Robert and Luke followed closely behind them. Robert closed the door with a soft nudge. The space amplified the door's soft *click*.

The building felt haunting with its silence. Robert lost himself in the quiet room, turning around and around in circles. Any sound made seemed to echo and originate from another place. Dez seemed less spooked, walking straight toward the doors to the sanctuary, and Luke investigated the receptionist's desk.

"What are you doing?" Dez whispered.

Luke stood, presenting a metal nail file. He ran the instrument over one of his nails, dashing it back and forth as Dez glared.

"You never know when you will need one of these," Luke said before he placed his hands on the top of the desk, lifted into a handstand, and flipped over to the front side. His feet landed soundlessly.

"Stuck the landing! And the crowd goes wild!" He wrapped his hands around his lips and silently cheered. Dez marched over and slapped him on the back of the head.

"Okay, you have lived out your cat burglar fantasy. Can we keep it moving?" Dez motioned toward the doors that separated the entry from the inner sanctum.

"Spoilsport." Luke stuck out his tongue.

Dez's hand snapped at Luke like a pouncing cat, catching his tongue between the tips of two fingernails. Luke squirmed in pain as she gripped the tip, piercing it with her nails.

"If you want to keep this tongue, you'll keep it in your mouth. Understand?"

"You're always so mean to me, Dezzy," Luke whined with his tongue outstretched.

"Waiting for verbal confirmation, Luke," Dez said, tightening her grip on Luke's tongue.

Luke nodded his agreement, and it was released. He rubbed the minor puncture points before they vanished. "Robert, kiss it and make it feel better," he said, turning to Robert with his tongue still extended.

"Pass," Robert said, holding out a hand to block Luke's attempt at another kiss before walking toward the large door.

"Everyone's so mean to me." Luke crossed his arms and pouted as he followed the group.

Without checking, Robert stepped aside and motioned for Dez to take the lead. "After you," he said with a slight bow.

Dez straightened her back and reached for the handle.

A harsh sizzle resonated through the atrium, and the stench of burning meat followed. Dez cried out as pain swamped her body. She released the handle and tore away her hand. A layer of skin was left on the door handle, cooking until it became ash and dissolved into the air.

"Lucifer on fire!" Dez cursed. Her fingers uncurled and revealed her blackened palm. Smoke wafted from her scorched skin, adding its horrific smell to the air. The inside of her hand blistered and swelled. The bright pink flesh welted like a third-degree burn. Dez flexed her fingers. Burned skin fell, and the welts oozed before another layer knitted in its place. The stench of singed skin faded as Dez's hand healed. Robert watched as her palm gradually returned to her smooth, dark complexion. Luke grabbed her hand and examined it as it recovered, pressing his fingers into her tender new flesh. Dez grimaced at the discomfort, while Luke showed no remorse. Robert waited for Dez to snap, but she dutifully sat as he turned her hand over.

Luke dropped her hand and squatted near the handle. Lifting a single finger, he pressed it into the metal. The metal reacted as it did with Dez's hand, burning away Luke's fingerprint. Robert's stomach tightened from the smell of cooking flesh. The stench grew as Luke repeatedly pressed each finger into the handle. One by one, his fingertips sizzled and cooked. He moved from the handle and found the same response over the door's surface and frame. He showed no interest in the pain or his charred fingertips, just a curiousness at the door.

"Fascinating." Luke *hmm'd* and *ahh'd* the entire time as he inspected different areas of the door, even asking Dez to lift him to touch the top of the door.

Robert sat stunned as he watched Luke work. He had seen many sides of Luke. There was serious Luke, friendly Luke, sexy/sultry Luke, but the inquisitive, nearly scientific side—this was a new one and the most surprising of all.

"Truly fascinating. It's some sort of infernal repellent," Luke observed.

"Clearly," Dez grumbled as she flexed her hand. "The question is, how do we get inside?"

Luke nodded toward Robert.

"Me?" Robert asked, pointing to himself. "I'm sorry. Did we forget I am the only *non*-superpowered person here? If I burn off a finger, it's not coming back."

"Understandable . . . *but*, if my hypothesis is correct, you, being a human, should allow you to come and go through this door as you please. Which means that you *should* be able to open the door and allow us entry into the sanctuary."

Robert was shocked on several accounts.

First, that they chose him to touch the door that flambeed both Luke and Dez, and second, Luke used the word *hypothesis*.

It must have been the expression on Robert's face that made Luke grin like the cat that caught the canary.

"Did I forget to mention that I have a Ph.D. in mathematics and theoretical science?" Luke nonchalantly offered.

Robert turned to Dez. "He's joking."

"He's not."

"Oh, and a minor in"—Luke struck a quick pose—"interpretive dance."

"And there he is." Robert laughed as the Luke he knew resurfaced. Luke danced away from the door, showing off his years of study as Robert hovered closer to the door.

Robert's hand hovered over the handle. Thoughts of losing a finger or burning his hands kept him stationary. But his fearful thoughts were cut short when Luke, twirling like a maniac around the room, 'bumped' his hip into Robert, forcing him forward.

"Oops!" Luke grinned.

Robert extended his hands, closed his eyes, and braced himself for the pain. But when he registered the grainy texture of the door and not the unyielding burns of celestial fire, Robert opened his eyes. He still had both hands and all ten fingers.

"Thank God," he sighed.

"Oh, that's good. I was sort of worried we would have to figure another way inside." Luke mused.

"You were worried," Dez quietly snapped. "You could have turned him into a well-done steak if you were wrong."

Luke raised an eyebrow accusatorially. "As I said, I was only *partially* concerned." Luke tilted his head to the side as his eyes again took on that scientific glimmer. "Were you worried, Dez?"

She squinted and turned away, looking at Robert instead of Luke's knowing gaze.

Robert clicked the door handle, closed his eyes, and pushed. He half-expected a bolt of lightning, a security alarm, or even some sort of angelic watchdog, but nothing happened. The doors just opened.

The three stood in the threshold, staring into the sanctuary. Headlights shone through the stained glass windows, spilling shades of red across the pews and the stadium. The scarlet color painted the room like the aftermath of a bloody battle—or a foreshadowing of one yet to come. Together, they stepped into the sanctuary and felt the heaviness of the air. It clung to them like cobwebs, weighing them down with every step. Robert's breathing became labored as the air thinned. At the base of the stage, Robert almost could not breathe.

"You feel that?" Dez asked. A frigidity wrapped around them, cocooning them in a warning.

"Yes." Luke's answer was enough to force Dez to act.

With a flick of her wrist, a knife slid from inside her sleeve and into her hand. Luke followed suit and withdrew a much shorter blade from one of his boots. Robert gave them both a look.

"Was someone going to tell me to bring a weapon?" Robert murmured. Dez flicked her other wrist, and an identical knife shot into her open hand. She tossed the blade briefly, catching it on its tip and handle before offering it to Robert.

Robert eyed the weapon.

"Take it," Dez urged. Robert accepted the blade and stared at the deadly point. "You know how to use one, right?"

Robert prepared a joke, but he swallowed it and accepted the blade.

"Good."

Luke approached the altar first. Candles, incense burners, and other religious paraphernalia sat atop a red tablecloth. Luke plucked each object off carefully, placing them on the floor before ripping the cloth away like a show person, tossing it into the air. Squatting, Luke examined the carved faces and engravings around the edge. He pressed a hand to the stone surface. To everyone's delight, there was no sizzle or cooking flesh.

"Your turn, Dezzy," he said, giving her a thumbs up before stepping aside. Dez stepped forward and gripped the slab.

The stone scraped against the floor, creating deep scores on the stage. Dez huffed and grunted as she tugged the structure from its position. Robert could see how heavy the altar must have been for Dez to struggle. And just as Luke claimed, it hid a well of darkness.

Luke peeked over the edge and stared into the empty depths. A gust of wind blew, throwing mildew-soaked air into their faces. Luke leaned forward, whistled into the pit, and listened as the sound traveled into the hole. Robert appeared at Luke's side, staring into the void and at the less than reliable ladder that led down.

"Ladies first?" Robert suggested, looking toward Luke and Dez.

"Well, if you insist," Luke leaned forward, took hold of the edge, lifted into a handstand, and with a simple push, Luke plummeted headfirst into the chasm.

"Holy shit!" Robert cursed, watching Luke disappear into the darkness. Robert waited for the sound of Luke's body crashing into the bottom or worse—a *splat*, but seconds passed without a sound. The continued silence became more concerning than a sound.

How far did it go?

"All clear!"

The two syllables restarted Robert's heart. But now Robert had to follow.

"Ladies first," Dez said, patting Robert's shoulder. "Just watch out, Luke gets a little handsy when he thinks nobody is looking."

Robert looked into the pit and prayed that Luke was the scariest thing in the cellar.

Chapter 21

The descent into the cellar was shakier than Robert would have preferred. The ladder jostled with every step. Robert and Dez both believed it was seconds away from collapsing. So they moved at a hesitant pace, which meant descending took much longer than necessary. Fifteen minutes into the climb, Robert realized Luke's swan dive into the cellar wasn't just for show.

Robert tried to occupy his thoughts, but then a rather unsettling creak would sound, and his attention would snap to the next rung on the ladder, waiting for it to crack. He hoped Luke was standing at attention if—and when—the ladder crumbled. Though beyond all reason, the ladder remained vigilant.

"Almost there," Luke called from the base.

"How deep does this thing go?" Robert whispered.

As deep as you want, Luke would say.

I'm surrounded by idiots, Dez would complain.

Neither answered Robert. Only the creaking, disturbing sounds of the ladder spoke.

They descended for another twenty minutes before a splattering of light appeared along the shaft's walls. The bottom was finally in view.

It does exist.

Robert released a sigh of relief as Luke waved at him from the bottom. The sight gave him the energy to climb faster, needing desperately to be on the ground.

When both feet touched the floor, Robert felt secure.

The cellar's chill stole the moment of relief before it invaded his body. The icy shock played along his skin. He could feel his temperature drop as the cold settled within him. Robert approached a nearby torch and held his hands to the fire. The flame was strong, but he felt no heat radiating.

"Fuck, it's cold." Robert shivered as he looked around. Endless could not describe the size of the cellar. Wooden doors with barred windows lined the sides of the hallway. Mounted torches were placed on either side, offering only enough light to illuminate the door. Gaps of darkness separated them, making the hallway even more foreboding.

If Hell existed, Robert imagined it would look similar.

"Where are we?"

A rush of air was summoned within the hallway, bringing a wave of screams—painful moans combined into a symphony of pain. Robert's hands flew to his ears, hiding from the agony. The sounds lessened as a voice rumbled beneath them. The voice was but a whisper, but carried the power to silence the cries within the corridor.

"Repent."

Luke bristled at the sound of her voice.

"Chastity." Luke turned toward the infinite hallway. His eyes focused as if he saw someone, or something, far off in the distance.

"Who?"

Luke's aura spiked, sapping the cheerful nature from his features. His blue eyes grew and contaminated the whites, releasing a different sort of power that Robert had not met. The gentle touch Robert associated with Luke's ability turned hostile.

"A torturer of souls. She warps people's minds. She creates husks that know only the pain she inflicts upon them. She's a foul, dark creature that wears a mask of innocence, but she is darker than any devil."

A cry of agony pulled Luke toward a nearby room. He paused at the door, pressing his forehead into the wooden surface. He closed his eyes as every painful emotion contained within the space ran through him.

"What's in there?" Robert asked, hearing the animalistic sounds and whimpering escape through the barred window.

"Who," Luke corrected. He lifted his head from the door and peered through the barred window. "Death save them." He backed from the door; his eyes reflected the horrors within. "Look and see what these . . . things do to innocents—to the supposedly *uncleaned*."

Against his better judgment, Robert approached and gazed through the window.

The cell was dark, empty of comfort or belongings. In the center stood a hunched man with his back toward the door. He rocked back and forth, whispering. Robert strained to hear his words, but they were too low and too broken to understand. Something dripped around the prisoner, splashing in a puddle at his feet. Robert pulled back, allowing a small amount of light into the room. The pool around the man's feet reflected the light and became red.

Blood.

Blood dripped from the prisoner's body. It flowed along the cracks of the stonework, spreading through the room like veins. It wasn't until the man turned that Robert's stomach tumbled into revulsion.

Two empty sockets found Robert in the window. Blood drained like tears along his features and onto his torso. The man raised an arm to wipe away the blood.

To Robert's horror, he raised only stumps.

"I'm sorry. I'm sorry. I'm sorry," the man cried as he wandered around the room in circles, stumbling in the darkness and begging for mercy.

Could this—could this be what happened to Becca?

The possibility turned Robert's stomach, forcing him away from the door before hurling. Robert's eyes watered, and blood vessels popped as his stomach emptied. The man's eyeless face was burned into Robert's mind, becoming something he could never forget.

"Why . . ." Robert gasped. "Why would someone do that to another person?" Robert wiped his mouth. Dez kept her distance from the door. She knew the horrors hidden within the cell and had no interest in seeing them.

"These aren't people we are dealing with, Robert. They never were human, like Katherine and me. They were born into their roles, immortals that have waged war against us and humankind since the beginning." Luke pulled the nail file from his pocket and fiddled with the padlock. "They are monsters. They search for order and obedience. No price is too high for them." He silently worked over the large door and did not stop until he received a soft *click,* and the lock opened.

Luke floated inside the cell, moving soundlessly towards the poor soul. Robert drew forward, watching as Luke approached the man. He placed a hand on the man's shoulder. The stranger screamed at the unseen person.

"No! Please! No more! Please!" He pushed Luke, believing him to be Chastity. Luke tried again, wrapping his arms around the bloody man. The prisoner fought Luke's every action, bringing the man's screaming face into his chest. His cries of fear became a sobbing penance. Bloody tears painted Luke's chest and soaked into his leotard.

"I'm sorry. I'm sorry. I'm sorry."

"It's okay." Luke stroked the man's scalp, pushing away his bloodstained locks.

"Please . . . no more."

"You don't have to worry. You can be free." Luke's hand disappeared for a moment and reappeared with his knife. "I am so sorry."

Luke leaned down and kissed the crown of the man's head. His cries paused, understanding the message within the tender moment. He embraced Luke, pulling himself tighter into his chest, and waited for what he knew was to come. "May the next life be kinder to you than this one." Luke lifted his knife and drove it into the base of the man's skull.

The man's breath hitched, then relaxed into Luke's arms. He was finally at peace.

Luke clung to the stranger, cradling his body until his heart released its last beat. Then, with a gentle hand, Luke laid the body on the ground. His hand drifted around the curvature of the man's jawline, imagining his face before he found his way into Chastity's dungeon.

Luke turned from the body with a clenched jaw, glossy eyes, and smeared makeup. He brushed the tears and blood from his face as he exited the cell. Dez and Robert moved away as Luke closed the door.

Dez approached Luke.

"We don't have time to save them." Her voice was soft, gentler than Robert had ever heard before.

"I know." Luke's voice was a thin note, a sound that was barely there when he spoke. He brushed past Dez, leading their walk down the infinite corridor without another word.

Robert approached Dez—her concern for Luke was clear. She worried for him. Robert chewed his inner cheek as he searched for the words to say to soothe her or Luke.

"Is he going to be, okay?" Robert asked, knowing it was a stupid question.

"It's hard for him—for all of them. People see them, see me, and think we're evil. We just want freedom. We want people to choose. Do good. Do evil. Do whatever the hell they want with their lives. It's all Eve wanted, to be free of Adam and God and be treated equally. Luke . . ." Her words faltered as she stared at the back of her friend's head. Her features softened as she looked at him. "Luke just feels so much more than any of the others. He is more connected to people and just wants them to be free to live and love. While Chastity . . . she wants submission. Those lost souls that fall into her web never come back."

Dez's words were finite and confident, making Robert worry about his sister's fate.

"She breaks people down until there is nothing left."

"But why?" Robert asked.

"It's her nature."

Robert remembered the ghostly howl that silenced the screams and the enjoyment that vibrated under her command.

"She'll sink her fangs into someone and twist until they don't know the difference between right and wrong. They could be the holiest person in the world, and she would make them believe they were nothing but garbage," Dez explained.

Robert swallowed a breath. "Do you think she did that—"

"We better get moving," Dez interrupted. "We have a lot of rooms to cover and don't know when Chastity or Charles may come searching."

"Okay," was Robert's response, not having the strength to ask a second time.

Silence settled over the three as they began their exploration of the hallway. Luke walked an invisible tightrope down the center of the corridor while Dez and Robert searched each room for Rebecca.

Each cell held a new indescribable hell. Missing limbs, scarred faces, disfigured torsos; each prisoner screamed their sorrows, begging for salvation from a monster who would never allow it. Chastity's voice vibrated along the walls and demanded their penance. Every so often, Luke stumbled when an excruciating scream was expelled from a cell, but he did not stray from his tightrope or speak.

Robert was unsure how far they had walked or how long they had taken. At one point, he checked his phone and saw that the clock had not moved since they had descended the ladder. He looked back to judge their progress. The ladder and beginning of the hallway had vanished, replaced with a mirrored vision of the corridor. There was no longer a beginning, and from what Robert could see, there was no end.

His current predicament worsened when the hallway unprecedentedly split into three directions. Each one stretched indefinitely in its appointed direction as the other two.

"Any ideas?" Robert asked.

"You go left. I'll go straight. Dez, you take the right," Luke ordered. Robert looked down his appointed hallway and felt uneasy about separating. He turned back to voice his opinion. But Luke had vanished, traveling so swiftly that Robert could not see him.

Apparently, I'm the one slowing the search.

"There's no way that we can search this whole place," Robert stated, surrendering to the reality of the situation. "There must be at least a thousand doors, if not tens of thousands."

"Probably more than that," Dez said matter-of-factly. "There's an infinite number of doors. Each room only holds one person. Once they die, the room is sealed and is never reopened. So, the hallway stretches, and more doors are added. Some of them have probably been shut for a thousand years."

"Thanks for that," Robert said, disheartened, as the facts weighed him down more and more.

Dez's lips went to the side.

"Try thinking about Rebecca," Dez suggested. "This place—it's different. Normal rules of reality don't apply in Chastity's domain. Hold the image of her in your mind and move towards her. Then at least, we will know which direction to go. Maybe your *uniqueness* will give us a hint of where to go."

"I'll give it a try." Robert wasn't sure if it would work, but it was better than walking for eternity.

Robert closed his eyes and imagined his sister. Her mischievous grin and curly brown hair. Her eyes that always had a plan churning behind them. Her firm stance and protective nature. He crafted her image within his mind's eye. He summoned the sound that encircled his stolen memory.

Robbie, she said.

"Becca," he whispered.

The image reached out to Robert. With eyes closed, Robert raised his hand to meet his sister and stepped toward her.

Space compressed around Robert as he launched through the hall. A high-pitched scream echoed behind him as he was dragged away by the unknown power of the corridor. His single step continued, uninterrupted, advancing miles forward towards an unknown location. The moment his foot connected with the pathway, the hallway became stationary, and Robert stumbled forward.

Robert's eyes opened, and the hallway spun. Robert braced himself against a wall as his face turned green. His stomach pushed for him to vomit, but he had nothing left to lose.

"Fuck." Robert groaned, lifting himself from his hunched-over position. He looked down one side and then the other. He didn't know how far he went, but Dez was nowhere in sight.

Did it work?

"Becca?" Robert called softly to the surrounding area. He waited for a sound, an acknowledgment, but heard nothing. Unlike the previous rooms, there were no screams of pain or torment, only stillness.

"Becca?" Robert cupped hands around his mouth and shouted. "Becca!" He walked forward. "Becca!" He called out for her repeatedly. "Bec—" Robert stopped mid-word when he heard a soft weeping.

The noise was unlike any of the previous cries for salvation. The cry was not painful or distressed, only filled with an overwhelming sense of despair. Robert went to the nearest cell and found it empty. He moved to the next one, and the next one, and the next one. Each cell was vacant, but the crying guided him onward. The louder the crying became, the faster Robert ran, no longer searching behind every door, instead running until the crying peaked.

The room was identical to the others, but Robert stopped.

He hung at the door, afraid to touch it as if it would burn him like the first door did Luke and Dez. He leaned forward, gazed through the barred window, and found a huddled mass in the corner. The prisoner shook in the darkness, crying into themselves. Shredded pieces of fabric hung off their skeletal frame. Dirt and dried blood covered their exposed back and legs. Robert squinted his eyes.

"Becca?" The form froze at the sound of his voice. They rotated their face, and in the shadows, Robert saw his sister. "Becca!" His hand shot through the space between the bars, reaching for his sister.

"Becca! It's me! It's Robbie! Becca, come to the door! Becca!" Robert shouted. It was her. It was Rebecca. She turned away from Robert, looking back to the corner, and began crying again.

What did they do to you?

"I'm going to get you out, Becca! I'm going to get you out." Robert withdrew his arm and tugged on the door handle. The large padlock bounced with each jerk.

Pulling the knife from his belt loop, Robert stabbed into the rotten wood surrounding the metal piece that held the lock. Piece by piece, Robert chipped away at the door. "Please be okay. Please be okay!" He leaned towards the window again and begged. "Becca, please say something!" But she remained muted, and Robert's efforts continued.

Stab. Rip. Stab. Rip.

Why couldn't Dez or Luke be here with him? Dez could have ripped the door from its hinges. Luke would have picked the lock in a matter of seconds. Robert was not crafty like Luke or strong like Dez, but he was determined. And a stupid door would not stop him after months of sacrifice and search.

With a deep stab, and some intense wedging, Robert ripped a large piece of the door away, and the padlock's hasp loosened. "Becca, I need you to move! We need to run when this door's opened."

Robert took hold of the metal piece, placed a foot on the wall, and pulled.

"Come . . . on!" Robert grunted as he tugged and tugged on the door, feeling it wiggle just a bit more every time he pulled. "Open up you . . . son . . . of . . . a . . . Fuuuuuuck!" With a last tug, Robert mustered his remaining strength and—

Crack

The metal piece snapped from the frame, and the door hurled open. Robert fell backward as the door slammed into the wall. A loud *crash* traveled down the walkway. Robert's head snapped to the sides, knowing that if someone—or something—were listening, they would investigate the sound.

Robert crawled to his feet, rushed towards his unmoving sister, and fell into her. His arms moved around her shaking body, pulling her into him. Her body tensed around Robert's touch, and did not look at him as he tightened his hug. Robert could feel every bone as they protruded through her paper-thin skin.

"It's okay. I'm here. I'm sorry, Becca. I'm so sorry it took me so long." Tears rolled down his face without restraint. He buried his face in her tangled curls. His sister showed her first signs of movement, twisting into him.

"I'm never letting you out of my sight again," he said, half laughing and crying.

His sister's hands brushed against his arms. Each finger was ice cold. Goose pimples erupted in their wake. She was so cold. So frail. Just holding her, Robert thought he would break his sister if he squeezed.

Her face dragged along Robert's chest and towards his ear.

"So long," she whispered, her voice harsh and fractured from months of screaming. "So long." She repeated.

Robert's soothing paused at the sound of the woman's voice. "Becca?"

"So long since I felt the arms of another." Even though the pained strain, the voice was deeper than Becca's, harsher, older. "Been so long since I have been touched by . . . a man." The voice slid into a sultry purr. Robert tore away from the woman, griping her shoulders. Her head fell back, throwing the frizz from her face.

She was not Robert's sister.

"Looks like I'm found out," the woman giggled, finding amusement in the lie. Her round face and pointed chin were covered in dirt, blood, and bruises. Her lips were full but cracked and reddened with dried blood. "What was that?" she asked the air, tilting her head to the side. "Shh, I know who it is. It's the brother," she said before giggling. Her eyes searched Robert's betrayed gaze, and a perverse smile flowered from her broken lips. "I know you." She looked at the ceiling, seeing something in the shadows. "I know you," she said once more. Her head snapped to the side as if an invisible person spoke beside her. "I won't tell him. I won't, I promise." She giggled madly.

"Won't tell me what?" Robert asked. The woman shook her head. "Who are you?" Robert asked.

The woman's eyes moved to the space above Robert's shoulder. Her smirk evaporated in a flash of fear. She threw herself from Robert's arms, slamming herself into the nearest wall. "I said nothing!" she screamed, crawling the wall behind her, seeking safety from whatever hovered behind Robert.

Needle-like fingers pierced Robert's shoulders and sank into his muscles. He jumped to his feet and spun, looking for the assailant as pain overtook his body. He twisted in the cell as the needles plunged deeper. Robert's hands flew to his back, swiping at what clung to him, but felt nothing. The needles curled happily within Robert, summoning pain from every nerve.

"Where are you?!" He shouted as it forced more pain onto his body.

An insect-like clicking sound reverberated around the room, bouncing off the walls as something crawled along Robert's back. Hundreds of tiny needles pierced his skin and retracted as it climbed. Robert's hands flung backward and finally made contact. The clicking sound came from the space above Robert's head, and he turned to face it.

A porcelain face looked down on him—not one of grace or beauty, but a hollow, ceramic expression with a pair of unfeeling eyes. The unemotional face stared down at Robert while its body clicked and snapped, digging its needle-like appendages deeper until he could no longer move.

Immobile and unable to fight, a voice whispered within his mind.

"Repent." And he fell into darkness.

Chapter 22

"Repent."

The words echoed through the dreamscape as Robert approached his old house, a three-story bricked condo. The edges of his vision were ghostly, the details of a memory that were unimportant to remember. Robert knew the memory he performed. He remembered how it changed the trajectory of his life.

Robert opened the front door and stepped inside. The air smelled of cologne and tasted of sweat. To leave and forget had crossed his mind; forget the scents, forget that his girlfriend's clothes were scattered across the floor, forget the man's voice he heard coming from the back of his home. Robert remembered wanting to turn back and forget this moment as he had so many others, but he investigated further.

Robert followed a trail of clothes that led to his bedroom; a discarded jacket, shoes, a dress, a pair of panties. He paused on the opposite side of his bedroom door. His insides screamed for him to leave and forget. He could forget about it. He could always forget.

"Turn back," his inner voice whispered, but Robert did not listen.

Robert pushed open the door.

"Victoria," Robert gasped from the doorway.

Two bodies intertwined beneath the sheets. Erik's muscular back lifted from the bed. Victoria's tiny hands dragged against his tan body. Neither cared nor acknowledged Robert's arrival. Rage boiled in Robert as he watched. Flashes of the memory played, him tearing Erik from the bed, Victoria screaming for them to stop, both parties blaming Robert as though they were innocent.

Every moment of the memory resurfaced as he stood in his bedroom again.

"So much anger within you," an icy voice whispered as it wrapped its fingers around Robert's arms. Its stony face pressed into Robert's head, tightening its grip on his shoulders. The needled fingers dug into his skin, playing with him like he was made of clay. "So much torment. So much regret. So much pain." Its lips, as cold as ice, pressed into Robert's ear. "Repent." The voice slithered through his ear like a worm, burying deep into Robert's mind. "Repent for your wrongdoing. Repent for your anger. Repent for your distress."

The voice cooled Robert's fury and replaced it with misery. Deep pools of regret and depression swelled, dousing the fire of his rage.

"It's all your fault," it whispered.

"It's all my fault," Robert repeated as his memory shifted. Foreign thoughts invaded Robert's mind, twisting what he knew to be true. He stared at Victoria, and instead of rage, he wanted only forgiveness.

"If only you had loved her more, she would not have done this."

"If I only loved her more," Robert repeated. The weight of his words warped his emotions and rewrote the scenes. Images of Victoria begging for Robert to love her. Visions of Robert ignoring her. Memories of Robert abandoning her. Moments ruined by Robert's inability to accept his emotions.

It wasn't her fault that she found comfort in the arms of another man; it was Robert's. It was his fault. He was to blame.

"If only you cared more, she never would have cheated."

"I'm so sorry," Robert cried to Victoria, but she would not look at him.

"That's right, Robert. It's all your fault. You could have loved her more if you wanted it. She would have never cheated on you. She would have never said those horrible things to you. You hurt her, Robert. You broke her heart."

Robert felt every syllable of the creature's poisonous words.

"I'm so sorry, Victoria. It's my fault." Robert fell to his knees and reached for her. The world pulled like taffy, stretching the room like a replica of the endless hallway. "Please forgive me. Please! I love you! Please don't do this to me! Don't do this to us!"

"This was your fault, Robert. I tried to accept you. But you are unlovable. It is your fault that nobody cares for you," Victoria's voice rang out as darkness swarmed Robert's vision, and another memory replaced it.

"You open?" a familiar voice purred as the door to The Rusty Nail swung open.

"Yes, ma'am, we are . . ." The words floated from Robert's lips as if spoken by another. "Dez," he gasped as she bounced into the bar with the same seductive stroll.

"Perfect," she responded, smiling larger and more brightly than ever. Robert remembered the moment she entered the bar.

"Repent," the bitter voice said, slicing through the happy thoughts that filled the memory.

"So, what's the house specialty?" Dez drummed her long fingernails along the bar top. Robert's eyes lingered longer than he remembered. Every curve. Every inch of skin. Every movement was like a spell on Robert.

"Well, we have vodka, vodka on the rocks, and then vodka with ice." Robert stared at her large, purple-tinted lips, wanting nothing more than to feel them against his own. Robert felt the memory slipping away as the edges began to unspool.

"Repent your sins. Repent your lust."

The creature's stiff fingers drifted along Robert's brow, digging into his mind again. The precious moment he shared with Dez froze as the creature took hold of the remembrance. A rigid body pressed against him from behind, directing him like a puppet and their creation.

"How would your sister feel if she knew this was how you spent your time while she was lost?" Lights within the bar illuminated scenes of Robert drinking his way through the night, using the bottle to cast out the nightmares that plagued him. The gluttonous nights spent eating more than he could afford. Hundreds of moments seemed to play before him as Dez sat tantalizingly in front of him. "What would she say if she knew these were the people you used to gain her freedom? How would she feel knowing that you found time for this . . . this thing . . . instead of looking for her?"

"It's not true," Robert whispered.

"Is it not? Just look at yourself. Lustful. Vengeful. Idle." The monster washed away the memory of Dez, and Robert was forced to stare into his reflection. His pale face. He had sunken cheeks. His empty eyes. Everything was wrong. "It's true, Robert. You are worthless. You are grotesque. You are unlovable. You will repent for your wasted life. You will learn the error of your ways. One act of penance at a time."

The creature unveiled itself, placing its doll-like face beside Robert's in the mirror. She pulled her arms from behind him, taking hold of Robert, wrapping around him like a carnivorous insect readying to devour its prey. Her overly jointed appendages popped and cracked with every movement. Robert flinched at every painful sound, but the creature's face showed no emotion. Her long fingers swept lovingly and carefully around Robert's face before she pressed her lips into his ear and whispered more of her toxic words.

"Are you ready to begin your penance?"

"No, please, no." Robert said, knowing the horrors her 'penance' created.

"But there is no other way, Robert." Her touch was tender and caring as her hands stroked Robert's cheeks. A tear rolled down his face as fear swelled. "Do not worry, my pet. You will learn, just as all my others do."

She twisted Robert's head and leaned towards him. Her ceramic lips parted and showed a horrific mouth of teeth. Dozens of rows and hundreds of long, pointed fangs threatened to devour Robert.

He panicked within her grasp as she inched towards him.

"Do not fight me, Robert, you—" The grotesque face turned to an unmade portion of the bar, sensing what Robert did; something was coming.

A flowery fragrance grew within his memory. A breeze blew through the bar, bringing warmth with the aroma. The scent battled the frigid cold and the worthlessness that swept over Robert. The creature hissed.

The perfume empowered Robert. The creature's body seemed to unhinge as Robert moved, forced from him as he moved towards the scent.

"What is that smell?"

"No!" The creature sunk its needled fingers into Robert again, but he did not feel the pain. It battled for control of the vision, but

Robert had already begun to slip from its hold. "Repent, Robert." Her calm, hypnotic tone became crazed—desperate for Robert to stay. "Repent! Repent with me, Robert! Learn the error of your ways! I am the only thing that will keep you from the darkness. Please accept me, Robert! Accept your penance!" Her fingers fell from Robert's skin.

Robert took another step. He couldn't see them but felt someone reach for him. Someone beyond his memory, and he stretched to touch them.

"Come to me, Robert." The warmth in the voice melted the ice formed from the creature's terrible words. Robert looked behind him and saw the ceramic creature fall from his back and vanish into the darkness, screaming for him to return. When surrounded once more by the nothingness of his mind, Robert closed his eyes and let the force direct where he needed to go.

Someplace warm, someplace—that smelled of lavender.

Chapter 23

Robert waited for someone to pull him from the sense of ease that washed over him, but nothing touched him. He could feel the horrible thoughts placed in his mind by the ceramic monster, still heavy on his mind, but he knew they were not his own. Slowly, Robert could feel them separating from his memories, and the truth in his recollection reformed.

After enough time had passed, Robert opened his eyes, and a blue sky greeted him. It was like a painting—a perfect blue sky with fluffy white clouds. He pulled himself into a sitting position and found himself atop a hill in the middle of a meadow. A field of wildflowers thrived around him, and acres of Lavender stretched beyond them, going as far as the edge of the memory. A breeze filled with flowers kissed his face. Robert inhaled and exhaled. This was peace.

"Beautiful, isn't it?" Dez asked, pulling herself from her hiding space within the flowers beside him. Purple petals and blades of grass decorated her dark curls. Dez gifted Robert with a soft smile before she turned back to the view.

"Where are we?"

"Someplace that Chastity can't reach you," Dez said, holding her eyes forward, staring intently at a foggy edge of the memory. "We're in one of my memories."

From the edge of the memory, a woman appeared, running through the fields of flowers. A man appeared seconds later, chasing after her. She squealed in enjoyment as the man shouted after her, following closely behind her. They jumped and skipped between the flowers, playing within the acres.

Several lifetimes separated the two, but Dez's laugh remained the same. The chase ended when the tall, simply dressed man tackled Dez into the wildflowers and kissed her. The real Dez sighed. Her fingers brushed against her lips, remembering the kiss, and recalling the moment. They watched from afar as the two kissed within the rolling fields.

"Is that Henry?"

Dez's eyes glistened. Her lips trembled, forcing a smile through her grief. "Yeah, that's him."

Neither spoke while they watched the two play in the lavender fields, chasing and laughing without a care.

"In all my years, I've never met a kinder person. He took in a woman who had nothing." She faced the sky and blinked away the

tears of the past. "He showed me compassion. He showed me his world. Showed me what it meant to be alive, what it meant to be human." *Robert inched closer to Dez.*

"What are you saying to him?" *Robert asked, seeing the past Dez whisper to Henry. Even at their distance, Robert could see Henry's cheeks redden.*

"That I wished this moment would stretch for eternity. That it could be just us until the end." *Dez's hand squeezed a handful of grass, ripped it from the earth, and searched for another handful. She pawed at the ground, needing something to hold—to center herself. Robert crept closer, fished his hand into hers, and gave a reassuring squeeze.*

"Time was harder than it is now. War was constant, food was scarce, and people feared anything different. And I was an outsider, I was a woman, and I was outspoken. I was worse than a demon to them. I was something they couldn't understand. But Henry was different. He supported my curiosity. He accepted me. All of me."

"So, he knew what you were . . . are?"

Dez nodded. "He knew, and he didn't care. He didn't see me as this evil monster. He saw me for me. I loved him, and he loved me. But the villagers didn't accept me or appreciate Henry for the freedoms he allowed me. They worried I would corrupt their women. So they took action." *The world shifted to night, and the smell of smoke conquered the flowery scents. Dark oranges and reds painted the sky, and fire erupted across the fields. Blazing flames grew along the edges and consumed the peaceful scape.*

"What happened?"

Dez rushed through the fires. The flames licked her heels and burned away her clothes, but did not scorch her skin. The further she ran, the more the world widened: a barn, a small cottage, a tree so massive that it outgrew the two structures. The figment of Dez froze before the tree. The world sharpened as a shape took form.

The man Dez loved so much swung from a branch.

Dez fell to the ground and released a scream that shook the world's foundation. Her pain materialized as a wave of ice. Hoarfrost sprouted across the dreamscape, extinguishing the flames. Ice coated the cinder-covered flowers and burnt lands. What life had not been claimed by the fire was encased by the tundra Dez summoned.

"They strung him up like some beast." Her hand tightened in Robert's. "I should've been there to stop them. I should've never left him."

Robert watched as Dez cut Henry down and placed his head in her bare lap. Night turned to day and back to night as Dez sat motionless beneath the tree. The world sped forward. Days flew by without movement. The ice remained even as the sun's warmth beat down on the icy wasteland. Though her tears stopped many days after, her sorrow remained. The frozen world she created remained.

On an unknown day in the future, hours before sunrise, Dez moved. She placed Henry gently aside, and beneath the giant tree, Dez dug a grave. Her fingers clawed through the ice and the earth, and finally, Henry was placed deep in the ground. Once more, Dez howled to the heavens before she disappeared beyond the memory.

"What did you do?" Robert asked.

"I slaughtered them," Dez seethed. "I tortured each of them until their bodies gave out. I inflicted every pain I could create. Forced them to beg for death, and when they were about to die. I'd let them heal and do it again. It was years until all three of them died. But it was not enough. I wanted more." The memory shifted. Dez appeared surrounded by discarded bodies at the foot of the tree, bathed in their blood. Every droplet shone underneath the starlight as she shouted words to the sky. "When they died, I called out to darkness. I bargained my freedom for revenge."

Shadows warped around her and took the form of a man. "I offered what I had, and he bound their souls to their dismembered bodies. I wanted them to rot beneath the ground until the day came that I died."

The dismembered people shuddered as life was forced back into their bodies. Horrendous screams boomed through the barren land. Once more, Dez clawed a grave, digging a hole deep enough that nobody would hear their cries. The crazed beast stared out at the fields that once birthed joy, now held only death and memories she wished to forget.

Dez faced Robert.

This pain was Dez's darkness, and Robert accepted it. He accepted all of who Dez was and who she had become. Robert saw her pain, and for the first time, Robert shared his darkness with someone.

"Becca saved my life once." The sentence was a fragment of a story he wished never to share, but felt it was finally time. "There was

a time when I felt so alone in the world. My parents didn't care, Victoria didn't care, and Becca—Rebecca was off living her wild and free life. And I just . . ." Robert's throat bobbed as he paused. "I just wanted someone to want me. For once in my life, I wanted to be enough for someone. I fell into this dark abyss and couldn't find a way out. Everything became too much. I just wanted to stop feeling so horrible. I wanted . . . I just wanted it to be over."

"Robert, you didn't."

Robert swallowed his fear and emotions and let himself release what he had bundled for so long. And with his words came tears.

"I did." Robert lifted his left arm. Two deep scars glowed against his pale wrist.

"I don't know if it was fate, but Becca came home that night and found me . . . afterward. An ambulance took me to the hospital. She didn't leave my side for weeks. She promised me she would always be there to take care of me, no matter how dark my world became." Robert smirked at how Rebecca mothered him when his mother hadn't come to the hospital even once. "Victoria bought me a watch to hide the scars. Unsightly was the word she used."

"She's a monster."

"She wasn't wrong," Robert said as he stared at the lines that would forever remind him of his weakness. "I just wish that I wasn't so weak—so afraid of the world and being rejected by it." Dez placed a hand atop his scars and looked deep into Robert's eyes.

"Do not hide what makes you human. You are perfect just the way you are. Never think otherwise." Dez gazed at the distance, seeing

269

her past. *"I have met thousands of people in my lifetime, and the most memorable were the ones who were afraid but chose to be brave. Just look at you, fighting angels and teaming up with demons."* Dez nudged him. *"I think that's pretty brave, if you ask me."*

Robert smiled, feeling an immense weight lift from his chest.

"Thank you." He whispered. Dez didn't reply, but he knew she had heard. The two watched silently from the hill as the corners of the memory curled up and vanished. The memory was ending, and they had to leave.

"Okay, enough time wasted on feelings," Dez said as she straightened her appearance and stood. Her internal switch flipped, and her emotions were gone. For once, Robert understood why. The amount of pain an immortal carried had to be crippling.

"I'm going to give you a push, and when you wake up, I need you to scream as loud as possible. Chastity may be with you, but I need you to scream for help. No matter where you are, Luke and I will come running. Do you understand?"

"What if she tries to pull me under again?"

"She can't, not at least for a short time. She's going to have to put in a little more effort than normally if she is going to break through the barriers, I put up around your mind."

"But how?" Robert asked. He still did not grasp the scope of Dez's powers.

"As I said, only the baddest of us have horns." Dez winked and then shoved Robert into the darkness before he could say another word.

Chapter 24

"Good morning, my pet." The porcelain smile that dragged Robert through his traumatic dreamscape welcomed him into the waking world. The unnaturally white face, colorless lips, and wide blue eyes hovered a breath's distance from Robert. A single brown curl hung free of a tight bun at the side of her face. "Did you sleep well?"

Robert threw himself away from the haunting smile, scurrying away until his head met the nearest wall with a heavy *thud*. The pain shocked through him.

"Oh, my." The woman reached for Robert. "Let me look, dear. I wouldn't want you to hurt yourself." Her voice was soft, but her eyes were hungry, eager to see Robert's self-inflicted pain. Her gloved hand stretched. The fingers popped as they reached for him. Robert plastered himself against the wall, fearing her touch and what she would do with just a brush of her fingertips. "Do not worry, Robert, I shall be gentle," she hummed. Robert pressed his face against the wall, fearing even the scrape of her fingers against his skin.

"Charlotte," a voice warned. "Behave."

Charlotte twisted away from Robert, looking towards the cell's entry. Footsteps sounded down the hallway as the person approached. Charlotte looked back at Robert. The hunger remained, but she obeyed—begrudgingly. She swept away from Robert. Her wide brown skirts awoke the dirt from the cell, sending the dust into the air. She took position beside the doorway as Charles appeared. He wore the same white dress shirt and slacks as before, and his hair was pulled away from his face.

"Charles," Robert growled.

Robert attempted to stand but stumbled as pain overtook his body.

His head pounded and bled from his recent collision, but an even more significant sting surfaced as the haze of his entrapment faded. He pulled away from the wall and looked over his shoulder. His shirt was shredded—hundreds of small punctures patterned the back. A handful of injuries were the size of knife wounds, some even more extensive. Blood leaked down his back, draining onto the surrounding floor. Gently, Robert pulled his shirt from his injuries.

"Fuck!" His chest tightened as the need to scream surfaced, but Robert contained it.

"Manners, Robert, we have a lady present." Charles wagged a chastising finger back and forth.

"Well, that fucking lady was just weaseling her way around my mind, so I apologize for feeling the need to curse." Robert gave a withering look to Charlotte. Her gloved hands pressed to her mouth, horrified by Robert's words and accusations—the face of a woman wrongfully accused.

"All I wanted was to help you, Robert." Her lips trembled as she lowered her hands and moved them together in prayer. "For you to learn the error of your ways. To repent. To become a child of God. Is that so wrong?" She wept unseen tears across her ghostly cheeks. "Please repent with me. Pray! Just give me more time, Robert. I know I can save you—I can fix you!"

"Nothing's wrong with me!" Robert shouted, repeating Dez's words. Charlotte shirked at his confidence, tucking herself inwardly. Her hands returned to her face, hiding her sadness as Robert continued. "I don't need to repent. I don't need to be fixed! I've seen what you do to those poor people. How you torture them and twist their thoughts until they have nothing left but bloody stumps with broken minds? You call that penance? I call it torture."

Charlotte's hands slid from her face, and with them came her mask. Her sobbing expression lifted, and something sinister slithered into place, something that enjoyed the carnage and destruction that she created with her penance. The reassuring voice that begged for Robert's salvation dropped several octaves and became an animalist groan.

"You are beasts. Insignificant insects to us. Does the boy with the magnifying glass not teach the ants as he burns them? Do they not

273

learn from their pain? The best lessons are taught through blood and sacrifice. Penance, agony, atonement, that is how insects are taught." She stepped forward. Charles held a steadying hand, knowing she would break Robert if given the allowance.

"You call us monsters when your cohorts are the definition of such creatures." Charles taunted Robert. "Do you know their plans for your sister if they find her? Ever wondered why they're so eager?"

Why?

The question had always been present in the back of Robert's mind. But why would he question the motives of the only people who offered to help?

Why hadn't Robert questioned their motives?

Charles nodded smugly; he knew Robert's answer.

"I guess not." His tone remained condescending. "Let me tell you, Robert, about the curse that condemns those beasts you call *friends*. They may act like they're immortal, but compared to us, they are seconds on a clock—moments that pass in the blink of our eye. So when the time comes for them to die, they must find their successor and pass on their curse before their untimely demise. Once plagued with their darkness, the innocent's soul will be pledged to the Devil and sentenced to an afterlife in Hell."

Charles paused, lips turning at the corner. "Any idea whose soul could be next? Any person you think would be a perfect match?" He squatted to Robert's level and impressed the truth upon him with a single look.

"No," Robert denied. "I don't believe you. You're a liar."

"Well, Mr. Monte, one of those monsters is dying, and soon the time will come when they must transfer their Sin to another, and your sister is their selection. They will force Rebecca to take up their blood-soaked crown, just like the rest of the long line of damned souls before her. And then when she dies, she will suffer an eternity in Hell tormented by the monster she will call Master."

"Your sister will be one of them. Lost from the light of the Lord," Charlotte bemoaned from her side of the cell. "And no amount of penance shall ever bring her back."

The crushing sense of betrayal overshadowed the pain in Robert's body. Charlotte glided down toward the floor, taking Robert's moment of weakness and feeding on it. Her hand slipped from her glove and grazed Robert's forehead. Her fingertips swiped away the fresh blood from his face. Charlotte savored the taste of his misery, groaning at the flavor. "And that is why we needed to take her. This line of darkness must end, Robert, whether at the cost of one life or thousands. We took Rebecca to keep her safe because, without her, they can do nothing." Charlotte reached out her hand, needing to touch Robert once more and taste his agony.

"Where is she?" Robert slapped Charlotte's hand from him. He braced himself against the wall and pulled himself to his feet. His ability to stand waned, degrading quickly as the blood drained from his back. Robert narrowed his focus on Charles. A hazy shadow surrounded his vision and grew.

Fight it. Don't give up.

"Somewhere . . . hidden far, far away. Someplace where you will never find her." Charles watched, undaunted by Robert, as he attempted to step forward.

"Robert, stop! Please, Robert! Just listen to us! We are doing this for her own good." Insincerity drowned Charlotte's features as she gracefully twirled toward Charles. Once again, her actions and her sentiments sat on separate sides of an emotional coin.

"Give. Becca. Back." Robert wobbled with every syllable but continued to fight.

"We have two pathways, Robert. Two choices." Charles lifted a finger. "One path that will lead to the death of your sister. It is unfortunate, but her death is the surest way for us to end the line of succession, but with her sacrifice, we shall snuff one of the Cardinal Sins."

"I won't—"

"Option two"—Charles raised a second finger—"we offer you a trade, and your sister shall be our bargaining chip." Charles paused, waiting for Robert to argue the point, but Robert remained silent. "There is an object that Katherine possesses, and I want it."

Robert's brows came together. "What is it?"

"I'm not sure. It would be something small. Easily carried. Potentially something that Katherine would always keep nearby or on her person. Something sentimental. It could be well-guarded or hidden in plain sight."

"Why do you want it?"

"That is none of your concern."

"Then no."

Charles shrugged his shoulders. "Then she dies. Best-case scenario is that your *friends* find her in time, but then—well, you know what happens if they find her."

Robert grit his teeth. "I won't let that happen. I won't let her die. And I won't let her become one of them."

"Oh?" Charles raised his brows in surprise. "You can barely stand. What good do you think you would be in a fight?" Robert did not answer again. Instead, he stared disbelievingly at Charles and his taunts. "Do not think we have kept your sister alive out of the kindness of our hearts. The time is not right, and we must be patient. The moment will come when her death is required, and it is a price I will willingly pay."

Charles presented Robert with choices, none were a risk he wanted to take, but he had to choose one. He had to decide what would be best for his sister.

"If I bring you whatever it is you want, you'll give her back?" Robert swallowed the bile that came with the thought of treachery, but it seemed Dez, Katherine, and Luke already had a taste for it.

"If you bring it to us, we will return your sister unharmed." Charles paused. "Though, I cannot promise your sister's safety for much longer—twenty-four hours at best. Our time for decision is encroaching, and we must decide. We cannot allow your sister to fall into their hands."

"But that's not enough time. I don't even know what I am—"

"Twenty-four hours, Robert. That is all that we can offer. Now, do we have a deal?"

Robert glared at Charles, wanting to say many horrible things to his sister's captor, but toppled before responding.

"I shall take your silence as an agreement." Charles turned away. "Come, Charlotte, I smell something *foul* approaching." Charlotte obediently rose from the ground and fluffed her skirts before leaving the room. "Remember what I have said, Robert." Charles looked over his shoulder. His human mask faded. Empty pits of anguish burned like white coals in his eyes, giving light to the bleak cell. "If you tell anyone of our deal, I will ensure that your sister meets her end by Charlotte's hand. She will break your sister so beautifully that you would never recognize her." Charlotte let out a squeal of delight before she skipped away with Charles, leaving Robert on the floor to bleed out.

The moment felt so familiar; powerless and in agony, collapsed on the floor while blood flowed around him. Robert pressed his face into the brick.

His breathing became shallow. The blood draining along his sides slowed with his heart. He wasn't sure if his eyes were open or closed any longer as blackness filled his vision. A muffled noise drew his attention, but it sounded so far away.

Something pressed into his back. "ROBERT!"

Dez . . .

"There's so much blood! Luke! Luke!" Hands moved across his body, pressing into his wounds. Robert knew he should have felt pain, but he felt nothing. His entire body felt as if it was wrapped in a blanket, cushioning any sensation.

"We need to get you out of here. Luke! Everything is going to be okay, Robert. Just stay awake. Don't go to sleep."

Don't lie, Robert wanted to say.

"Everything is going to be okay . . . don't worry . . . just stay with me. Please, stay with me." Her voice drew further away as Robert sank into the welcoming darkness, ready to meet death.

Chapter 25

The afterlife was more painful than Robert imagined, painful and itchy. As he floated in the darkness, something kept irritating his back. He tried to touch it, but he could not move. His body was both weightless and heavy.

When he opened his eyes, expecting to see cold, welcoming darkness or a light at the end of a tunnel, he faced a familiar popcorned ceiling.

I'm not dead?

He blinked at the ceiling.

I'm . . . home?

For a moment, Robert thought it all was a dream. The cellar. The memories. The moment shared with Dez. He looked at his bedside table and saw his phone. Everything was as it should have been. Everything felt so real. He reached for his phone, and unyielding pain shot through him.

"Fuck!" Robert cried as he fell back into bed, slamming into the mattress. Moving awakened and amplified the pain hidden in his body. Every inch was raw.

Definitely not a dream.

"Try not to move," Dez called from the kitchen.

"Could have used that advice earlier!" Robert groaned, closing his eyes as he waited for the pain to ebb. He listened as Dez crossed his apartment and stood beside him. Robert opened his eyes and saw Dez's bright purple makeup and curly hair.

He was not dead, and he was not in the cellar. Robert sighed in relief. But the moment was snatched away when he recalled Charles's threat and revealed truths.

"Becca!" Robert shot forward without thinking of the wounds. Warmth spread down Robert's back as he bent over in pain. "Jesus Christ!"

"You stupid child. I say for you to stay still and what do you do? You throw yourself around your bed like a mosh pit." Dez pushed him forward with little care. Robert winced. "Hush, this is your fault." Dez lifted the back of his shirt and *tsk'd* as she examined the rows of stitches that stretched along his upper shoulders. She pressed into a sensitive area, and Robert shuddered. "Luckily, nothing ruptured. A stitch popped open, but it was just one on the end of one of your . . . uh, injuries," Dez explained, selecting the least abrasive term to describe the massacre that was Robert's back. She lowered the shirt gently before entering the kitchen and returning with a cup of coffee. "I know you're probably thirsty."

Robert took the mug, and Dez searched for food. Robert stared into the black liquid, contemplating Charles's threats and his revelations. His stomach growled, but hunger seemed unimportant when betrayal already filled him.

"Why do you want to find Becca?" Robert asked, staring into the coffee like a psychic gazing into a crystal ball. Dez's back tensed for a moment before she resumed gathering the food on the counter together.

"I think you should talk to Katherine about that," Dez said to the kitchen wall. She returned with food from a cafe down the street. "Here." Dez offered a sandwich. "You should eat."

"No. I'm asking you." Robert repositioned himself even as the stitches tugged with every motion. "Why do you want to find my sister?"

Dez heard the intensity in Robert's question and noted his resolute expression. He wasn't just asking a question; he wanted an explanation.

"It seems like you already know the answer, Robert. So why are you asking?" Dez carelessly dropped the sandwich onto Robert's bed before she returned to the kitchen and brought a chair to the foot of his bed. She took a seat and motioned for him to speak. "Give me the courtesy of not playing games and say what you must."

"Are you going to make Becca one of the Seven Deadly Sins if you find her?" Robert held his breath, hoping Dez would deny it. He wanted her to deny it. He wanted Dez to tell him Charles filled his head with lies and that there was an even bigger game afoot. Robert needed Dez to say that they were just pawns and meant nothing more in their elaborate game.

Dez held his gaze, pursed her purple lips, and nodded.

"Yes." The single syllable was all Dez needed to tear apart Robert's reality completely.

"Why?"

"Why what, Robert?"

"Why her?"

"I don't know."

"Not good enough, Dez."

"Well, I don't know. I'm not in control of the cosmos. Contrary to what you or I want, neither of us gets to choose. She's next. It's that's simple." Dez bit back.

"She has to have a choice; there has to be a choice."

"Death or acceptance," Dez answered simply. "It's accept the universe's grand scheme or die defying it. That is her choice." Dez checked her purple nails as she spoke about Rebecca's demise as if she spoke of the weather, sliding back into her unemotional and straightforward way of talking.

"You're lying." Robert's hands tightened into fists. "Charles said that she would be safe if—"

"Oh, Charles said? You saw what they did to those people down there, Robert. Now you are trusting them?"

"At least those monsters aren't trying to be something they aren't." The hidden meaning under Robert's words was clear. "Why trick me? Why make me think you wanted to help me save her when all you wanted to do was turn her into one of you?" Robert's heart thumped faster with every question. His cheeks flushed red as his anger bubbled. Dez's lack of expression only made him that much angrier. Did she even care how much he was hurting?

"We wanted to help Robert! Why won't you understand that!?

"No! You were using me, just like you want to use Rebecca!"

"Is that what you think we are doing?" Dez raised her brows. "*Playing*? You do not know what is at stake here, Robert."

"My sister—"

"Screw your sister!" Dez interrupted. "There is so much more at stake than just one person's life!

"It's not like any of you wanted to explain anything to me. At least Charles had the decency to tell me what you all kept from me."

"Do not side with them, Robert."

"I am not on any side. I just want to find Becca and to get the fuck out of this city and away from all of you."

"That is not an option."

"I'll make it one."

Dez laughed a mocking chuckle. "With what power, Robert? You were caught like a fly in a spider's web when Chastity had you. Luke could put you in his thrall without trying. I had to save you from bleeding to death. Without us, you would not understand where your sister is. You're *weak*, Robert."

Her words hurt Robert more than any wound inflicted by Charlotte.

"I won't let you have her." Robert declared. "I'll die before I let either of you have her."

Dez clicked her tongue and raised from the chair like a wraith ready to attack.

"If we do not find Rebecca, she will die. If she does not accept her role, the world is fucked. Everything will tumble into chaos, and the balance will tip. So, if you think for just one moment that we did this for shits and giggles, then you have not understood a single thing any of us have attempted to explain. And if you get in our way, Robert, I will not ask for forgiveness for what I must do to keep the world spinning and out of the Virtues' control."

"What are you gonna do to me? Torture me as you did to those men who killed Henry?" Robert landed his final blow. Emotion cracked through Dez's expressionless face. Anger. Sadness. Betrayal.

"We're done here, Robert." Dez turned away.

"The hell we are." Robert pulled himself to the side of his bed. Every movement caused an upsurge of pain, but his anger pushed his body to move. "I need to speak with Katherine."

"The fuck do I look like? Her secretary?" Dez collected her belongings and walked toward the door, showing no interest in staying a moment longer.

"Desdemona!" Robert shouted. Dez froze at the door, fingers tightening around the doorknob. "You will do this for me. If there is any truth to your words, you will help me. You will get me in contact with Katherine." Dez held herself like a statue, staring at the door. She released the knob, opened her purse, and withdrew a business card.

She twisted at the waist, flinging the card with the dexterity of a knife. It embedded in the headboard, landing a hair's length from Robert's ear.

"Do it yourself." Dez opened the door and slammed it shut, shaking the walls with her anger.

Robert pulled the card from the wood and read the red lettering of Katherine's name and her number below it. He tapped the card against his palm and didn't wait before taking action. His heart ached for what he had said to Dez, but Becca's clock was ticking, and there was no time for feelings when so much uncertainty was left.

Chapter 26

Katherine answered the phone on the second ring and threatened to end the call five seconds later. She brushed off Robert's demand to meet, pushing it to some unknown date in the far future, but Robert's assertive tone intrigued her.

"Tonight. Eight o'clock. I will have a driver at your apartment building at half past seven. If you're late, I'll advise him to leave without you." She ended the call with no further conversation.

Robert sunk into his mattress with a deep sigh. Regret weighed him down, and pain kept him immobile. His back ached. His head throbbed. He did not know a part of his body that did not pulse with pain.

The following two hours, Robert rested. Sleep eluded him, but the lack of movement allowed the pain to recede and Robert to stir. Every action was slow, but the stitches that held his back together remained intact.

His back throbbed slightly with every movement, but it was bearable until the water struck it. The shower he desired was too painful to endure and became a towel bath, forcing him to confront the massacre. Hundreds of pinpricks coated his back—each a minor wound with a bead of dried blood. The largest of his injuries were three deep red lines, each at least half a foot and oozing a modicum amount of blood between the stitches. He bandaged himself up with what medical supplies Dez left and hobbled into his bedroom. Robert's stomach grumbled at the sight of the sandwich. It taunted him with the necessary calories his healing body required.

Begrudgingly, he ate it, crumbs and all.

The intensity of his resentment simmered as the day progressed. Whenever his hands were not busy, he thought back to Dez's face—how horrified she looked when Robert all but outwardly called her a monster. He regretted his choice of words, but had no way of taking them back.

Hours remained until Katherine's driver would arrive, so Robert did what he could to best prepare. He reread the book lent to him by Luke, hoping to find a secret hidden within the parables, one that he could use to save his sister.

*   *   *

As Robert expected, the car arrived on time. He waited atop the stoop in a pair of dress pants and shirt bought from his shopping spree with Dez. Robert hunted for something else in his closet, but even his most acceptable T-shirts seemed like the wrong choice. The driver opened the door as before, nodding to Robert as he took the same spot as he did days prior. As the car drove away, it forced Robert to stare into the now empty seats across from him. The back felt overly vacant without Luke's constant innuendos, Katherine's taunting, and Dez's threats.

In another life or another place, Robert felt that he could have been friends with them. Robert turned away from the empty seats and stared at the traffic. His thoughts drifted through the last weeks of his life, the church service, the afternoon lunch, the entire day he spent with Dez. The sense of friendship that had grown between the four of them.

It couldn't have all been fake, could it?

A horrible voice—one not planted by any other—whispered, telling him it was a charade. That these relationships were just like all his others, hollow. That he was nothing to them, nothing beyond a way into the church.

Once again, Robert had nobody in his life; without Rebecca, he would truly be alone.

Robert watched the buildings transform. Blinking casinos and tall hotels replaced the crumbling buildings of Naked City. Empty sidewalks and bushes became palm trees, and tourists crowded the walkways. Once the glitz and glamor of Las Vegas enchanted Robert, but now, he could not stop thinking about the darkness that hid within the city's bright lights and magic. The vehicle turned off the main road, going into a short roundabout before pausing at a hotel's front door. Robert gazed out the window, instantly recognizing the large doorway and the fountain out front.

"You have got to be shitting me," Robert cursed as the driver opened the door. "She lives in the Bellagio?" The driver nodded, leading Robert into the grand hotel.

Opulence surrounded Robert as he walked through the main entrance. They polished the tiled marble floors to perfection, reflecting every object within the space. Art sculpted from blown glass hung from the ceiling. Each check-in counter was staffed by an identically dressed young woman, each with not a hair out of place and a hollow yet welcoming smile on their face. Large vases of fresh flowers were strategically placed around the entrance, masking the horrible smell of smoke from the casino opposite the welcome area.

The first night together, Rebecca pulled Robert into the hotel, wanting to see every landmark. He remembered taking pictures of the glass sculptures while Rebecca beelined for the slot machines.

The driver coughed, pulling Robert from his memory and leading him towards the elevator.

"Ms. O'Donnell is in the presidential suite. She is expecting you. Just walk inside when you find the room." The driver pressed the top floor button. Robert thanked the man for his help and waited while the elevator ascended. The gifted blade warmed in his pocket, reminding Robert of his purpose. The weapon would do little for him if the encounter became violent, but it gave him an inkling of protection.

The doors opened with a soft *ding*. A short hallway with a red runner led to a pair of doors. Scenic paintings hung on the walls and above small end tables. Large vases with fake flowers flanked the tables' sides.

"For Becca."

As Robert entered the apartment, a blast of bread-scented air wafted into the hallway. He expected to hear Katherine inside, barking orders at whoever cooked or had entered her home; instead, he heard a gleeful hum. Katherine decorated with warm fabrics and rich colors, opposite her cold nature and structured appearance. Dozens of unique art pieces decorated the twenty-foot-tall ceilings, each bright, vibrant, and composed of varying mediums. Mismatched furniture filled the sunken-in living room; each piece placed awkwardly around the open concept. Some were patterned and upholstered in fabric, while others were worn leather. Floor-to-ceiling windows occupied the main wall, giving a view of the entirety of Las Vegas, while the other held overflowing bookcases placed around an unlit fireplace.

A long glass table dominated the dining area. Each chair was a work of art in its own right, each dramatically sculpted out of a combination of glass, leather, and wood. A buffet filled the glass table: glazed hams, roasted birds, bloody steaks, and bowls of cooked vegetables. Steam drifted from freshly baked bread, drawing Robert closer. Robert's stomach grumbled. Everything looked homemade and begged to be devoured.

"Surprised to see you're on time." Katherine walked from the kitchen.

Broad streaks of gray painted her curly red hair as it flowed from the messy bun on the crown of her head. Deep wrinkles crept around her eyes and lips, deepening as she smiled. Freckles splattered across the bridge of her nose and her cheeks. She looked almost human. She looked as if she had aged twenty years since Robert last saw her.

What is happening to her?

Katherine wiped her hands on the stained apron around her waist, adding to the multitude of blemishes baked into the once-white fabric.

"Surprised to see you know how to cook," Robert countered as he leaned against a wall, feeling dizzy from so much movement. He waited for her typical snide remark, but instead—she laughed. And it wasn't the elegant, high-class sneer but a bark of enjoyment at Robert's bite.

"You're learning. That's good. It shows you know how to survive."

Robert pulled himself from the wall, ready to ask his first question, but Katherine stopped him. "Give me a moment. I want to change, and then we can have this meeting you were so eager to make happen." Katherine took off her apron and hung it on a nearby hook before disappearing into the back half of the suite.

Robert wandered into the sea of ugly furniture, staring at the bookshelves. An odd collection of books and knickknacks lined the shelves, items ranging from old baseball bats to an extensive collection of dictionaries. Robert's fingers grazed the spines of the books as he read the titles, recognizing some while others were in languages he did not know.

The Art of War . . . fitting.

"Anything interesting?" Katherine asked as she reappeared in a pair of loose-fitting green palazzo pants and a billowy cream blouse. She walked soundlessly across the stone floor, staying on the tips of her toes as if she wore a pair of invisible heels.

"My father always said you could tell a lot about a person from the books they keep in their homes," Robert said as he looked at a book besides an oversized leather couch.

"And what do my books say about me, Mr. Monte?" Katherine questioned as she situated herself on an ugly velvet chair trimmed with gold accents at the end of the dining table. Robert examined the book on the table and then the ones on the bookshelves.

"It seems like you read a lot. Most of the spines are broken, saying they aren't just for show, but this one seems to be your favorite." Robert lifted it and examined the spine, seeing the repeated creases created from rereading the book. "Wouldn't think you were a fan of poetry."

Katherine smiled a reserved, seductive grin before dipping her head toward Robert.

"Neat little party trick, Mr. Monte. Please sit, eat." Katherine motioned toward the chair sitting at the opposing head.

"Didn't expect a 'please,'" Robert said, taking his chair and staring out onto the piles of prepared food.

"Do not get used to it."

The shadow Robert had seen returned to Katherine's eyes for a brief moment but was blinked away as quickly as it came.

"Now, don't be shy. Eat your fill. Nobody else in this place actually eats any food, so it is a treat to cook for someone besides myself." Katherine reached into a bowl of steaming green beans and heaved a healthy scoop before moving towards a platter covered in meat. Robert followed suit, piling food onto his plate. After months of takeout, Robert was more than greedy for something not deep-fried. It was nearly twenty minutes of ravenous eating before Katherine placed her fork and knife on the table and dabbed her lips.

"To what do I owe the pleasure, Mr. Monte?" Katherine poured herself another heavy glass. An idea had formed as he watched Katherine continuously drink, a plan allowing Robert to search Katherine's suite uninterrupted. All he needed was for Katherine to continue to drink.

"Why do you want to find Becca?" Robert asked, testing the waters with a question to which he already knew the answer. Robert needed to know if Kathrine was going to lie or, for once, answer his questions.

"She's next in line." Her voice remained flat, unsurprised by the question. "I assume you know from your rather—direct question, or you wouldn't be asking." She sipped from her glass, painting her lips with a fresh layer of red wine. "Next."

"Choose someone else," Robert said firmly.

Katherine's eyes widened, and brows raised. The wrinkles of her face dug deep crevices into her cheeks and made her already unsettling grin that more malicious.

"That is not a question."

"I wasn't asking one."

"Choose someone else?" She said the words, tasting them as if they were a flavor she could not discern. "Do you think this was a choice for me or my predecessors?" Katherine's voice was light and airy as her fingers played an invisible piano, playing with the ghosts of the past. "Do you think any of them wanted this life?"

"You seem to enjoy it well enough." Robert motioned to the luxury surrounding him. "I'm sure you can find someone who would kill for this. Go find them and leave my sister alone."

Katherine rolled her neck, cracking it several times before running her finger around the wineglass. She licked the residue from her finger, tipped the rest of the wine into her throat, and relaxed further into her chair.

The alcohol was already showing its effects.

"Fascinating how you think any of this means anything to me." Katherine flicked the glass, shattering it across the table. "Do you understand what we give up for this?" She waved one hand lazily around the room. The broken shards of glass vanished, and a fresh glass took its place. "Do you understand what I had to give up to keep the world safe? To make sure that those monsters don't take control of humanity?" Katherine poured herself another glass of wine and swallowed it in one mouthful. "Years pass, the world changes, but I stay the same. Loved one's die. Friends forget. The world continues to turn while you are a rock vigilantly standing against the rushing river of time."

"Then why do it?"

"Why do you think there is a choice, Robert?"

"It's just not—"

"Fair?" Katherine finished. "What part of the world do you think is fair? Do you think it is fair for a child's mother to abandon her? Do you think it is fair people are chosen and forced to give up their life to save a world of people who couldn't care less? Well, Robert, life isn't fucking fair. There was no choice." Robert parted his lips to ask a question, but Katherine continued. "If I offered you the choice to live or die, which would you choose?"

"To live," Robert said.

"Exactly, and for your sister. Would you prefer she lived or died?"

"To live."

"As any brother would. This *job,* as you call it, is not just a job. This is a purpose. It is a calling that was created before we were even born. I represent the wrath felt by the first woman—the one who birthed this emotion into the world. We not only represent the sin but also embody it—contain it. Without me, without my brothers and sisters . . . there would be catastrophe." Her tone turned haunting. She turned to the large windows that occupied the wall behind the table. "And I have given up too much to allow that to happen."

"There has to be a way around it," Robert said, fishing for some solution, some cosmic loophole that he could use to get his sister out of the line of succession.

"Potentially," Katherine said before she turned back to Robert. "I don't know of one, and one has yet to be found in the last—oh, three thousand years. But who knows, maybe the great Robert Monte will be the one to end the endless cycle of good and evil." She poured what remained of the decanter, spilling most onto the floor. "Once we find Rebecca, she will take her place, whether or not you like it."

"I won't let you."

Katherine did not miss Robert's change in tone. Her eyes observed Robert as something danced within her foggy irises. A secret? An answer? Another riddle?

"I know you have wondered why you are so different. Why you aren't as susceptible as others to our influence? Would you like to know, Robert? Would you like to know why everyone is so intrigued by Robert Monte?"

Robert froze, unsure of what to say. He came to Katherine for Rebecca, not answers to his questions. But Katherine knew the morsel she dangled in front of him and how Robert could not resist being able to learn the answer to the question, "What are you?"

He gave a slight nod.

Katherine leaned forward, intertwining her fingers beneath her chin. "You are a descendant of Eve and Adam." She whispered the answer as if she feared someone was listening.

"But aren't we all descendants? If the Adam and Eve story is true, wouldn't we all be descendants?"

Katherine laughed at Robert's ignorance.

"You think *they* stopped with just one garden?" Katherine laughed again. "No, there were dozens more—hundreds, if not thousands of more gardens. God repeatedly attempted to craft the perfect human who would obey without question." She knocked her head back and forth as if she shifted the memories free from some past life. "Some ended like Adam and Eve—cast from Paradise—but some obeyed. Some were gifted eternity within his hallowed halls. Though the number was far less than he would ever admit." Katherine placed her hands together in prayer and tilted her head, giving her face a disturbingly serene expression, a look reminiscent of Charlotte's peacefully disturbing face.

"But Adam and Eve were the first and the strongest. A mistake he did not make twice when he made his second batch of mortals. But their blood, the blood of the original man and woman, flows through you and your sister."

"But aren't there more people like me? Like Becca?"

"You and your sister are the product of two bloodlines meeting. Both your father and your mother are descendants of Adam and Eve. Two powerful ones, from what I can tell. Never has a person such as you existed, Robert. You aren't just different. You are special. You are a chess piece both sides want—someone who could tip the scales."

Robert thought back to how he broke free of Captain Russo's memory wiping, Katherine's rage, and Luke's lustful influence. Robert wasn't a Sin, but he was closer than anything else before him. And it wasn't just the Sins that Robert could fight, but the Virtues. Robert had fought Charles's will and Chastity's torture; he lost both fights, but could he potentially beat them with practice?

"Now, Robert, our cards are on the table. You need us just as much as we need you."

I don't need you. I don't need any of you.

Robert did not answer her plea. He knew he wouldn't be able to lie. He was not here to join her side but to steal. Katherine sensed Robert's apprehension.

Did Robert see their failure in the cellar as a reason to lose faith?

Knowing Robert's significance, Katherine offered one more piece of information. She closed her eyes and released a breath. "We are running out of time to find your sister, and I am running out of time." The shadow Katherine battled settled on her face, and she did not fight it. She yielded to it. The luminescent glow in her skin dimmed and finally died. Her cheeks sagged, and her skin grayed. Imperfections appeared on her cheeks, scars, acne marks, and age lines. Her lips thinned. Her intense eyes turned hazy, growing cloudy with age. The years rushed through her body. Her grays overtook the red, leeching the color until it was gone.

It became clear why she was so intent on finding Rebecca.

"You're dying," Robert said breathlessly as the final missing puzzle piece fell into place. The one who was dying was Katherine.

"Yes, Robert. I am dying. I have lived longer than I have wanted and through much more than I thought I could survive. This life is hard, Robert. It takes pieces of you and forces you to break them again and again and again."

Katherine's words were no longer a confident monologue or powerful stream of taunts or jabs but an elder's warning. A foretelling of his sister's future and what she would endure if Robert allowed her to become a Sin.

Robert needed to stop it from happening.

Abruptly standing, "Where is your bathroom?"

Katherine weakly motioned down the hallway, uninterested in answering his question if he would not answer hers.

Robert went down the single hallway, hearing Katherine loudly swallow more wine. It was sad to see Katherine in such a way, withering away before his eyes.

Turning on the bathroom lights, Robert saw a ghostly vision of himself in the mirror. The blood loss, the lack of sleep, and the conversation all took their toll on Robert's face. Beneath the bright fluorescent lighting, he looked closer to death than Katherine. He turned on the faucet, splashed cold water on his face, and looked back in the mirror.

Robert didn't look any better.

"They don't care about you or Becca." Robert splashed water on his face once more.

His choices were few, let Rebecca die, let her become the new Katherine, or he could believe in Charles and make his trade.

Leaving the water running, Robert opened the bathroom door. He listened for the clang of silverware or Katherine's rather loud slurping but only heard the rhythmic sound of her snoring. It was time. Robert slipped across the hall and into Katherine's bedroom.

The homey decor continued into her room with large quilts on the bed and photographs on the walls. One caught Robert's eye. A faded photo of a portly man and child sat on her bedside table. The resemblance was uncanny: the sharp chin, the curly hair, and the toothy grin. It had to be Katherine as a child and her father.

Efficiently, he worked through Katherine's bedroom. He searched the closet, looking inside every hatbox, shoebox, and jacket pocket, but found nothing. Her clothes were designer, and her jewelry was opulent, but each piece seemed . . . mundane—expensive but mundane.

Robert found the same in Katherine's bedside tables and her dresser.

"Where is it?" Robert said, sliding against the side of the bed and onto the carpet. "What is it?" He looked at the photo and stared at the child: her poor clothing and wild hair. Robert's attention moved to the man and his jolly grin. He held open his suit jacket, revealing his ample gut, and a gun holstered around his waist. Robert leaned closer, eyes settling on the weapon. Though small, he had seen the same pearl inlaid handle before.

"Of course."

In all the time Robert spent with Katherine, what was the most out-of-place object? What did she hide with ease? What had Katherine shown to Robert that could have any sentimental value?

Robert's eyes bounced around the room, thinking of where she would have hidden her gun. His eyes went back and forth between the image and the room. He checked the closet. He had checked her drawers. He looked had searched every potential place within the bedroom. He stared at the image's industrial background, the little girl, and the older man.

"That's it." Robert realized what he was doing wrong. Katherine wouldn't have hidden something important, like someone born in the 21st century. Anyone who survived the Great Depression hid their valuables in two places, the freezer or under the mattress. Robert gripped the edge of the bed and lifted it. Like unearthing treasure, Robert found Katherine's gun.

It looked so ordinary, but somehow, Robert knew this was what Charles wanted.

Large pearls embedded the wood handle. The metal and wooden pieces shined from a recent polishing. Just staring at the object, Robert felt a tingling in the back of his head. Like a dull electrical current seeking a place to ground. He reached for the gun, brushing his fingers around the handle, and excruciating pain exploded within every receptor in his body.

Fire tore through his system and forced Robert onto the floor. His hand unconsciously clenched the gun as he dropped. Every neuron felt set ablaze with gasoline. Robert writhed as the pain became everything he knew. He opened his mouth to shriek, but could only release a silent scream as the inferno burned. His hand tightened around the gun as something crept from within the weapon's core. A darkness-like ink dripped along his consciousness, filling him. It showed no care or kindness, as its every touch sent unbearable pain through Robert.

Who are you? Every syllable was a spike driven into the space behind Robert's eyes. It was like Katherine's touch, but with no concern for Robert.

I'm . . . a friend.

Friend, it hissed in response.

The firestorm flared at the answer. Robert's vision filled with stars; the pain his mind felt was too great to understand. The world around him disappeared as the creature within the gun fed on its captive. Robert pulled at whatever force that had kept the Sins' and Virtues' power at bay, throwing it against the monster. The thing brushed against his mental defenses, testing the blockade. The pain paused. The creature's touch turned inquisitive, tasting the thing within Robert, seeing it as something familiar.

Friend, the thing said.

Yes, friend!

The force within the handgun threw waves of pain at Robert. His body jolted upward, spasming as his mental defenses protected Robert from ultimately succumbing to the creature.

Friend. I am your friend.

The monster retreated slightly, withdrawing from within Robert.

Friend? it asked, pausing a second time.

Yes, friend.

Robert thought himself a fool but allowed his mental fortitude to fall, opening himself to the creature. He waited, expecting the monster to seize the moment and devour him whole, but the creature did not attack.

Friend, the monster repeated as it inched away from within Robert. It collected itself within the gun, pulling away from Robert and taking the pain it caused with it. When the last vestige of the gun's protector withdrew, the pain vanished.

Robert relaxed, but his back muscles remained tight. He licked his lips, tasting blood. With no time to relish in his survival, Robert stood, feeling his shirt peel from his back. He looked over his shoulder; blood dotted the shirt and stained the carpet. The gun that had caused so much pain had fallen silent. He felt nothing, no power, no anger, no dark foreboding presence. Whatever attacked Robert had silenced itself, seeing Robert no longer a threat. He wasn't sure if that was a good sign, but if it were to awaken again, that would be a problem for Charles.

With any luck, I'll be out of the city with Becca before it happens.

Robert tucked the gun into his waistband, pulling the back of his shirt over the weapon before he returned to the dining room.

With several loud, aggressive stomps down the hallway, Robert announced his return to the dinner. Katherine's even snoring hitched and stopped as Robert turned the corner. Katherine positioned herself across the chair, staring at Robert as if only seconds had passed, not fifteen minutes. She forced her eyes to remain open to appear awake, but Robert noted the fatigue tugged at her features.

"I'm leaving." Robert's voice shook, hiding behind his chair. His declaration sent a bolt of energy through Katherine, pulling her further from slumber.

"Robert, you can't do this without us," Katherine warned.

I hope you're wrong.

Robert said nothing as he turned from her and walked out the front door. He hobbled down the hallway and the stairs, not wanting to spend another moment near Katherine, fearing she would learn of his deception. One painful step at a time, Robert fled from the penthouse and then the building. His pace quickened when he reached the sidewalk.

For a moment, Robert believed himself safe, but a stirring in the air proved him wrong. A gale passed through the streets, carrying a wail of fury. Robert paused, turning towards the penthouse suite of the hotel. Though he could not see her, Robert was certain Katherine had realized his deceit. The wind's strength grew, becoming a tempest fueled by her rage. Robert turned away, hastening his stride as he trekked to the church, knowing that any second wasted was another moment Katherine could find him.

Chapter 27

The distance from the hotel to the church was further than Robert had hoped, but he couldn't convince himself to stop for a taxi. Katherine's influence stretched far, and Robert didn't know if anyone could be trusted. With every alleyway he passed, Robert expected Katherine to leap from the shadows and punish him. But she never appeared. Pain begged him to slow, but fear hastened his speed.

It was late into the evening when Robert finally stumbled up the church's stairs. The lights within the building were dim, but silhouettes moved behind the colored glass and gave him hope that someone would be working. He banged on the front doors without care or courtesy for the late hour. A frail woman in an orange dress answered Robert's aggressive thumps.

"Do you know—" she began to ask, but Robert pushed past her and into the main hall. "Excuse you!"

On each visit, the sanctuary changed. The building felt alive and cheerful the first time; the second visit appeared empty; now; the building felt as if it were sleeping. Like it waited for something to occur, for a reason for it to awaken. The lights were low, and the inner sanctum was quiet as Robert rushed toward the back office. His haste drew the attention of several praying worshipers. Robert followed suit, sending a prayer to whoever listened as he descended the stairs and entered the back office.

Charles sat in the same position as before, muttering to himself as he wrote within a large tomb. Charlotte hovered over his right shoulder, reading as he wrote. They dressed in entirely white outfits, like contemporary angels—a dress for Charlotte and a dress shirt and slacks for Charles. Their attention broke as Robert entered the office, greeting him with smiles so warm that they unnerved him. The blank expression made Robert feel worse.

He made a deal with a devil and now had to honor it.

"Ah, perfect timing, my friend." Charles capped his pen and placed it on the desk.

"I had hoped we would lead you down the path of righteousness, Robert. I knew my prayers would be heard!" Charlotte's voice was overly sympathetic, but Robert could see the darkness hidden within her words.

The face of an angel but the heart of a fiend.

"Did you bring what we discussed?" Charles drummed his fingers. He was anxious, hopeful that Robert had succeeded in a task he could not.

Last chance.

He could still run away. He could return the gun to Katherine. He could find another way to save Rebecca. He could do a lot of things, but he didn't.

Robert lifted the back of his shirt, withdrew the gun, and dropped it on the desk. Charles's eyes widened to an unbelievable size as he gawked at his prize.

"You did it!" Charlotte clapped and jumped. She reached to touch it, but Charles swatted away her hand.

"Careful, my dear." Charles extended a finger, pressed it into the hilt of the gun, and chaos erupted.

Robert covered his ears as the gun's protector screamed like a kettle whistling. Darkness erupted from the gun as the creature took physical form. Black tar bubbled from the weapon and swelled. Oily shadows rolled across the desk. Everything it touched was eaten, dissolved into the nothingness of its inky surface.

Charles showed no fear. His eyes became pearls, bleached of color and glowing with power. Light outlined Charles's body and grew and illuminated the space.

Friend, the thing hissed within Robert's mind. The voice quivered with distress as its advance halted.

FRIEND, it screamed to Robert for help.

Robert stayed frozen, repeatedly blinking as the light around Charles grew stronger. Charles became a sun, pushing the shadow back into the weapon. Thick tendrils grew from the blackness, reaching Robert, begging for help. Robert stepped back from the living shadow. He couldn't help it.

Charlotte stepped to Charles's side, placing a hand on his shoulder. Her eyes transitioned into the same frightening, pearlescent shade. The endless white within their eyes radiated power as it slammed into the shadowed being, forcing it back. Robert could hear the agony in its cries. Slowly it was swallowed back within the confines of the weapon, taking with it the whistling and its pleas for assistance. Once the living shadow was no more, the virtuous light surrounding Charlotte and Charles dimmed, and they returned to normal.

Charles lifted the gun with ease and a look of disgust. He twisted it, examining every angle of the weapon.

"Superb job, Robert. Truly superb." Charles opened a drawer, dropped the weapon inside, and locked it, placing the key in the spine of a nearby book. "Thank you for your cooperation." Charles gave Robert a nod of thanks before pulling a stack of papers from the floor and placing them on his empty desk. Seconds passed without words before Robert felt the courage to speak.

"My sister," Robert croaked.

Charles lifted his head and gave a look of confusion. "Oh yes, your sister." Charles tapped the end of his pen on top of his paperwork. He looked at Charlotte and then back to Robert. "We do not have her."

Robert's heart stopped.

No.

"What? No! That can't be true! You said you had her! Give her back to me!"

"We do not," Charlotte said as her features twisted into the creature that enjoyed agony. "Charles spoke truthfully when you first met him. We never had her," she said, nearly giggling. "The penance we shared for our lies was so delicious." She rolled up her sleeves and revealed several long gashes. Deep wounds ran along her forearms, even bleeding still as Charlotte showed Robert. "We didn't even let our bodies heal afterward. We shall heal as slowly as humans. Every moment is pure torture. The agony I feel just from moving makes me . . . makes me . . . UGH," she groaned, relishing the pain that she had unleashed on herself.

"No. You're lying. This cannot be true." The room spun as the lies settled. The space seemed hotter—the air thinner. Robert's heart pounded so frantically; he thought it would explode. "What do you mean, you never had her?" Robert gasped. "Katherine said you had her! You said you had her. Who—who else would have taken her! Where is my sister?" Robert slammed his hands on Charles's desk.

"I request you remain calm, Robert. Unfortunately, that is beyond my knowledge," Charles said evenly.

"I believed you! I threw everything away. I betrayed the only people who were willing to help me! Look what you made me do!" Robert shrieked.

"People? You think those things are people?" Charlotte laughed. "You saw what crawled from that gun. Would you want that inside your sister? Crawling around her mind, feasting on her soul. We saved her. We saved you. Without the gun, Katherine cannot transfer the Sin of Wrath to any other innocent soul, and your sister shall die without it. Be thankful for that—"

"Give me back the gun!" Robert shouted, but stopped midair when Charles raised a hand of warning.

"Now, Robert, I cannot do that." Charles's answer was short and without explanation. "I am sorry that you feel deceived, but it is all for the best—I assure you." Charles looked back at his paperwork, disinterested by Robert's pleading.

"You don't even care. Look at me." Charles ignored Robert's command. "Look at me!" Robert swept his arms across the desk, throwing what remained of the papers and Charles's knickknacks onto the floor, bringing his attention back to Robert. "You made me think what I was doing was right." Robert wept. "You twisted my hope and made me betray the only people who wanted to save my sister. You are no better than the monsters you despise. All of you are just selfish, with no care or worry for the people in your way!"

"Robert, I can understand you being upset—"

"Upset! You think I am just upset? I'm enraged! You two are disgusting! You toy with people who look to you for help, only to further your own desires."

Charles stood from his chair. He seemed taller as he rose, stronger, mightier than the man Robert saw standing on the church's steps. "The Lord sacrificed his son to get what he wished. Sacrifice is a necessity for good to prevail. Do you think one human life is not worth sacrificing?"

"You want us cowering. You want us afraid. Mindless husks, like those tortured souls in Charlotte's dungeon!"

"Soon," Charles whispered, his voice becoming a rumble. "Soon, all of you will be on your stomachs, cowering like beasts. We will return to a simpler time without these thoughts and sins. Soon enough, all of you shall be punished as Adam saw fit. But all with due time. For now, I will thank you for contributing to our cause. I would ask if you have considered my offer of a partnership in our future endeavors, but it appears now would not be the time. Robert, you must understand. Everything has happened as it was meant to. Now I must return to my work. Please do not hesitate to ask if you would like a service for your sister when her body turns up. We would be more than happy to do something exceptional for you and her."

Robert clenched his fists, ready to withdraw his knife and plunge it into Charles's chest to see if a heart truly beat within, but Charles extinguished Robert's anger with one last threat.

"Do not take kindness as weakness, Robert. You have set our plans in motion, and for that, I am thankful. So, I shall spare you on this day. However, my grace will not extend further than this last warning. Charlotte, if you wouldn't mind, please help our guest to the door."

Charlotte's face shifted, taking on the empty doll-like expression as she stepped forward. Robert backed away.

"Allow me to show you the way, Robert. We can even light a candle for your sister's safe return." Charlotte raised an arm. It snapped and cracked, extending further than possible, stretching like it did within Robert's nightmare.

This can't be happening.

"Come with me, Robert. Let me help you." Charlotte crept forward like a spider approaching its prey, hungry and deranged.

Robert twisted from her reach and did what he did best—he ran.

Chapter 28

Aimlessly, Robert moved through the city. He wandered into the streets, disregarded traffic signs, and collided with people. Life blurred in Robert's vision; he saw nothing and everything.

He sentenced his sister to death.

He had damned her.

He had damned the entire world.

Everyone would pay for his mistake, because he made one terrible decision to trust the wrong people.

Robert walked until his legs were ready to give out, and blood drenched his shirt. Without thinking, Robert's body directed him to the one person who might help him.

The door to the Queen of Hearts was open and unmanned. Loud crashes and guttural screams professed an internal battle. Robert knew he should turn away, but he went forward. Katherine's deranged voice rang atop the sounds of furniture breaking and glass shattering.

"How did he know about it? What did you tell him?"

"I didn't tell him anything about your gun!" Dez shouted back. The sound of a fist contacting pulled Robert towards the main floor, revealing the destruction his mistake had caused.

No space was unmarked by Katherine's rage. Shattered glass decorated the floors. Piles of broken furniture amassed at the sides of the room. Robert gaped as Katherine held Dez against the wall; blood covered both. Dez thrashed and kicked against her captor, attempting to break free of Katherine's hold. One arm attacked Katherine while the other hung uselessly at her side, broken.

"LIAR! I saw how you looked at him! How you looked at each other! You are weak, Desdemona! WEAK!" Katherine lifted Dez from the wall and hurled her across the room, crashing into a pile of broken furniture. She screamed as the sharp edges of a fractured table pierced through her flesh.

"Dez!" Robert cried out, drawing the room's attention.

Robert became stone, petrified by Katherine's scorching eyes. The inhumanity of her gaze held Robert. She had given into the wrath that she embodied and basked in it.

"YOU!" she screamed like a banshee as she flung herself at Roberts with arms extended, dripping blood and torn flesh. Robert raised his arms in defense as Katherine's hand reared back to strike. A blue blur shot from the corner of the room, throwing Katherine at the last possible moment. She impacted the stage, demolishing the front. Blood gushed from her torso as a large plank speared her. She howled in anger as she lifted herself from the destruction, pulling wooden pieces from her body. Katherine's rage did not diminish.

"Katherine, you will pull yourself together," Luke commanded as he positioned himself in front of Robert, protecting him from Katherine's rage. Luke looked over his shoulder and gave a half-smile. Long scratches covered both cheeks. He winced as his smile twitched his now crooked nose. Luke hadn't just protected Robert; he had suffered Katherine's attack before diverting it.

"It's his fault! His fault! His fault!" Katherine frantically repeated to herself as she paced in front of the stage. "He ruined it. I tried. I'm sorry. I did all that I could."

"Katherine . . ." Robert began, wanting to explain.

Her head snapped to Robert, her attention back on him. She flexed her fingers and charged. Before she could prepare an attack, Luke struck her with the back of his hand, sending her into a far wall.

"Katherine! CONTROL YOURSELF!" Luke shouted. His cheerful speech slid into something powerful and ancient as his voice was layered with others as he spoke.

"He took it! I know he took it!" she screamed before attacking again. Luke raised his hand. Katherine ducked and took hold of Luke's wrist and squeezed. A horrific *crunch* sounded as his bones snapped within Katherine's hands. Luke dropped, twisted, and slipped from Katherine's grasp. His feline movements continued, spinning around her before slamming the back of his leg into Katherine's side. The blow sent her back into the wall.

"I will not ask you again, Katherine," Luke warned as his power spiked and gathered around him, eager to be unleashed.

"You think you can fight me, Lust?" she snarled, spitting Luke's title. "I am fury! I am rage! I am Wrath!"

"You forget, Kitty Kat; lust gives way to many delectable sins." Luke licked his lips as if he could taste the power that dripped from his skin. "Anger, passion, and my personal favorite—madness." Luke looked back at Robert and winked a sapphire eye before he disappeared in a haze of quickness. Katherine charged at her unseen foe, striking the air in hopes of contact. "Too slow, Kitty." Luke reappeared in front of Katherine with his hand around her neck. Katherine fought Luke's hold, slashing against his arm as he lifted her and pinned her against the wall as she had done to Dez.

Katherine fought like an unhinged beast. She kicked, clawed, and snarled at Luke. Her deadly nails scooped away large sections of Luke's skin. His grip tightened, staying vigilant in containing Katherine.

He leaned closer and whispered into her ear.

"I can taste it on you, Katherine." He placed his tongue on her neck and dragged it along her skin, licking away the lines of blood that ran down her neck. She shivered as Luke spoke. "The pleasure that fills you when your monster is unleashed . . . so mouthwatering is your need for release." He walked his free hand along her shredded clothes, dancing along the areas of exposed flesh. Her body twitched underneath his fingers. "That ache you feel every night as your last

317

breath draws closer. The emptiness that you wish to *fill*. Do you want to give it a final go, Kitty Kat, one more time before you die?"

"Let me go!" A wave of red energy blew from Katherine, furthering her destruction. The building shook as her energy coursed through the earth, forcing the remaining bottles to fall and the structure to quake. Robert fell into the nearest wall, clinging to it as the ground vibrated. Luke showed no weakness.

"CONTROL YOURSELF, KATHERINE, OR I WILL MAKE YOU!" Hundreds of voices spoke from Luke's lips.

"What, are you going to love me to death? Make me orgasm? Scream your name? You pathetic piece of trash! Without me, you are nothing. You would have fucked yourself into an early grave if it were not for this fucking curse!" Katherine spat a wad of blood at Luke's face. Luke's powerful, stern expression softened as he stared at his friend. His voice became a singular entity again as he spoke to Katherine.

"I'll use it."

Katherine's call for chaos paused as she stared at Luke. Shock mixed with the rage in her bloody eyes.

"You wouldn't."

"To protect Dez. To protect Robert. I would. As of now, we're already fucked, so what would one more mistake truly cost us?"

Katherine's gaze relaxed. Slowly, her irises floated to the surface of her inflamed eyes. She leaned her head against the wall, took several deep breaths, and caged her rage. When she looked back at Luke, her green eyes had returned.

"There's my Kitty Kat," Luke said as he lowered Katherine to the ground and rubbed the blood from his face.

The two collected themselves, acting as if a battle to the death had not just occurred. It wasn't until Robert heard a painful groan that he remembered the additional casualty of their struggle. Robert rushed to the pile of broken furniture.

Dez cried as she pulled a large piece of wood from her midsection. Blood spilled from her in large gushes. Her hands covered the wound, but blood still seeped through her fingers. Robert moved to help.

"Here, let me—"

"Don't touch me!"

Robert shied away.

When the blood finally stopped, Dez lifted her hand from the hole in her stomach. Pink flesh covered the wound and then darkened.

"I was just trying—"

"Don't." Dez motioned to their surrounding area. Robert's mistake destroyed The Queen of Hearts, forced Katherine and Luke to fight, and Dez—Dez was broken, body and spirit. "How could you do this? You ruined everything!"

Robert made a mistake that he could never appreciate, but one that would haunt him.

"I didn't mean . . . I was just trying . . . Charles said if I helped him, they would give her back," Robert whispered. "They promised they—"

"And you think we weren't trying everything we could to make that happen?" Katherine interrupted across the room. She brushed the mixture of dirt and blood from her face. She pulled her graying hair from her face and tied it. "What do you think we were doing this whole time?"

"I just thought . . . I thought you were trying to use her." Robert searched for the right words, but they didn't seem true even as he said them.

"We don't have a choice, Robert! What part of that do you not understand!?" The ground shook with Katherine's anger, remnants of her influence. "This—all this—is destiny. Lucas, your sister, me, none of us get a choice. You either take the job, or everything goes to shit. And now they have my Piece of Eve, and we are fucked!" She walked over to a wall and punched it, adding a hole to the crumbling structure. "Do you know what my father used to say to me, Robert? *Family before self.* To put the greater good before ourselves to preserve what must be preserved."

"I just didn't—"

"Didn't what? Want her to become one of us? One of the 'bad guys'? Shouldn't that be her choice, Robert? I don't know why I was chosen, and neither does Luke. Maybe there's some master plan that we don't know about. Maybe it's because we were people who sought freedom when the world tried to restrain us. Or maybe it was just fucking luck that we could make a difference. Do you know what Wrath is, Robert?"

"Anger."

"Exactly, anger. Wrath fuels the change in the world. I am what forces a woman to fight back finally. I am what makes a child stand up to their bully. I am what propels the world forward, Robert. Without anger, why would anyone fight? We embody and hold safe those emotions that Adam wished to deny."

"So you aren't Lucifer's puppets? Robert asked, his voice so quiet that he could barely hear himself.

"Christ, Robert, have you heard nothing we have taught you? No, we are not. Eve is a part of us. We are the freedoms, she realized. We have no further connection to Lucifer than we do to God. Yes, we are at times on his side of the chessboard, but we are not his slaves."

"I didn't know."

"Exactly. You didn't know. And instead of confronting us, you went behind our backs and ruined everything." Katherine exhaled a sigh. "Sometimes I'm afraid to die. Afraid of what is on the other side." Tears edged Katherine's cloudy eyes, but they did not quench her anger. "I'm afraid my father won't be there to greet me on the other side. I'm afraid that all my horrors have purchased me a ticket for an eternity in Hell. And other times, I am just fucking over being alive and ready for the torment owed to me."

"Don't say that." Luke placed a hand on his friend's shoulder. Katherine squeezed his fingers.

"I know it's a hard truth, Lucas, but time is short, and we have even less now. We have to prepare for the worst now that they have my gun, and we don't have Rebecca."

"What is it? The gun?" Robert asked.

Katherine's eyebrow twitched as her eyes flashed red before she turned away, allowing Luke to answer the question while she searched for a much-needed drink.

"It's called a Piece of Eve. Think of it as a conductor for our gifts. It supplies us with what we need to extend our lives and contains our Sin's heart, the thing that takes us from being human to a member of the Seven Deadly Sins. But it is also a weapon—the Hail Mary of weapons. It can only be truly released by its owner, and if done so properly, it can kill anything. But it comes at a cost; if we use it—we die. 'Tis the ultimate temptation for a person whose purpose is to entice. I guess it's the cosmic way of teaching us to remember restraint." Luke flicked the gemmed earring that dangled from his lobe. "This isn't just pretty costume jewelry, Robert. I could kill anyone within this room if I unleashed the power held within."

"Then why haven't you? If you can end all of this, why haven't you?"

"You still don't understand. We don't want a fight. Charlotte, Charles, the whole lot of them, they were the ones who threw the first punch. It's been a millennium of jabs and parries, but now it appears they have tired of the games," Luke explained. "We aren't meant to fight; we are representations of Eve's freedom. All we wanted, all Eve wanted, was freedom: freedom to choose, freedom to live, freedom to love. We represent the will to live and choose, and now that choice is about to be taken away." His cheery tone darkened. "You have damned not only your sister, Robert, but the world."

"And now they have my gun and your sister," Katherine shouted as she rummaged around the bar, looking for something she did not shatter.

"Charles said that he didn't have Rebecca," Robert said.

"Of course, Charles said that! He may not have her, but one of them does. And now I don't know if I will even have the time to find her." Katherine gazed at the shards of mirror on the ground, staring at the old woman reflected. Her wrinkles were more profound, her eyes glossier, and the grays in her hair began to turn white.

"I can fix this. Let me help. I can—"

"Robert, what do you not understand? There is no time! I am getting weaker by the second. And this little spat didn't help." She looked around her and regretted the devastation. "With my Piece of Eve, I could have siphoned power from it to last weeks, maybe months, but now—I don't know. If I don't transfer the role of Wrath to Rebecca, she will die when I die. She will wither away like me, and there's no stopping it." Katherine bit her lip in thought. "We just don't have time to worry about you."

"Please! Let me help!" Robert begged.

"Just go back to your life, Robert. It's up to us to find her now." Dez brushed past Robert, ignoring his pleas. "We need to talk about our next step, and you can no longer be trusted."

"But I can help. They trust me!" Robert said, begging his case. "I can get the gun back; I can give us more time. I can—"

"I SAID LEAVE!" Dez howled as she turned and faced Robert.

A pulse of frigid air empowered Dez's demand. The humid space turned crisp as the temperature dropped. The air became cool. Spilled liquors and leaking pipes froze as she freed her power. Her horns pushed through their curly hideaway, twisting and curling around her head. Her hair lengthened and grew wild. Her brown skin deepened until shadows and darkness painted her body. She blinked, and her eyes became the infinite galaxies that had once bespelled Robert. Each footstep forward burned the carpet with her subzero temperature.

Dez stopped a foot from Robert. Her frozen aura stole the heat from his body, begging to be unrestricted so it could feed on what remained within him. Robert stared into her vortexes and did not see anger; it was pain.

"Leave," she ordered in the softest, most commanding voice she could muster. Robert did as he was told; he walked away, knowing that he had damned the world.

Chapter 29

The emptiness that burdened Robert for months had returned. The feeling of worthlessness, laziness, and idleness filled his every waking hour. Robert didn't sleep that night or the one that followed. Robert welcomed the isolation. The consequences of his actions hung in his psyche, feeding his hopelessness.

When the will to move appeared, Robert returned to the Queen of Hearts. The bouncer denied him entry and did not care how much Robert begged.

So Robert waited. He sat on the curb for hours, waiting for Katherine or Luke to appear so he could plead for their forgiveness. But nobody ever emerged. After two days of waiting, he decided the best thing to do was to obey Dez. Nobody wanted to see him or hear his apologies. He needed to accept it. He was unwanted, no matter how much he sought to help.

*   *   *

It was early Sunday morning when Nathan descended from his apartment above the Rusty Nail and found Robert standing behind the bar, counting inventory. Nathan gave a raised brow as his greeting. Robert waited for the verbal lashing he deserved for missing so many days. Nathan collected his topmost paper and sat at the bar.

"Think you're just going to put in some overtime, and all will be forgiven?" Nathan questioned.

"I thought I should show up at least once this week." Robert looked down at the stack of doodles of Dez collected under the bar and threw them in the trash. "I want to apologize for not showing up. The last week has been—difficult. I had a lead about my sister, and things just got out of hand. I know that's not an excuse, but I'm sorry." Robert expected Nathan to launch into a long string of threats or snide remarks, but he uncharacteristically accepted Robert's apology.

"Not a problem, my boy. Life is a fickle friend. It gets ahead of us and runs wild and free until we reel it in." Nathan took his rolled-up newspaper and bopped Robert on the head.

"Where are you going, so dressed up?" Robert asked, noting his boss replaced his usual oversized Hawaiian shirt and jeans with a fine suit. Nathan combed his graying hair and shaved his face. The smile on his face was disturbing, to be frank. This man couldn't be the same man who tossed glasses at customers and cursed at a girl scout. That man shouted at children and flirted shamelessly with young women. This man seemed like someone's grandfather, who had pocketfuls of caramels for his favorite family members. It wasn't just odd seeing Nathan cheerful; it was downright absurd.

"Out," was Nathan's response as he marched to the front door, pushed it open, and practically danced down the sidewalk. Robert watched through the front glass as Nathan disappeared in one direction, grinning as if he had just won the lottery—or a lifetime supply of free newspapers. With Nathan gone and Robert's livelihood somewhat secure, he turned to his work list.

Robert started with the counter, washing and polishing the wood. He chiseled off the gum stuck to its underside and then washed down the barstools. Moving onto the bottles of alcohol, Robert dusted the shelves and wiped down the glass. He avoided the area beneath the bar with every task, unsure if any images of Dez remained. But the list was shorter than Robert had hoped, forcing him to look.

One sketch was left behind, unburied by paper towels and trash. Robert lifted the sketch and gaped at his image of Dez.

"I'm sorry." Robert had ruined a friendship that had just begun. Robert couldn't stop hating himself. He dug through the trash, pulling out the rest of his artwork, remembering each sketch.

"If only we could have had more time." An idea formed as he stared at Dez's mischievous eyes. "More time."

If Charles didn't have Rebecca, that meant she was still out there, somewhere unknown but safe from him and Charlotte. He could give Dez, Katherine, and Luke more time to search. All he needed was to make some foolish decisions.

With a handful of stolen cash, Robert locked the front door and hailed the nearest taxi. He slid into the back seat, yelled the church's address to a stunned driver, and then dialed Dez's number.

The phone rang once and went directly to her voicemail.

"Don't immediately delete this message. I know I am the last person you want to hear from; just hear me out. I know I fucked up. But I'm gonna fix it. I'm going to the church to get Katherine's gun back, give you all more time to find Rebecca, and fix my screwups. None of you even have to talk or speak to me, but I will get it and bring it to the bar. It's the only thing I can do to help, and I will do it. I'm sorry for everything I did. You don't have to accept my apology. I just hope you will accept my help."

He prayed Dez got the message and sent the cavalry. Robert envisioned her standing at the church's front steps with her arms crossed, slicked-back hair, and an entirely purple outfit. They would enter the church together, ready to take on Charles and Charlotte.

But reality never aligned with Robert's hopes. He exited the taxi and found the steps empty.

No Dez. No Katherine. No Luke. No cavalry.

Halfway up the stairs, Robert realized—he didn't have an actual plan. He wasn't stealthy enough to sneak into the office during the service or strong enough to barge in fists first and demand Katherine's gun back.

Robert paused at the front entrance and listened as the organ played. He nudged open the door, and the entry was empty. The thick walls muffled the priest's voice. Robert listened as he went inside; the priest spoke of forgiveness, how it was divine to forgive and move past the troubles that one causes another.

Hopefully, it is also an infernal quality.

He searched the atrium, piecing together a plan. Maybe he didn't have to be sneaky or strong; maybe he just needed a distraction? He needed to let humans do what they did best. Robert went to the wall behind the front desk, staring at the bright red lever.

"Get in. Go get the gun. Get out. Easy." Robert opened the plastic case and held the fire alarm. "Easy." He repeated and pulled.

Loud sirens and flashing lights filled the high ceilings. The reverberations amplified the sound to an ear-splitting level. Worshiper's screams quickly followed and then overshadowed the sirens. The panicking congregation threw back the doors and charged forward. Robert hid behind the front desk and watched the stampede of people move out into the street.

They pushed. They shoved. People fought for their lives from a nonexistent threat. Charles stood out among them, calling for everyone to remain calm and to watch for the children. His voice remained peaceful in the chaos, though the churchgoers were driven further into madness. People's true nature showed in disaster. Watching people scream "fire" and cough from 'smoke' inhalation was odd.

When the last person 'escaped,' Charles slammed the door shut, hoping to contain the fire. With the building empty, Robert charged into the inner sanctuary, unsure how much time he had before they returned. Pamphlets, Bibles, and several large hats were left behind, forgotten as people fought for safety. Robert hoped Charles had the same mindset.

His office was open.

Robert closed the door and began his search.

"Where is it?" Robert asked as he tried to recall the book Charles used to hide the key. Was it red? Blue? It was hard to remember the book's color when just seconds before, an oily monster erupted from Katherine's gun and then found out Rebecca was still missing. It was like trying to remember what piece of hay the farmer wanted from his haystack—and the haystack was on fire.

Thousands of options cluttered the room, and every book was identical in Robert's eyes. So he selected the stack nearest to the desk. He opened the first book, dangled it, shook it, and tossed the book into a space on the floor. An action he repeated again and again and again. He moved from one pile to another, constantly shaking and throwing the books to a corner of the room.

"Where did he hide it?"

The door jiggled, and Robert's heart stopped. Not five minutes into the search, and now it had ended.

"No. No. No. The fire trucks haven't even arrived yet. Why are they already coming inside?" Robert slid behind the door just as it opened. His heart jumped in time with the footsteps as the person crossed into the office. Robert reprimanded himself for not bringing a weapon—not that anything he had would be of any use against Charles or his cohorts.

With nothing but absolute foolishness in his hands, Robert slammed the door into the stranger, and they released a painful yelp of surprise. Robert jumped from behind with fists raised but stiffened at the sight of purple.

"Dez?"

"What the hell is wrong with you?" she growled, rubbing the red bump on her forehead.

"Well, I thought you were Charles or Charlotte," Robert said as he shut the door behind Dez and then returned to an unsearched pile of books.

"And you thought you would win a fight by hitting them with the door?

"Well, I had to do something." Robert lifted a book, shook it, and threw it aside.

"What are you even doing?" Dez asked, gawking at Robert's endeavor.

"The gun's in the desk, and the key is in one of these books. Grab one and start—"

"Move," she commanded, pushing past Robert before reaching for the drawer. "Lucifer!" she cursed. Dez ripped her hand free and stared at her scorched palm. Black flakes dropped from her hand as she flexed her fingers. It did not heal immediately like her previous burns.

"You good?" Robert asked as he held a large novel in two hands and shook it.

"I'm fine. Where did you say the key was?" Dez asked, hiding away the pain that throbbed from her burned hand.

"In here somewhere." Robert threw yet another unsuccessful book onto the pile. "Those I have already checked." He nodded. "Those I haven't."

"Can you be any less clear?" Dez stood near a stack between the chairs and began her search. The two diligently worked through piles and shelves, finding nothing besides tucked away receipts and notes between the pages. Robert felt the urge to talk—to clear the air between them—but he held his tongue and searched. This moment was not for him. It was to right his wrongs.

With every unsuccessful book, Robert's heart raced faster.

How much time do we have? Was the key even here?

Robert pushed himself to search faster. But even with Dez's enhanced speed, they had only searched through a small portion of Charles's collection before the fire trucks arrived. The tiny flame of hope Robert cultivated with his plan flickered weakly, dwindling, and soon, it would extinguish.

"Robert? What are you doing?"

The familiar voice tore Robert from his stack of books and towards the door.

"Nathan!" Robert said, surprised to see his boss standing at the door of Charles's office. "What are you doing here?"

"I'm here for church. Why are you in Charles's office?" Nathan questioned as he looked at Robert and Dez. "Robert, come with me. The firemen say it isn't safe to be inside. We need to leave." Nathan extended a wrinkled hand to Robert.

Robert stood from his nest of books. He looked at his surroundings, the hundreds of books he searched, and the potential thousands he had yet to touch.

It's not here.

Something inside him spoke, telling him the key was not there. Robert knew it to be true. He looked at Dez as her face contorted into something he could not decipher.

I failed again.

Reality dowsed his flame of hope. He stepped over the discarded books and reached for Nathan's hand, accepting his failure.

Before their hands could touch, Dez's burnt palm intercepted Robert's hand and tugged him away. Nathan gave a puzzled expression.

"Robert. Enough games; it isn't safe here," Nathan said.

Robert stepped toward Nathan again, but Dez pulled him back and held him firmly.

"What?" Robert mouthed.

"How-how do you know him?" Dez stuttered. It was fear that he saw on Dez's face—genuine fear.

"Nathan? He's my boss. You've met him before? At least a handful of times." Robert thought back to the times that Dez had visited the bar. Every moment that she came, Nathan had found one excuse or another to be away.

"No, he's not." Dez squeezed his hand tighter, filling their palms with ice. "That's Patience: leader of the virtues."

Robert looked at Nathan, his face full of disbelief. Dez had to be mistaken, but Robert was again proven wrong as light vibrated along his skin, identical to the one that radiated from Charlotte and Charles.

"Well, fuck."

Chapter 30

Nathan wrapped a hand across his midsection and bowed deeply at his waist.

An unfamiliar face settled on his features as his back erected, standing straighter than Robert had ever seen. The wrinkly face Robert had stared at for hours was refreshed. Years vanished from his cheeks and his eyes. The sagging skin beneath his jaw tightened, becoming a strong jawline. His hair became more salt and pepper as black strands appeared. The glow that outlined him seemed to envelop his body, fixing his hunched-over appearance and the spare tire around his waistband.

"Pleasure to finally meet your acquaintance, Desdemona. Robert's little sketches do not do justice. You are much more of a monster than his sketches could ever capture."

Robert struggled to breathe.

Was everything in his life the result of another's deception?

"Now, let me ask you once again, Robert. What are you doing in Charles's office?" Nathan looked around the room, examining the scattered books and the even more disorganized state of the room. "Looking for something, are we?"

Robert and Dez said nothing.

"Going to make me guess, Robert? You know I don't like games." Nathan shook his head. "Could it possibly be this?" From his front pocket, Nathan withdrew the key to the drawer. Robert's body tensed. "Or could you possibly be looking for this?" Nathan reached into another pocket and, wrapped in a handkerchief, Nathan removed Katherine's gun. "Such a disgusting piece of filth."

"Give it back," Dez growled. From the corner of Robert's eye, he could see her skin begin to shift, darkening. Her horns peeked from within her curly hair as she stepped forward, releasing Robert's hand.

"Or what, devil child? You'll fight me?" Nathan laughed. "This thing is of no use to us. Today Katherine shall die. I have seen it. She will die, and so will your pathetic sister."

"You son of a bitch," Robert cursed, moving forward. Dez stretched out a hand and stopped him.

The darkness bloomed across Dez's skin, transforming her as before, but her transformation continued. Robert had not noticed before; it was not shadows that enshrouded Dez's skin, but a vision of the night sky. Tiny starbursts appeared across her body, glowing and sparkling like diamonds. Her horns grew more prominent and heavier. They twisted inwardly toward her face, shaping around her forehead like a crown. Dez flicked her hands, and her nails extended. Shadows dripped from the tips; the substance burned like acid, eating through the books and carpet within seconds. She was not some horrible monster—but a beautiful dark angel, a goddess of judgment.

"Where is she?" Dez's voice scraped the inside of Robert's bones, causing him to shake with pain.

Nathan laughed at her attempt to inflict pain, waving it off like a pestering gnat.

"My, my, you are a persistent one." Nathan laughed. "You will have to do more than some pathetic mind trick if you want to cause me any genuine pain." Nathan dabbed the corners of his eyes as tears of laughter appeared. "God! You do not know how long I have wanted to answer that question. I'm practically itching with anticipation!" He turned to Robert. "Every day, I watched you search and cry and wish for your sister's safe return. But I knew patience earns the sweetest victories. So, I waited. I watched. And now that it's here, the look on your face is the ultimate reward."

"Where is she?" Dez growled, repeating her question.

"Oh, just a few feet away from Robert this entire time. Just one floor above him, to be exact." Nathan pointed upward. "Just lying and waiting for her brother to save her." Nathan pushed out his bottom lip, mocking Robert's misery.

Robert's face fell, realizing the answer.

"That's right. You were right next to her this whole time, Robert. I wonder, do you think she heard you laughing, flirting, and drinking while she was held captive? Do you think she had given up hope you would ever rescue her? I mean, I sure would have by now. Seven months is an awfully long time to be held by Charlotte. Do you think Charlotte broke her weak little mind into so many fragments that she wouldn't even recognize you if you got to her in time?"

"Upstairs . . . as in . . . ." Robert couldn't finish his sentence.

"Right in my apartment. Oh, how I hoped the day would come when you would burst through the door and find us lying together. Every day that passed, I grew more anxious and more excited. But I knew this moment would come and how sweet it tastes to see your face." He smacked his lips. "Delicious!"

"Go, Robert," Dez commanded as she moved closer to Nathan. "I'll handle him." Less than a yard separated the two. Nathan only smiled as Dez forced her gaze upon him. White light radiated from him as he prepared for whatever Dez would throw at him.

"How?" Nathan taunted.

A dazzling blue flame sparked to life between the points of her horns, floating between the two like a gem within her crown. The same fire ignited along the rest of her body. Small flames kindled among the stacks of paper as the temperature escalated, reaching unlivable levels within seconds. Robert backed away from the safety of her shadow as the blazes grew around her, eager to devour.

"Hellfire, my dear?" Nathan asked, clearly unamused by her show of force. "You think that will stop me?" Nathan stepped forward, unafraid, as the white light condensed around his body and focused within his fists.

"Hellfire may not stop you, but a brick to the head will at least slow you down."

"What?"

Dez raised her hands, and blue fire unleashed from her fingertips. The flames corralled around her body, traveled up her legs, and shot from her fingertips. Floors melted, wood burned, and mortar softened as blue flames scorched everything within its path.

Nathan could barely register Dez's plan before the building above collapsed, burying him beneath a thousand pounds of rubble.

"GO!" Dez screamed, breaking Robert from his trance. She halted her flames for just a moment.

"Dez …"

"Shut up, Robert. This is not the time! Now GO! I won't be able to hold him for long. Call Katherine! Get to Becca!" Dez shouted. The rubble slightly shifted as Nathan moved beneath, forcing his way free as more debris tumbled atop him. "Move it, Monte!"

Robert jumped into action, running towards the rubble. His eyes caught a familiar sight at the edge of the wreckage.

It wasn't buried.

Before he jumped across the threshold, Robert reached and stole back Katherine's gun. He dove as light spilled through the cracks in the debris.

Robert just hit the staircase before light erupted behind him like a flash grenade. Dez released another howl of anger as heat blasted along the corridor.

"YOU THINK YOU CAN STOP ME WITH THAT!" Nathan bellowed.

Another loud crash behind Robert gave him the strength he did not know as he ran down the middle aisle. A loud crack echoed in the sanctuary. Robert turned just in time to see a portion of the stage collapse inward, burying Dez and Nathan. Both light and fire erupted from beneath, throwing the rubble skyward into the rafters and the pews.

Chapter 31

Fire popped like gunshots behind Robert as he ran down the church's steps and hunted for Dez's purple dinosaur. As expected, she illegally parked the vehicle at the base of the stairs. He dropped into the front seat, finding the car keys in the ignition. Fireman approached the vehicle, barking for him to move out of the fire lane. Robert happily obliged, throwing the car into drive and launching forward into pedestrians standing in the street. Most dove out of the way in time, while one rolled down the side as Robert sped away In the rearview mirror, Robert watched firefighters race towards the building with hoses, ready to douse a ravenous flame.

"Please be okay," Robert whispered as he wove in and out of traffic. Robert caught Dez's large purple purse as it rolled on the passenger seat floor. With a single hand on the wheel, Robert dug for her phone and dialed Katherine's number. "Pick up. Pick up. Pick up."

But it was just his luck; the call went straight to voicemail.

"Katherine, it's Robert. Becca is at the Rusty Nail. Get there quickly! Dez is fighting Patience, and I don't know how long she can"—a loud explosion halted Robert's speech and furthered his worry. The car's mirrors filled with smoke and flashes of orange and red. Dark clouds spill into the peaceful blue skies of Vegas—"just get to the bar! Quickly!" Robert threw Dez's phone into the passenger seat as several firetrucks flew past.

"Please be okay," Robert said, but this time, it was for Dez.

Robert took every sharp turn, sped through every yellow light, and drove through any opening, if only to chisel away seconds from his clock. When the Rusty Nail was in sight, Robert floored it and slammed on the brakes seconds later, leaving the car running in the middle of the street. He went through the front door and charged up the back staircase. Robert prepared to break down the door, if necessary, but the door opened with the gentlest turn of the doorknob.

"It's not even locked." Robert cursed his ignorance.

He stepped inside.

The room looked abandoned. Robert had thought old newspapers and fast food wrappers would have overwhelmed the space, but it was clean. The only piece of furniture was the bed at the far end of the room and the body lying atop it.

It's her.

Tears washed over Robert's face as he went towards the body. She slept like some fairy-tale princess, dressed in a white gown with her brown hair delicately laid across the pillowcase. It was a picturesque moment. He touched her cheek. She was ice cold. Frozen.

The longer he stared at her, the more he saw how time had changed her. Her cheeks were no longer round, and her lips were now a frosty shade of blue. Her hands, clasped together against her stomach, were mostly bone. It was clear to Robert that whatever cosmic force was killing Katherine did the same to Rebecca.

"Becca." Robert's voice was scratchy as he continued to cry. "Becca, wake up." He gave her body a soft shake, but she did not move. "Becca?"

Fear rose within his mind. Robert had found his sister, but was he too late?

Please. Please, just be . . . please, Becca. Please.

Robert unlaced Rebecca's hands and pressed two fingers to her wrist. He felt his heartbeat several times as he waited. His lips became a thin line as the world crashed around him. He closed his eyes, feeling grief rise.

"Becca . . . please done leave me."

Thump-thump.

Robert fell forward onto his sister's chilled body.

She was alive.

"Thank God!" Robert wept as he melted into the floor, holding his sister's arm. The heartbeat was weak and slow, but it was there. The gentle *thump* only appeared every two to three seconds.

She was alive, but for how much longer, Robert did not know. As Robert cried into the comforter, a hand came to rest on his shoulder.

Robert launched into the air. "I won't let you—"

"Calm yourself, Robert," the voice croaked.

Looking above himself stood a crone. Thin strands of white hair flowed along her wrinkled face and skeletal shoulders. The angles of her features seemed almost painful in the way they protruded, threatening to pierce through her paper-thin skin. If not for the green eyes, cloudy as they were, Robert would not have recognized her.

"Hello, Robert."

"Katherine," Robert whispered. She nodded before falling into a fit of coughing. She turned from Robert, covering her mouth, but blood spewed between her fingers.

"Katherine, what's happened to you?"

"Do not worry about me, Robert." Katherine hobbled to the other side of Rebecca; slow and painful were her footsteps. She laid a hand on Rebecca and nodded. "We must wake her."

"I tried."

"We must try harder." Though Katherine had aged rapidly, her voice still held authority.

"I have something that belongs to you." Robert withdrew her firearm, and surprise rushed across her features. She reached for the gun. Life came to her cheeks, just a fraction of the lightest blush of pink.

"Thank you, Robert." Katherine held the gun to her chest, squeezing it tightly. Robert understood the gun's importance but also knew of its significance. She placed the firearm on Rebecca's chest, covering it with one hand while placing her other on Rebecca's forehead.

"This will hurt her, but it's the quickest way. Do you trust me, Robert?"

"Yes." He answered. Robert should have always trusted her.

Katherine closed her eyes and released a breath, drawing the last bits of her power. Her eyes opened, showing the blood-red shade Robert had come to fear. A red haze surrounded Katherine, bathing the room in the deepest hue of scarlet. The surrounding air spiked and sizzled with power. Her white hair dragged against her face as Katherine summoned phantom winds. Her eyes focused deeper on Rebecca, biting hard as she fought the creature within Rebecca. Energy whipped around them. Katherine doubled over, coughing blood onto the floor as the strain took its toll on her body.

"Katherine!" Robert shouted above the storm of her power.

Katherine did not respond. Instead, she moved her hands toward Rebecca's wrists. She gripped both firmly, digging her nails so deeply that blood painted the front of Rebecca's dress. Rebecca's mouth parted slowly, and hope trembled within Robert.

"Katherine, it's working!"

Rebecca's lips parted further. Robert leaned closer.

"Becca, it's Robbie. I'm here! Wake up!"

A wail of agony tore from Rebecca's mouth, throwing Robert back. A horrible cry of pain and grief spewed from Rebecca as she thrashed in the bed. Her back arched, throwing her midsection toward the ceiling. She was possessed.

"HOLD HER!" Katherine commanded.

Robert launched toward Rebecca's legs, pinning them to the bed. Rebecca's wails ceased, and she finally spoke.

"STOP! You're hurting me!" Rebecca's voice croaked through chapped lips. "Robert, please stop her. It hurts so much!"

"Don't listen to her, Robert! She's trying to trick you." Katherine blazed with ghostly flames as she spoke. "Charlotte has taken root inside your sister like a parasite. And I will burn that bitch out if it kills me!" Katherine's fiery aura flowed down her thin arms and poured onto Rebecca.

"You will break her, Katherine!" Charlotte mocked through Rebecca's lips. "You will break her poor, feeble mind! So much sin, so much regret. An eternity of it waits for her if you allow this to happen, Robert. An endless realm of darkness and pain for her. You want that for her? Let her die, Robert. Let her be at peace! Let her die, Robert!"

"No!" Robert grasped his sister's wrists and felt something pull him forward, tugging him into his sister's subconscious with Katherine.

*   *   *

Robert found himself standing in an ocean of darkness.

Ink black water surrounded him and stretched in all directions. The sky was onyx black, but Robert could somehow still see within the world. Images raised around him, drifting to the surface and sinking seconds later. Robert squinted at the nearest one. It was a memory, a vision played out through Rebecca's perspective. He searched around him. Hundreds of memories settled on the water's surface, playing continuously like television channels.

"Robbie."

Robert looked far into the distance and saw Rebecca standing, frozen like a statue. A centipede-like creature encircled Rebecca, wrapping itself around her thrice. White fabric stretched continuously around its body, hiding the deadly claws that Robert had met firsthand. Its ceramic face nuzzled Rebecca's frozen features before meeting Robert's gaze.

"Becca!" Robert ran, splashing within her ocean of memories, but the distance never decreased.

"Focus, Robert!" Katherine said, appearing at his side, radiating her red energy. He faced her, seeing the woman he admired. Her skin shone with power, glowing like a moon in the darkest night. Her hair danced and moved like fire personified. She stood beside him as she did the first day they met, powerful. "Fight for her. Fight for your sister!" Katherine closed her eyes, and like a phoenix rising from the ashes, her aura lifted and threw itself at Charlotte.

"You will not save her! She is ours, Sin! You shall never beat us, for we are immortal! We are eternal. We shall win the war and rule!" Charlotte screamed into Katherine's assault.

Katherine poured herself into her attack, throwing herself at Charlotte in a rush of fire and rage. Charlotte laughed as the power flew into her, showing only the briefest discomfort.

Robert watched his sister's lips part, fighting against Charlotte's hold. Her lips moved, forming words, but made no sound. Her lips moved again, mouthing the exact words repeatedly.

"Help me, Robbie." Rebecca's voice whispered in Robert's head, speaking the words that had haunted him since the night she was first taken.

Once, Robert was powerless to save his sister. He was too weak to make a difference. But he wouldn't be that way again.

"I'm here, Becca!" Robert called out across the black ocean. He stepped forward and took Katherine's hand and felt something stir.

Rage flared within him.

"Wrath is not evil. It is what fuels the world to fight."

Robert's fury set ablaze as he narrowed his gaze on Charlotte. The emotions he hid from the world came alive. Months of pain and regret. Years of rage, of anger, of sadness. Everything went to the surface, and for once in Robert's life, he let go.

"GET OFF HER!" Robert demanded before he threw every ounce of himself at Charlotte.

White light exploded from Robert, throwing a wave of power in all directions. The power buried within him mixed with that of Katherine's, creating something potent enough—something strong enough to peel Charlotte from Rebecca.

Bestial screams met the rush of energy as they burned Charlotte from Rebecca's body, and Rebecca began to move. Her shoulders tensed, her legs moved, and her face turned from desperation to anger; she became Medusa incarnate. Her lips released a powerful command that vibrated across the sea of memories.

"GET OUT OF MY HEAD!"

With one final push of their combined strength, they cast Charlotte from Rebecca's mind, and the three fell back into the waking world.

Chapter 32

"Robbie." Rebecca's eyes opened as she inhaled the words.

"Becca!" Robert rushed to his sister. Katherine collapsed onto the bed, drained of what had been keeping her alive.

"Fuck, my head hurts," Rebecca groaned.

Robert began to laugh at the sound of her voice. She was alive. And she was free. Robert hastily wiped away the tears that formed. She reached out her hand, brushing away one he missed. "I knew you would find me." Her hand cupped Robert's chin. "I just knew it." The two locked eyes, silently speaking. They were both okay.

Painful coughing tore through the silence, drawing their attention to their fallen ally.

"Katherine!" Robert reached for her. She swatted away his concern.

"Get off me. I'm fine." Katherine fell over, coughing more blood onto the bedspread. "We do not have time for pleasantries." She turned to Robert's sister. "Rebecca, I'm so sorry. I wish I'd had more time to explain. To teach you what we are—what you are. You are meant for so much more in this life, Rebecca. And I can give you that chance to make a difference. We are what oppose that monster that had captured you, and I need someone who will fight. But there is no time for me to"—Katherine coughed again—"you need to trust me."

Rebecca gazed at the dying woman and then at Robert.

"Do you trust her?" Rebecca asked.

Robert nodded. "With my life."

Rebecca pulled herself against the headboard. "If he trusts you, then so do I."

"What I am about to bestow upon you is a gift. A lineage handed down from Eve. She birthed the power held within me; now, it is yours. Your life will not be without struggles, but trust those closest to you, Rebecca. You are to become Wrath the Vengeful. You are the spark that kindles change. Do you accept this gift?"

"Yes."

Katherine made a puzzled look. "But now, we require a vessel to hold the Sin of Wrath—something that can act as your connection between you and Eve."

"I have nothing . . ." Rebecca's words floated from her lips.

"You have me. Use me." Robert's declaration drew Katherine's gaze. She examined him with her deep, colorless eyes.

"Are you sure, Robert? This will be binding you to her. To us. Not just in this life, but in the next." Katherine's lips pursed in thought. "I don't know what will happen to you, what your life will become if we do this."

"I don't care. If it saves Becca, then I'll do it."

"Robbie, please don't—"

"No, Becca," Robert said firmly. "You saved my life once before. Now, I'm going to do the same for you."

"I can't let you give up your life for me."

"I'm not giving it up. I'm letting myself live. I will be there with you, with my friends, to fight for the freedoms that Eve brought into the world."

Rebecca watched her brother, seeing how he had changed in the months since her abduction. She nodded her agreement while Katherine continued to stare at Robert.

"I think we could have possibly been friends in another life, Robert. We could have ruled this city," Katherine said, sharing a smile that did not hold a single ounce of her trademark malice.

"Are you afraid?" Robert asked. Katherine shook her head.

"I have seen the darkest parts of this world. And if the next is anything like this, it should be more afraid of me than I of it. Are you ready?"

Rebecca and Robert nodded. Katherine reached for Robert and Rebecca's hands, taking both within her soft withered palms while the siblings grasped each other's hands.

"I am ready to die." With her final words, something beyond their plane of existence snapped into place around them.

A sensation wrapped around the siblings, binding them and the preceding Sins together. The strings of destiny unwound around Katherine, releasing her from her role and tightening around Rebecca and Robert. Katherine's aura arose one final time, radiating around her as the energy left her body. Her heart slowed while Robert's and Rebecca's hearts became one—connected as the Sin of Wrath and the Piece of Eve.

"No!" Nathan's voice cut through the transference of power, drawing three pairs of eyes. Nathan fell inward into the empty apartment. His skin was charred. His shredded clothes hung across his flickering body. Blood dripped from his face as he attempted to hold himself together. "I won't let this happen!" Weakly, he raised a hand and slashed through the air. A blade of white light shot toward Rebecca with deadly accuracy.

The moment slowed as the ethereal blade flew through the air. Robert moved to protect his sister, but Katherine, using the last vestiges of her mortal strength, pushed Robert from the blade's path. Her lips parted in a soft gasp as the tip found its home in her heart. Robert shouted as Katherine collapsed onto the bed and spoke.

"Kick his ass."

The sounds that followed were indescribable.

Hell erupted from Katherine's gun. A surge of living darkness wrapped in fire spewed from the weapon, filling the space. Nathan was thrown onto the floor while Robert flew into the nearest wall as the Essence of Wrath sought its new home. It tasted Robert as it had once before.

352

Friend, it said, as it found the connection between Robert and the new Sin of Wrath.

"Friend," Robert agreed.

He wasn't sure how, but he was confident that the creature smiled as it fell over him. Robert braced himself for the burning sensation he had once endured, but felt no pain. The essence sank into Robert, filling its new home while it fed Rebecca wrath's power. Robert watched as the blazing red aura shrouded Rebecca, bathing her with the power of Wrath.

The Sin of Wrath burned away her weakness. It healed her wounds. It brought her back from the edge of death. She lifted herself from the bed, tilting the same bright red eyes at Nathan as he screamed obscenities.

"I will not allow another devil to walk!" Nathan shouted as he stood, summoning another dagger of light into his hand.

Rebecca faced him without fear. She squinted her eyes, and Nathan flew across the room and held aloft against the wall.

Rebecca stepped from the bed and stalked toward Nathan. He sent repeated pulses of white light at Rebecca, all of which she extinguished with a wave of red-tinged energy. Her furious aura pulsed larger, feeding on the sweltering rage within her.

"Becca, stop!" Robert called over the clashing energies summoned by Nathan and her. "Becca!" His sister turned and faced Robert, and he saw the same monster that escaped from Katherine the night she destroyed the Queen of Hearts.

A being of fury that fed on revenge and cultivated rage.

"Becca! Remember who you are! You are not a monster!"

"You can't kill me! You won't do it!" Nathan's voice lacked certainty, especially as Rebecca formed a dagger of fire and shadows. She examined it, watching the blackness drip from her dark creation.

"I may not be able to kill you, but I could hurt you," she said as the dagger grew sharper and longer in her hand. "I could make you feel what I felt every night. Fear. Desperation. Horror. I could make you cry for death."

"This isn't what I wanted for you. I wanted to help you, Rebecca! I wanted to save you!"

"You wanted me dead. I remember every moment you draped your disgusting body around me and whispered your horrible secrets into my ear. What future you saw for me. For my brother."

"The future is not my fault, Rebecca. I only see the choices that were to be made. Please let me go! Please, I'm only doing as I'm told!"

Rebecca studied the weak man.

"No, I don't think I will." Rebecca raised the dagger.

"Please!" Nathan screamed, fighting against her hold.

The dagger flew toward Nathan as he shrieked for mercy.

"BECCA, NO!" Robert pleaded.

At the last second, the blade turned and stabbed into the wall beside Nathan. The sharp edge slid along the curve of his ear, splitting the skin. Blood ran along the blade's edge.

"Leave now, or you never will," Rebecca ordered as she withdrew the blade from the wall. Nathan fell to the floor and scrambled toward the door like an animal desperate for freedom. Robert could taste Nathan's fear and contempt as he paused at the door.

"This isn't over!" Nathan warned, returning to his air of confidence. "I have seen what is to come, and I know my time will come again." And just like that, Nathan was gone in a blur of burnt skin and fear.

"Becca?" Robert hesitantly asked. The energy within the room died, and the air went silent. Rebecca stared at the wall as if unsure about her decision to allow Nathan to escape. "Becca? Are you okay?" Robert reached out to her. His fingers grazed her shoulder.

Slowly, Rebecca turned to Robert. Her human eyes returned, and she smiled. "Can we go home?"

Robert shook his head and took her hand, leading her away from her prison and toward her new life.

Epilogue

"Are we ever going to reopen, or is all this cleaning and redecorating just for fun?" Dez groaned as she single-handedly lifted a beer keg and placed it on top of one of the other four, she had already brought inside.

"Dezzy, as I said, I am not reopening this place unless it's perfect!" Luke replied as he dangled his legs over the bar like a child. "It's not like you need the money." Luke turned to Robert. "Did she ever tell you she was rich? Like *suuuuuuuper* rich."

"How rich are we talking?" Robert asked with a raised brow.

"Answer that, and I am throwing one of these kegs at you," Dez threatened. "Also! Are you planning on helping us today? Or are you just going to lie around and bitch?"

Luke stuck out his tongue and hopped off the bar top. "I'm management, sweetheart. I'm managing," he said before he skipped to the back office.

Dez rolled her eyes and went back outside to the delivery truck while Robert took inventory of their most recent shipment.

Life had been unreasonably calm since Katherine's death and Rebecca's ascension. The following days moved by quickly, but in hindsight, everything seemed so slow.

Dez was okay, a little worse for wear from her battle, but she healed—slowly. She made it a point to say that Nathan fared much worse than she did. Robert found she had not only burned down the church, but had taken the entire city block with it. She said it was an accident, but nobody believed her.

Luke took Katherine's death the hardest, demanding the most fabulous Irish funeral money could buy, which to him meant hot Irish lads in kilts, ladies in skirts, and an ungodly amount of food.

While Rebecca, being dealt the sourest hand of all, seemed to handle most things in strides. Rebecca's first night of freedom was spent in the Rusty Nail, drinking, talking, and eagerly asking about the past six months, especially focused on the past few weeks. Luke arrived late into the evening and was beyond angry that he missed all the 'fun' but was more than eager to welcome Rebecca into the family.

Everyone watched and waited for Nathan's return, but he never revisited the apartment or bar. All the Virtues had vanished from the city. It was a positive, but the idea of them hiding concerned Robert.

"They will show themselves if they wish to be seen," Dez had explained. "They always do."

It was the *when*, not the *if*, that troubled Robert.

"Dez!" Robert shouted. "Dez!" He called a second time but heard no response. "Jesus freaking Christmas tree," he grumbled as he placed his clipboard on the bar and walked through the back exit. "Please tell me you're not torturing the delivery man again! We can't keep getting blacklisted from all the providers in the city!" Robert expected to see Dez verbally assaulting yet another driver, but he found her standing silently with her head down next to a man in an all-black suit.

"Robert," the man welcomed cheerfully. "Great to finally meet you."

The man's smile was wide and full of overly white teeth. The man's grin was disturbing, too perfect, and too friendly to be anything but a façade. His skin was tanned, and his hair was oil black, slicked back, and smoothed over.

"Hello," Robert said, swallowing once before he spoke again. "Dez, we need more cider. Do you know where the delivery man went?"

"Upfront," Dez spoke to the ground, choosing not to look up as she uttered her one-word response.

Robert had never seen Dez so docile before. She shrunk in on herself like a dying flower while the man placed a hand on her shoulder, giving her a reassuring pat. Just the touch seemed to make her shoulders slump further.

"Desdemona," the man began. "Go ahead and talk with the delivery driver. I want a moment alone with Robert." The man dismissed her, and she obeyed. Before entering the bar, Dez shot a worried glance at Robert.

"I suppose a thank you is to be expected since you helped keep my little family together," the man in the black suit said.

"It was nothing. I needed—"

The man appeared in front of Robert, stopping Robert's sentence. "I said I should thank you; that does not mean I will." His breath was like fire as it hit Robert's face. The sulfur smell was heavy on his breath and swaddled him like some horrible cologne. "You were almost the reason that all of this," he motioned around him, "came to an end. So, I will just call it even."

Robert held his tongue, though his dark companion—the Wrath's Essence—begged for a fight.

"I could choose to punish you for the trouble caused, so I recommend you thank me, Robert, for my kindness and generosity." The man pressed a blistering finger beneath Robert's chin, tilting his face up, forcing Robert to meet the man's gaze. His brown eyes became pitch black—wormholes threatening to pull Robert into the soundless world of darkness. Robert lost himself in the infinite voids. Robert had seen infernal eyes, and he had seen Virtuous eyes, he had seen the eyes of the Seven Deadly Sins, but these—these were something far older.

"Thank you," Robert grunted in pain as the man's finger burned the underside of his chin.

"There we go." The man turned his back to Robert and paced as he spoke. "Forces are gathering, Robert. Things that have slept for a millennium are waking. Things much older and far worse than I. Things far less . . . sympathetic than I." Vagueness thinly layered the stranger's words. "Friends will be needed, Robert. Infernal, mortal, and those lucky few that fall between the lines." He eyed Robert over his shoulder. "We all may need to band together one day to fight what comes from beyond the horizon."

"You need me," Robert said, knowing the significance he held as a descendant of Eve and now as a Piece of Eve.

"*Need* is such a heavy word, Robert. It would be mutually beneficial," the man corrected. "You remain with us, obedient and un-trying, and I won't torture your sister until the end of time." He said his threat so carelessly, so easily, as if torturing an innocent soul meant nothing to him.

"Leave her out of this." Robert clenched his fists.

Release, the Essence of Wrath whispered.

Robert contained the voice and the power that simmered within him. It was not the time to fight; perhaps one day, but not today.

"Oh, but she's a part of this. You are a part of this. There is no telling what creatures will crawl from the abyss, but a friend would be nice. Especially one in very low places." The man extended his hand, and Robert felt he was reliving his first interaction with Katherine. The moment where she offered Robert a partnership and changed his world forever.

"I doubt you have friends."

The man laughed. "I befriend people who are useful."

"So do I." Robert extended a hand.

Their hands clasped. Heat flared within the stranger's hand, but Robert did not flinch. He did not yelp. He did not pull away. He made no show of strength. Katherine had taught him well.

I am not weak. Not anymore.

"You will be a fun one, Robert. I shall remember to keep an eye on you," the man said as he walked into the shadows of the delivery truck. "Oh, and Robert, remember to behave around my daughter."

"Your daughter?!"

The man's laughter filled the alleyway as he merged with the shadows and disappeared, but his taunting laughter remained. Robert stood alone in the alleyway as he absorbed the interaction: dark creatures, an upcoming doom, and Dez's familial connection with Lucifer. Robert wasn't sure which ranked highest on his priority list.

"Knock knock," Rebecca called from the entrance to The Queen of Hearts.

Robert tucked his questions and thoughts away before slipping on a smile and walking back into the building. Dez stood behind the bar, nervously organizing bottles, until Robert walked through the back entrance. She looked at him. He gave her a subtle nod, signaling that everything was okay.

"You know, most people knock before coming inside, right?" Robert said as he moved behind the bar with Dez, arranging the cider delivery.

"Whatever, Robbie." Rebecca rolled her eyes. "I brought a present." She shook something behind her back.

"What is it?" Robert asked.

Rebecca smiled so brilliantly that Robert's heart melted. This was his sister.

"Ta-da!" Rebecca presented the secret. It was a shadow box lined with black velvet with Katherine's gun mounted on the inside. They pinned a small engraving beneath it. "I thought it would be nice to pay tribute to her. Since she sort of saved me."

Robert felt a tug on his heart as he looked at the gun and read the engraving.

"Katherine O'Donnell, one hell of a bitch."

"Well, you got the engraving right." Robert held the shadow box, staring at the gun. Most of Katherine's belongings had been collected, sold, or donated. Luke kept a few of the more sentimental pieces, but most were gone. "Weird to think that's all we have left of her."

"Oh, she's still here," Luke said as he returned from the back office in a different outfit. A fluorescent pink romper paired with a neon yellow fanny pack. He nudged his hip into Rebecca. "We've got you here. You're basically a Ouija board with legs," Luke said with a wink. "Just make sure you don't listen to her too often; she doesn't give the best advice. I could tell you the stories about the trouble she got us into in the '90s!" Luke teased. Robert's ears perked in interest. "Two words, Robert: home perm."

"I would pay a lot of Dez's money for that picture." Robert laughed, and Dez gave a soft chuckle behind him.

Robert beamed; he loved the sound of her laughter.

"You ready to go?" Luke asked, and Rebecca nodded.

"What? You just got here. Where are you two going?" Robert asked.

"Well, the family wants to get a look at the new girl," Luke said as he clapped Rebecca on the back.

"Good luck," Dez said. "Did he warn you about Russo?"

"Lord," Robert groaned, remembering the stench that still haunted his nose. "Just sit downwind. You'll thank me later."

Rebecca looked at Luke and then back to Robert.

"What? What's wrong with him? Who's Russo?" Rebecca asked cluelessly.

"Don't worry, I got you," Luke said as he wrapped his arm over Rebecca's shoulder. "I'll be your guiding light through the darkness. Your personal, Sherpa." He placed a hand on his heart. "It is a burden that I will carry."

Rebecca, Robert, and Dez gave a collective groan.

"I think I can handle myself." Rebecca released a small pulse of her power that touched everyone.

She didn't like Robert's constant worrying, but he couldn't help it. Robert knew she was still working through the trauma, but Rebecca was strong—especially with Katherine guiding her from the great beyond.

Luke and Rebecca left shortly after her arrival, leaving Dez and Robert alone for the first time since they were in Charles's office. He stared at Dez as she placed the liquor bottles on the shelves.

I wonder if she would say yes to a date.

The thought made Robert quake. He had faced bloodthirsty nuns, a church fire, and several pseudo immortal beings, but it was asking Dez out that really made him sweat.

The longer he stared, the more he felt the fluttering return to his stomach. Robert didn't know if Dez would ever forgive him for what he called her or entertain anything beyond a professional relationship, but he wouldn't know unless he tried.

I think I can afford one more mistake today . . .

Robert pulled open a box, withdrew two glasses, and set them on the counter.

"Want a drink?"

"Always," was Dez's answer

Acknowledgments

First, I would like to thank anyone who has listened to me talk about writing this book over the last five years. Thank you all for listening and nodding while I ranted about my dreams of one day publishing a book. I want to thank my husband Tyler for shouting, "Five pages a day," constantly at me and believing in me every step of the way. I want to thank my friends who read the rough drafts of A City of Sin and Virtue when it was just two hundred pages of nonsense and grammatical errors. Thank you to my father, mother, stepdad, and stepmom, who purchased me every book I could have ever wanted as a child and supported my love of fantasy and being creative. And lastly, I would like to thank you, the reader. I couldn't be a writer without you, and I hope this book brought some joy into your life and that you fall in love with the characters as much as I have.